The Ring bearer

Deborah Emery

Dedication

To those who love to leave the present and escape to a world of imagination. To my loving family who encourage and support me.

Adventure. I heard it once told that just about everyone loves an adventure. People climb mountains, sky dive, scuba dive, and sail. They drive fast cars, go to amazing locations, the premise is endless. Adventures build memories and great stories. Most people plan their adventure. I, however; had my adventure thrust upon me. I remember it clearly as if it were yesterday. I was a mere 26 years old and it was the end of May.

My friend Ali and I were spending most of our free time together. We were and are still great friends. My adventure began with one of Ali's and my routine days. My name is Emily and this is my adventure.

Chapter 1

The sound of the ringing telephone went unheard as I continued my long hot shower. I loved to allow the warm water to cascade down my head and shoulders. The scented soap always adds to the enjoyment of the shower. It wasn't until the water ran cool that I finally stepped free of the tub. My continuous bouts of insomnia were getting the best of me. I couldn't sleep at night and went through my days in a fog from the lack of sleep. Even the doctor and his prescriptions couldn't help me to attain a restful night of sleep.

I was towel drying my hair when the telephone rang again. "Hello".

"Did you get any sleep last night?" asked Ali.

"I think I dozed off for about 45 minutes".

"Are you going to feel up to going today?" questioned Ali.

"I'll be tired, but what else is new?" I replied.

"Then I'll drive. I don't want you falling asleep behind the wheel", demanded Ali.

I knew I wouldn't fall asleep behind the wheel, but driving when I was tired did make my reflexes a little more hyper.

"Ok, pick me up in a half hour, I'll be dressed by then", I stated.

Ali and I spent every weekend driving to flea markets and finding deals on the various craft materials we needed to make our one-of-a-kind quilts. We loved the flea market. It was open every Saturday and Sunday. The flea market itself was a collection of buildings with tables set up inside the buildings as well as on the outside. The flea market was huge. It must have been well over two acres or more and every person in the county came shopping there at one time or another.

Ali's favorite spot at the flea market was at the end of the outside tables. The woman who sold there had always managed to have copious amounts of material on bolts. Ali and I found materials that would have been out of our price range had we purchased them in a regular material store.

I had taught Ali to quilt. My quilting skills had begun when I was a child. My grandmother had spent hours, teaching me the ins and outs of quilt making. My grandmother came from the generation of idle hands are tools of the devil generation and she used quilting as a way to entertain me while babysitting me. I had no idea that my grandmother was actually passing on her sewing skills to her only granddaughter, me.

I loved going to my grandmother's home. I can still close my eyes and smell her scent. She smelled of pound cake and coffee. She always found time to spend with me. I knew my grandmother had health issues, but as a child, I never noticed. Thinking back, I can recall her fingers were a little slower to thread a needle. She didn't move as quickly as she had when I was really young. She would ask me to bring the sewing supplies to her as she sat in her comfortable brown chair. I loved my grandmother and was devastated when she passed.

After my grandmother died, making quilts made me feel as though my grandmother was still with me. I realized the memories that my grandmother and I made together working on a quilt could never replace today's generation of techno kids.

Ali and I met at church. I was new in the area and thought what better way to meet people than to donate my quilts to help those in need. When Ali and I met, she voiced she admired my quilts. I suggested she come visit me and I could teach her how to sew. Ali came over and we had such a grand time sewing we decided to meet every Saturday and sew.

Ali and I kept my grandmother's tradition of working on quilts alive. We donated the profits from the quilts we made to the local church. I knew how difficult it was to survive in the economy back then. Even the church was finding it difficult to find extra money to help her needy families. Ali and I spent every Saturday morning searching our local flea market for inexpensive material we could use for our quilts. I am still remembering it so clearly, me walking past one of my usual sellers.

"Hey, Em, I have a couple jars of buttons for you", yelled Charlie. I walked over to Charlie's table. Two large jars sat full to the brim with various buttons. I smiled. I buy material. Buttons had never entered my mind. When I saw Charlie's desperate face, I decided I would buy them and try to fit them into a quilt somehow.

"I'll give you five dollars apiece for them".

Charlie frowned." If you look through the jar, you can see there are a couple brass buttons on the top of the one jar and the jars look really old. They may be antiques".   I figured those buttons alone would be worth a lot more than five dollars".

"I'll go as high as ten dollars for each jar, but that is my limit", I told him firmly.

Charlie knew I was on a tight budget. Charlie nodded his approval. As I turned the jars of buttons around, I questioned myself, "What am I going to do with two jars of buttons?"

Ali ran up to me and breathlessly stated, "There is a table at the end of this row that has tons of bolt material. They are practically giving it away. Come on Em".

With that said, Ali turned and ran back the way she came. Again, I could only smile. I paid Charlie the twenty dollars and slid the two jars of buttons in my large shoulder bag.

"Thanks, Charlie", I said and began to briskly walk in the direction that Ali had recently gone.

Ali was right. The woman at the end table had out done herself. She had material of all colors. The prices were a steal. Ali and I bought all the extra bolts of material from the seller. After she and I had lugged all my bolts of material up to my apartment, Ali said she was heading home. I admit, I was exhausted after all the walking and lifting. I just wanted to sit and start cutting up squares of fabric for my next quilt.

"Are you sure you don't want me to ride home with you and help you carry in those heavy bolts of material?" I asked.

"I appreciate your offer, but then I'd have to drive you back home, and I'm exhausted", replied Ali.

"Ok, then call me later", I suggested. Ali nodded her agreement and flung a wave toward me as she trotted down the steps two at a time.

I yawned. You know one of those back stretching yawns. "Boy I am tired". I sat on the edge of my bed and slipped off my shoes. I took the jars of buttons out of my purse and sat them on my night stand before collapsing onto the bed.

"You know you won't fall asleep, but it won't hurt to rest my eyes", I whispered to myself. I rolled onto my left side, and without realizing it, almost immediately had fallen deep asleep. I slept so soundly. I hadn't noticed the strange disturbance that was occurring next to my bed. A large green glow illuminated the room and one of the jars of buttons fell over. The top opened from the fall. I slept through it all, and yet, my adventure was just beginning.

The room was dark when I woke up. I couldn't get my bearings when the telephone rang. I groped around and finally found the receiver.

"Hello", I stated trying to focus my eyes.

"Em? Were you sleeping?" asked Ali.

"Um, yeah, I guess I must have dozed off. What time is it?" I asked.

"Almost ten fifteen. You should have called me before you went to bed. I feel badly waking you up" admitted Ali.

"I didn't know I had fallen asleep"

"When did you lie down?"

"What time did you drop me off?"

"Two thirty. Did you fall asleep after I left?"

"I must have. I remember taking off my shoes and needing to rest my eyes".

"Wow… that is the most sleep you've had in months. What did you take?"

"I didn't take anything. Maybe the lack of sleep finally caught up with me".

"Do you think you can go back to sleep or did I ruin the rest of your night for you?"

"I feel like I can go back to sleep. It's weird. Maybe all that lifting today wore me out".

"Call me tomorrow if you want me to come over and help you cut your fabric", said Ali.

"Give me a call when you get back from church".

"Want to go to church with me?"

"I think I'm going to try to sleep in while I am tired enough to sleep. You don't mind do you?"

"Of course I don't mind. I'll call you tomorrow. Good night."

I remember slowly wandering into the kitchen. I grabbed a glass and filled it with orange juice. The cool beverage felt good to my dry parched throat. I made a quick bathroom trip and raced back to my bedroom. I slipped out of my street clothes and put on my night gown.

"I should brush my teeth, but I am too exhausted. I'll brush them double tomorrow morning". I climbed back into bed and rolled over. Surprisingly, I fell back to sleep.

What I didn't realize while I slumbered and snuggled into my pillow, the light green glow began to illuminate the room once again. I slept on, but I felt a warm embrace encircle me as I slept. It is difficult to describe but somehow I felt safe and secure. The clock in the living room chimed the time each and every hour. The light musical chimes that were my absolute favorite sound, fell to deaf ears as I slept throughout the night.

Chapter 2

The sunlight slowly flickered and bounced around the room. I always keep my windows locked and the blinds closed but somehow the little slivers of light managed to dance around the room. I yawned and glanced at the clock. "Eight o'clock. I slept through the night... till eight o'clock. I can't believe it." After I finished my shower, I made a light breakfast and then set up the bolts of fabric for cutting.

Twelve inch by twelve inch squares were the first cuts. If I decide I wanted smaller squares for my quilts, I could always cut them down to four inch squares. This saved me from wasting any material. I loved to design new quilts. Quilting was more than just a hobby. My latest idea was to make a quilt with buttons, thanks to Charlie. It would be a decorative quilt and I envisioned it would be a master piece. I went to get the jars of buttons.

"I must have knocked you over in my sleep", I said aloud as I scooped up the buttons that had fallen out of the jar and replaced the lid.

I had purchased large clear plastic bins on wheels to house my materials. I sat one jar of buttons in the bin with the squares of fabric. I took inventory on the amount of quilting thread I had. I would need to purchase a few more spools in the coming weeks. I sat and looked at the various colors of fabric. Yes, I think I have a plan for my new quilt.

I took one jar of buttons to my work area. I must have inadvertently opened the jar of buttons that had remained sealed on my nightstand and began sorting them. First I placed all the flat buttons in one pile. Next I sorted the round buttons, then on to the odd shaped buttons. Buttons with material would be separated into yet another group. Although the flat buttons were different because some had two holes for thread while others had four, the colors nicely matched my quilt fabric and would lay flat against the material. I compared the button color to that of the fabric. Many were complimentary and others would contrast. I would have to decide what role I would want the buttons to perform. Compliment the chosen fabric or contrast and draw attention to the buttons.

It wasn't until my stomach began to growl and ache for food, that I realized it was noon. I pushed aside my fabric, and walked into the kitchen. A light lunch with soup and a sandwich would do the trick. Ali would be out of church and home soon. I gobbled up my lunch then called Ali.

"You won't believe it, but I actually slept until 8 o'clock this morning. I have no idea why all of a sudden I could sleep, but I feel great".

"Want me to come over and help you cut up your fabric?"

"Actually, I'm almost done. I started this morning and have been working until about a half hour ago".

"Then the race is on", stated Ali.

Ali and I always started a quilt at the same time and raced to see who would finish first. It usually took us months to complete. Once finished, we would appraise each other's works and decide whose quilt would be the best design between the two. In the past, it had been my créations that had won most of the competitions. My ability to design quilts was phenomenal, even if I have to say so myself. "Wait until Ali sees my button quilt", I said to myself smiling.

Ali and I continued to work on our perspective quilts. We still made time to get together every weekend and shop at the flea markets. I was making great progress on my quilt. Matter-a-fact, I was almost finished. I was sewing on the buttons one night when one button broke. Looking in the almost empty jar of buttons, I searched for a matching color but had no luck. "Well, time to open the other jar of buttons, I guess". I poured the buttons onto the table, when suddenly; I saw a very old ring slide free from the mound of buttons.

The ring was large and looked really old. It looked like a man's ring. The stone was deep red and had been chiseled into the shape of a knight's shield. A bar of what looked like gold crossed over the stone. The gold bar must have resembled a sword at one time. The top appeared like the handle of the sword, but the end point had been worn down and was now a rounded shape. I grabbed my magnifying glass and went to my bedside table. I turned on the reading lamp and inspected the ring for further details. There was nothing inside the ring to indicate if it were 24 or 18 karat gold. No initials were inside. Of course, if the ring was that old, I wasn't certain if people had put their initials on their rings years ago.

"I'll need to ask Charlie if he knows where he bought the jars of buttons. I know he wouldn't have let this antique go for ten dollars. I'd hate to have someone lose a family heirloom".

I sat the ring on my bedside table to remind myself of my future task. My thoughts keep returning to the ring. There was something about that ring.

Saturday like clockwork, Ali and I made our rounds through the flea market. Charlie was nowhere to be seen.

"That's odd", I thought, "Charlie isn't here today. I've never known him to miss a day".

"Maybe he's on vacation", replied Ali.

"Maybe", I replied a bit skeptical.

Ali and I had planned to shop at the flea market then have lunch at the new restaurant nearby. We drove around the area but was disappointed to find the restaurant had yet to open.

"I can make us a nice salad. I found that if I added salsa to the top of a mixed lettuce plate, it tasted great. It also means less calories. With me sitting and sewing so often, I noticed my pants are a little snugger", I blushingly admitted. Ali agreed and we were soon on our way to my place.

Chapter 3

"I'm sorry; Mr. Potter isn't in at the moment. Mr. Potter is my uncle. I am in charge here when he is out of his office. May I be of service?" stated the clerk to the weatherworn soldier.

"I have a message for Mr. Potter from my Captain".

"It shall be my pleasure to pass on any messages to my uncle", the clerk conveyed.

"Let Mr. Potter know that he hasn't much time to prepare".

"Prepare?"

"The enemy is advancing and has broken through the city of Sowerville defense lines. He needs to prevent enemy troops from attaining the monies in his vault or they will use the money to pay more men to fight against us. I was sent ahead to warn all the shop owners or citizens of wealth".

"How much time would you say we have before they arrive here in Thatcher town?" questioned the clerk.

"Who can say, with fresh horses and good weather, maybe only hours?"

"I'll pass on that message on to my uncle immediately" replied the clerk.

The soldier hesitated for a slight moment, then left to speak to the merchant next door. Daniel knew his uncle would not want to contribute to the enemies assets, but his uncle was still at home with breathing problems. Daniel raced to his uncle's office.

The office had all dark oak paneling. One window was opposite the door. The window was always locked. Wooden panels were attached to each side of the inner window. When the office was closed, the wooden panels would be locked to prevent anyone from entering the office. Although the town was usually safe, Daniel's uncle made certain that theft of any monies placed in his possession would be safe.

Daniel searched through his uncle's desk drawers. Retrieving the key from the top right drawer, he raced to and opened the locked money cabinet. A pile of fabric bags sat on the lower shelf of the money cabinet. Collecting every bit of coin and placing the monies in a fabric bag, Daniel readied himself to take the monies to his uncle's estate for instruction. Daniel's uncle's estate was on the east side of the city park. It would take time to get there, but Daniel would have to manage.

Daniel climbed into his carriage and slowly guided the horse toward his uncle's estate. He did not want to make it seem as though anything was wrong in the event an enemy spy was lurking about. Daniel looked around the streets. The other business owners were collecting what valuable belongings they didn't want confiscated and placing those belongings into their own carriages or they had already locked up their business doors.

Only a small child and the drunkard were on the streets. Surely neither could be spies. The drunkard had an almost empty bottle of ale. The drunkard was sitting and leaning against a building. He didn't seem to notice that the businesses were closing early.

The small child was pulling a small puppy on a rope. The puppy was whimpering and laid down on its stomach. The child was having a difficult time dragging the puppy home. Daniel wondered if the child had found the puppy or if the child was taking the puppy out for a walk. The puppy didn't seem to care for either circumstances. Daniel snapped the reins when the horse reached the edge of the city park, and the horse began to gallop more quickly. Darkness was falling upon the streets. A man with a long stick was walking down the street lighting the street lamps. The park was not well lite but Daniel's horse knew the way to his uncles. Daniel kept a watchful eye out for anyone or anything suspicious.

Daniel hoped he could make it to uncle's home in time to be able to finish taking care of this matter before the enemy made it Thatcher town. When Daniel arrived to uncle's estate, the hearse was in front of the home. Daniel felt his heart grow heavy. The breathing problem must have taken his uncle. Daniel left the fabric bag with the money, inside his carriage and entered uncle's home. Soulful weeping could be heard. "Poor auntie", thought Daniel. She must bear the burden of facing life alone now. Daniel sought out his aunt. "Oh, Daniel, I'm so glad you are here. He is dead", wept his aunt. "When?" was the only thing Daniel could reply.

"He died an hour ago. I think the doctor called the mortician. It seemed they were here before I could even take my next breath. Daniel held his aunt within his arms as she quietly sniffed and wept. "What did the doctor say?"

"The doctor said your uncle" sniffed Auntie, "Died from pneumonia".

Daniel's mind was racing. "What shall I do with the monies? "He thought.

Daniel poured his aunt a small sherry.

"Auntie, I have some of uncle's business to handle. It is urgent that I complete the transaction. Shall I have Marjorie come and stay with you?" Marjorie was a longtime friend of Daniel's aunt and uncle. Marjorie also worked in the church which often aided to give comfort to those who needed a spiritual boost. Auntie could only sniff and nod yes.

Daniel instructed the butler to send a message to Marjorie informing her of the death of uncle and the need for her presence at the estate to help his grieving aunt. Once this task was taken care of, Daniel climbed into his own carriage and headed back toward the town.

Chapter 4

Ali and I finished our weekend with no purchases from the flea market, but found that tasty little café to treat ourselves to. It had opened and surprisingly was not packed with patrons. I explained to Ali about how I had found an old ring in the jar of buttons and felt the right thing to do was to return it to Charlie.

"Are you kidding me?" replied Ali. "That man has made enough money off of you for years. It surely isn't his ring. He wouldn't give it back to the owner, if he even knows who the owner may be.

"Maybe he would remember who he purchased the buttons from and I could find the family" I injected.

"Charlie buys from estate sales and anywhere else he picks up auctions. I even think he has been buying merchandise from some websites on the internet. I heard he has bought a lot of Chinese merchandise until his customers began to complain. I think he has been buying from Ireland and England lately. With all the different people he buys from, do you really think he is going to remember where a couple of jars came from?" asked Ali.

"Maybe not, but don't you think I should try? I would hate to have something of my parents sold off without having the chance to recover it", I confessed.

"Why do you think everyone is as honest as you? You don't even know if it was a family members ring. It could have been some rich spoiled child's play toy".

"I don't know, Ali. The ring looks pretty old. I must say though, it is in pristine shape for being old".

"Suit yourself. I think Charlie will be all the richer if he finds out you found a ring amongst those buttons. He likes his cash and won't let you get any further than him when it comes to that ring. Mark my words on that".

I was more confused than ever.

"Maybe I'll just ask Charlie where he bought the jars of buttons; after all, if my quilt turns out as great as I think, I may need more buttons. I won't be lying; I simply won't be offering him all the information", I thought to myself.

Chapter 5

I was just stepping out of the shower when I heard the telephone ring.

"Em. It's me, Ali. I can't make it today. I have a really bad head cold. If you see anything I may like, pick it up for me, and I'll reimburse you when I see you. Sorry to cancel out on such short notice". Ali's voice was quite hoarse and I could tell her nose was stuffy.

I toweled dried and dressed. I put on my yellow slacks with a crisply ironed white blouse. I had stumbled across a pair of yellow pumps that were just my size at the flea market last month. They matched my slacks perfectly. I pulled my hair up into a pony tail. I was going to tie a yellow ribbon around my pony tail but felt I may look a bit childish so tossed the idea away.

I was disappointed that Ali was not able to make it. I had hopes Ali and I could wander to that nice little café again. I took my time gathering my large shopping bag, enough cash to purchase any fabric, but was finally ready. After finally putting off long enough, I put the ring inside my purse and headed out. I climbed into my car and drove toward the flea market.

"I'll try to find Ali something special", I thought. "After all, she isn't feeling well".

Charlie was not at the flea market. When I asked the other sellers, no one knew where Charlie lived or how to get in touch with him. I hadn't notice the three men who were standing nearby. I continued to wander through the flea market picking up a few trinkets that may add to my next quilt. I still had not found anything that I felt would be a good cheer-me-up gift for Ali. When I completed the length of the flea market tables, I turned to find the three men blocking my path.

"What did you buy from the old man?" asked one of the men.

"I beg your pardon", I stated. I was totally confused on what the men were talking about.

"What did you buy from Charlie?"

The man was very fat. He had a sour odor about him. He didn't look like he took very good care of himself. His hair looked greasy. His shirt had food stains, and even though he wore a tie, it wasn't fastened appropriately and his shirt hung opened and loose.

"Oh", I replied.

"Don't make me ask you again" stated the man stepping closer.

"Who are you?" I asked.

"It doesn't matter who we are. What did you buy from him?"

"Fabric, I buy fabric and make quilts. Where is Charlie? I haven't seen him here in weeks. Is he sick?" I asked boldly.

The men smirked. "Yeah, he's real sick".

The smaller man of the group had a sickly grin. He wore glasses and had dark hair. He was cleaner than the fat man. He didn't wear a tie but did wear a dress shirt with the collar unbuttoned. His pants were black but looked like they had not be cleaned nor pressed in a long while. The color looked a bit faded too as though the pants had been through a lot of wear.

I could feel fear growing within. I looked past the men, long enough for them to think someone was behind them. They glanced back long enough for me to dart under one of the tables and race towards the flea market stores. The men were larger than I and had difficult climbing over the table. I raced onward. I found an area full of fabric bolts and slide in between a few of the thicker fabrics. I ducked my head down and prayed. I must have been was hidden well, because when I did poke my head up, I could see the men race past me. I had to remember to breath. Fright was strong. I could feel my stomach twisting. I thought I was going to vomit, but I made myself breath slowly. When I saw the men turn the corner, I slid out from my hiding spot and raced in the opposite direction of them. I headed quickly toward my car.

I only glanced back once before climbing into the driver's seat. I ducked down low and waited a few minutes before starting the engine. I had to make myself drive cautiously and slowly so not to arouse any suspicion. I turned out of the parking lot and onto the road. As I glanced through my side mirror, I noticed the three men heading away from the flea market stores.

"They must still think I'm hiding somewhere inside", I whispered to myself.

I made it home before my hands began to tremble. I called Ali. I had to speak to someone before I broke down in tears.

"Charlie wasn't there again today".

"Emily, did you see this morning's paper?" asked Ali between coughs and sneezes. I could hear the roughness in her voice.

"No. Why? " I asked.

"Charlie is dead".

"What? When? How?" I inquired.

"Well, I felt so bad, I decided to stay in bed. I had some tea and toast. I thought I would read the paper then take a nap".

"Tell me about Charlie. How did you find out about Charlie? Was he in the obituaries"?

"He's not in the obituaries. There was an article written about a man that was killed. Charlie was assaulted in his home. He apparently has a shed that he stashes all his merchandise in, and someone ransacked his house and the shed too. That's what the article says".

"You don't think they were looking for this ring, do you?" I asked, hoping Ali would say "No".

"Why would you think who ever ransacked Charlie's place was after that ring? "Questioned Ali.

"Ali, three men followed me today at the flea market. I had stopped by Charlie's booth to see if he was there. Of course, Charlie wasn't there. I didn't notice them until I was at the end of the rows of tables. They blocked my path. I had to run and hide from them. They were still searching for me when I managed to get to my car. Do you think they can find me here?"

"Why would they follow you?" asked Ali.

"They wanted to know what I bought from Charlie. I told them fabric, but I don't think they believed me"

"I don't see how they could find you. No one keeps receipts. We pay cash every time we buy something. I don't even think they take charge cards, do they? " asked Ali.

"Just for safety sake, I think we need to avoid going to that flea market" I stated.

"Maybe we shouldn't go to any flea markets for a while. It seems odd that those men would follow you after you stopped by Charlie's table. They may be smart enough to know we may go to other flea markets. If they know what you look like, you may be in danger if they spot you".

"Do you think I should call the police?" I asked.

"What would you say?"

"I don't know. I don't even know if those men were going to harm me. Why would they chase after me if they weren't up to something? I really felt unsafe. I guess maybe I'm being paranoid, but I had a gut feeling, you know?"

"All the same, I think we should take some precautions, just in case", stated Ali.

"I think so too ".

So we both agreed to refrain from shopping at the flea markets until we were both out of supplies for our quilts.

It may have been the fright, but I began to have vivid dreams. "I have been having dreams of a thirty something year old man who I know is somehow connected to or involved with those dangerous men. The odd thing is, the man didn't look as if he belongs here. He wore a suit that had a vest and a matching jacket that was long. Down to his knees kind of long. No one wears things like that today, do they? His hair was blondish brown and he had the richest brown eyes. He was tall. He must be at least six foot 2 or 3 inches. He didn't wear shoes but boots. These dreams are so vivid. But it's the same dream, night after night. What do you make of that?" I asked confiding to Ali as she and I enjoyed our Saturday lunch.

"I think we need to get you a date" giggled Ali.

"Ha ha" I replied as I felt my face grow hot.

Ali sipped on her ice tea as I finished the final touches on the button quilt.

"Well, I guess it's time to go back to the flea market" stated Ali. It had been weeks since Ali and I had gone to our flea market. We refrained from shopping at other flea markets in the area too. Just in case. I could only look at Ali and nod hesitantly.

I have to confess, I was nervous just thinking about going back to the flea market.

"I'll pick you up tomorrow morning, but we'll need to have a plan just in case those men are there. You are sure those men followed you, right?" questioned Ali.

"I didn't imagine it. I had to hide in the bolts of fabric until they passed by and turned the corner. I wasn't certain I would get away without being seen", I confessed. "I can still recall how hard my heart was beating out of fear".

"Ok, then if we see them, we'll leave and go straight to the police department" stated Ali.

"What if they see us and we can't get to the car?" I asked. I was growing more nervous by the minute.

"We separate and each run for help" exclaimed Ali.

So that was our plan. I prayed very strongly that we would both be safe when we went to the flea market.

Chapter 6

The next day was warm and sunny.

"Well, we picked a good afternoon to go shopping" I stated while trying to control the fine tremors of my hands. I kept praying to myself that it had been my imagination. I just couldn't convince myself that we would be safe.

We drove down the parking lot and looked through rows of tables to see if the men were there.

"I don't see them" I said. Ali parked her car and we both got out. Ali grabbed our shopping bags. My mind had turned to mush and I wasn't thinking straight.

Ali began walking quickly toward the end of the long tables.

"They always have wonderful bolts of fabric down at this end of the market and fantastic prices too". I followed Ali to her favorite spot at the flea market. As Ali and I lifted and sorted through the fabric bolts, movement caught my eye. It was them.

"Ali, it's them, "I whispered.

"What do you want to do, we're trapped at the end here" stated Ali.

"You go to the car, they won't recognize you. I'll run the other way and guide them away from you" I plotted.

"Ok, but I'll meet you at that big oak tree at the end of the property" stated Ali as she pointed to the northeast corner. "If you aren't there within fifteen minutes, I'm going to the police station". All I could do was nod. I briskly walked toward the end of the row and ducked under the table. I then mustered up all the speed I could and raced toward the stores. I ran down the aisle I had the last time I had the encounter with these men. I ran and turned left. I felt badly pushing people out of my way as I headed for the back doors of the market. I heard a woman yell that someone had stepped on her foot and run off. A man I pushed landed up against a table full of plates and glasses. I could hear the breaking glass as I continued to run. I made it past the storage areas and into the trees. Suddenly one of the men grabbed my arm. It was the third man. He was stocky and stood about five foot ten. His hair was brown and he wore a short sleeved shirt. He wore khaki pants with a brown belt. His brown shoes were loafers and they were well worn. I was panting from all the running but I managed to fight for my freedom.

"Let go of me", I yelled.

"You're going to take me to your house and show me everything you bought from Charlie", stated the man.

I pulled hard and the man pulled back. My shoe slid on the wet foliage and I fell hard against one of the trees. My arm hit the rough bark of the huge tree. I could see I had a nice abrasion that was beginning to bleed. The man grabbed my hair and pulled me upward. Suddenly, Daniel, the man within my dreams was there. Daniel grabbed the man and tossed him with an unbelievable force into the bushes. The man didn't get up. I could only stare in disbelief. Daniel helped me to my feet. I continued to stare. How can this be? How can he be here? Daniel began guiding me toward Ali's car. He even helped me in the front passenger seat. When I looked back at Daniel, I became extremely dizzy and must have fainted.

When I woke up, I was still sitting in Ali's car, but we were parked outside of my house. "I'm glad you woke up, I wasn't sure how I was going to get inside" confessed Ali.

"Did you see him? Did you?" I asked.

"Yeah, he grabbed you and pulled your hair. You fought like a mad woman", admits Ali.

"Not that man, the other one".

"There were two?" asked Ali.

"Didn't you see him when he helped me in your car?" I asked.

"You staggered to the car. No one was with you. Let me see, "stated Ali as she fingered through my hair," Did you hit your head?"

"No, I didn't hit my head" I was exasperated.

"Emily, maybe you started hallucinating from fear." Ali stated as she helped me into my house and then poured me the largest glass of whiskey I had ever seen. My hands continued to tremor so I began to sip the dark caramel colored and throat burning beverage.

"I can't believe how real he seemed" I couldn't help myself, I kept repeating that same sentence over and over. "He did, he seemed so real".

"You've had a shock. You need to rest".

"Ali, I think we should contact the police. Obviously they had something to do with Charlie's death" I declared.

"Maybe they are trying to find Charlie's murderer too" suggested Ali.

"I don't think so. They wanted to know if I bought something from Charlie. I think they may be after that ring I found".

"If Charlie didn't know it was in the jar, how would they?"

"Just a feeling" I said as sank back and into the sofa," they are after something valuable. Charlie may not have known it was there, but I have a feeling those men do".

"Let's sleep on it and discuss it more tomorrow. Do you want me to make you some dinner?" asked Ali.

"I am too upset to eat. I'll finish this drink and try to lie down and relax. I'll call you tomorrow around 10 a.m."

"If you want me to, I can stay the night. I can bunk on the sofa" offered Ali.

"I think this drink will help my nerves and put me to sleep. Funny, I usually forget about having alcohol in the house unless I have a bad cold. You know what a light weight I am" and with that I began to giggle.

"Ok, but remember, you can call me anytime you need me "stated Ali as she picked up her things and headed for the door.

I remember I had turned on the living room lights then laid back down on the sofa. Suddenly I jumped up and raced to the door. "I thought I forgot to lock it" I chuckled to myself as I checked to ensure the lock was set to the lock position.

By the time I emptied that glass, I felt myself slow down. My eyes lids felt heavy, I could feel my breathing seemed slower and deeper. The room seemed to have gotten much warmer. I plopped myself back down on the sofa and I laid my head upon the largest throw pillow. Funny how alcohol can cause your coordination to slow. It can make your body feel heavier than it really is too. Before I realized it, I was soon asleep.

Unknown to me at the time, the illuminating green glow enveloped me. Daniel kneeled down beside me. He brushed the stray hairs from my face.

"You are such a beauty. I am a cad to have not stopped that assailant sooner", whispered Daniel.

I stirred slightly. "I will keep you safe. I promise" stated Daniel.

I am not certain when I fell asleep, but I began to dream. I was home. It was my home. I found myself looking around to confirm my judgment. I had fallen asleep on the sofa. The music was playing softly. The handsome man appeared beside me and I wasn't afraid. It was odd though, because I couldn't move. The man had a look of concern on his face. I could only stare. The man brushed stray hairs from my vision. His touch was gentle and yet electrifying. My mind was confused. I was home and yet he was here. I didn't know him and yet felt strangely safe in his presence. I was lost in thought when suddenly I realized he was so close. Was he going to kiss me?

Chapter 7

"Auntie, you must listen carefully" whispered Daniel. "I'm joining the local forces to fight against our enemies and I fear we may be out numbered. I may not survive. You have a grave responsibility. I have hidden uncle's money. I had the gold smith put the coordinates on my ring. They have been added to the gold behind the stone. You must prevent anyone from finding the money. Our enemies could use the money to pay mercenaries to fight against us. Once this battle is over, I can reclaim the monies or you can have someone to retrieve the money; assuming I do not survive".

Daniel could see the look of fright on his aunt's face.

"I just lost my husband. I cannot lose you too" she cried.

"Auntie, you must be strong. You cannot tell anyone the secret of the ring, especially the servants. They could rob you while you slept".

Daniel's aunt sniffed. "I will hide the ring where no one will find it, but you must promise me you will come back".

"I will do my best, auntie" smiled Daniel as he kissed her forehead.

What Daniel did not know was that the gardener had been eavesdropping on their conversation.

"I don't need your old ring, "spouted the gardener to himself, "I'll find out what I want to know from the gold smith". His hand rubbing the sheathed blade that was secured to his belt.

Auntie watched from the doorway as Daniel mounted his dark black steed and rode westward. Auntie dropped Daniel's ring inside the jar of buttons she had been collecting. She pushed the ring down until it was completely hidden by buttons. She placed the jar within her sewing basket. When everything was in place, she called for the maid.

"Isabella, I need you to fetch my purse from my dressing table. Take my sewing notions upstairs to the attic. I'm bored with sewing".

Isabella arrived. Isabella was a thin young woman. She had a messy wad of hair that she kept pinned on top of her head. Her uniform was clean but her apron displayed stains and spots. Isabella took the sewing basket upstairs. She soon returned with auntie's purse.

"Tell James I'll need the carriage", instructed Auntie. Soon auntie stood beside the bank of the Knop River. Making certain James and Isabella were watching, auntie tossed her purse into the churning waters of the River. The river was full and wild. The recent rains had caused the water to swell to the top of the banks. The rapid flowing water created a multitude of eddies.

"James, the misses dropped her purse in the river". Before James could move, auntie replied, "Stop James, let God hide Daniel's secret. I don't want our enemies getting any help from Daniel and me". The purse blended quickly into the rapid swirling water and was now nowhere to be seen. Isabella and James just looked at each other. Each uncertain what to do or say. Auntie climbed back into the carriage and Isabella followed. James took the reins and headed the carriage toward home.

Chapter 8

The next morning, I could barely open my eyes. The alcohol had turned my mind to mush. "I need coffee".

I slowly sat up. My head pounded like someone was using it for a drum. I rubbed my temples in efforts to ease the pain. The daylight flooded the room adding stabbing pains behind my eyes. The hot coffee did little to help curb the drowsy feeling that clung to my brain. I took some aspirin and put an ice pack on my throbbing head. The telephone rang. I thought I would die from the pain it caused. It was Ali checking in on me.

"Drink water", stated Ali, "you are dehydrated. That is what gives most people that awful hangover headache after a night of drinking". Ali arrived a short time later. I sipped on the glass of cold ice water that Ali had sat in front of me.

"He was here last night", I stated.

"Who was here?" asked Ali slightly alarmed.

"Daniel, the man I have been dreaming about".

"I think I poured you too much alcohol", stated Ali with a sly grin.

"I think he was going to kiss me, but I must have passed out".

"Ok, now you have my attention" said Ali as her grin blossomed into a smile.

"I'm serious. I have no idea how he managed to get in here. I don't know what his business is. Maybe he is after the ring too, only he thinks he can romance it out of me".

"Will you listen to yourself? No one knows you even have the ring for certain. How do you know this man's name is Daniel and why would you believe, this man named Daniel, is attempting to romance you?" questioned Ali.

"I don't know. Funny, isn't it? I just have an odd feeling about his name".

The truth was, I didn't know how I knew the man's name. I didn't know if he had truly been here or if he was a figment of my imagination. I was getting to the point where I didn't know what was a dream, the truth, or real life anymore.

"Well, I've been thinking about this ring thing", stated Ali. "If we go to the police, they will confiscate the ring and hold on to it. That will not solve your problem. It will make you more vulnerable in the event those goons from the flea market manage to find you."

"How so?" I asked, attempting to follow Ali's logic.

"If those men find you, you have nothing to give them. You won't be able to give them the ring. If the police have it, they won't release it to you either. It may get lost in the bureaucratic process. I have heard stories of evidence disappearing of police custody."

"Ali, that is only in the movies. Police are very thorough and I believe very honest. Geez", I said as I rolled my eyes at her, "but seriously, what am I going to do? I can't keep looking over my shoulder the rest of my life for those thugs."

"We're going to have to think hard about this situation and come up with a really good plan" stated Ali.

Every plan seemed hopeless. "I guess we will need to stop going to flea markets all together", stated Ali." We may have to resort to buying our notions from fabric stores on line. A few of my co-workers buy on line all the time and have had no problems. This would actually solve two problems. One, we wouldn't have to worry about those guys trying to attack you every time you went looking for fabric and notions. We could also save time and gas money by shopping on line", stated Ali.

"Do we really want to have some thugs control our lives?" I inquired.

"No, but if we aren't alive may be a point that should be considered here", stated Ali.

I could only sigh in frustration.

"I honestly have no clue what to do". At least Ali did see there were thugs after me and I hadn't imagined that.

"Do you know anyone that may know a policeman? We could ask how they would handle a situation like this", claimed Ali.

"No. But you were right. If we stop going to the flea markets, there would be no way they could find us. It does mean changing our way of shopping for deals but our safety should come first".

Ali waved goodbye as she drove away. I have to confess, I was worried. Those men could harm anyone that may have purchased anything from Charlie. Anyone could be in danger.

"I'd feel awful if someone was hurt and I didn't try to stop it from happening". I finished the dishes and tidied up the living room. I stretched my aching shoulders and headed off to the bathroom to brush my teeth before heading off to bed. I had only just opened the medicine cabinet and removed the tooth paste when a brief movement caught my eye. As I closed the cabinet door, my breath caught as I saw Daniel's reflection in the mirror. He was standing in the doorway behind me.

"I'm not sure what you want but I can assure you I have nothing of value here", I confessed.

"Ma'am, I am not here to rob from you" stated Daniel.

"I don't understand".

"I don't quite understand the situation myself, Madam", stated Daniel.

"Why are you here? How did you find me? How did you get into my home?" I questioned.

"Those are all excellent questions. I wish I could give you answers. I am afraid I do not have any answers for you. I found myself here. I am not certain where this place may be, why I am here, or who you may be."

"You are the man from the flea market. You helped me into my friend's car. Somehow you must have followed us to my home….here", I couldn't control my speech, and I sputtered out fact after fact but my breathing and nervousness was impairing my words.

"I do remember protecting you from that thug. I did assist you to get away. I have no clue as to what a car is."

I gathered what little courage I had and slowly walked toward Daniel.

"What do you mean you have no idea what a car is?"

"What is a car? "Asked Daniel.

I thought by talking to him, I could distract him as I reached for the telephone.

"I suppose you have no idea what this is either?"

Daniel looked puzzled. "Ma'am, what does that device have to do with the situation?"

I dialed 9-1-1. "This device is known as a telephone. It is a communication device. Don't you have them where you live?"

"I'm afraid not. We have to use messengers to communicate"

This had me more puzzled than ever. "Messengers? Like men on bikes?"

"What are bikes?"

I listened for the sirens of the police as I continued to distract this intruder.

"You don't know what bikes are and yet you have messengers?"

"That is what I am stating Ma'am. Messengers take our correspondence to the intended by way of a horse or a carriage. You confuse me, Ma'am. Pray tell Ma'am, what is a car and bike?"
Suddenly the lights of a police car could be seen flashing blue and red into my home. I ran past Daniel and flung open the door. I pointed toward the bathroom and stated with a quivering voice, "He's in there". As police raced into each room, I tried in vain to calm my pounding heart.
"Miss, there is no one here", stated the lead police officer.
I could feel blood drain from my face.
"How is that possible? He was just here, standing in front of the bathroom door when I opened the door for you and the other officer to come inside".
I noticed the officers gave each other *that* look. The look one will give a friend or co-worker when someone is not quite making sense.
"Would you mind staying until I check all the windows and doors?" I asked as I tried to force back my tears.
"We'd be happy to miss", replied the officer.
All the windows and doors were locked.
"I don't understand. He was here. How did he get in and out with the windows and doors locked?"
"Here is my card. You can obtain a police report in 48 hours. Please let me know if you notice anything missing. That can be added to the report", Stated the officer.
"Thank-you, I'll check my valuables and let you know if anything is missing", I replied.
I made certain to lock the door after the police officers left.
"How did you get inside?" I questioned out loud. I dialed Ali's phone number.
"Emily, I'm coming over and staying with you. I'm not certain what is going on, but if he finds his way in again, you'll have a witness".
I actually sighed with relief when I heard Ali knocking on the door.
"I hate dragging you into this thing, but I am so glad you came".
"I'm really worried about you. We need to figure this thing out."
Ali and I were sitting on the sofa sipping tea when the mantel clock chimed one o'clock in the morning.
"We'd better get some sleep or we'll get our days and nights mixed up", mentioned Ali.
"I'm sorry for keeping you up so late. I guess all the excitement got my adrenaline pumping".

"So, do I take the couch or do we play it safe and sleep in the same bed?"

"I'm not sure I can sleep. Why don't you take my bed and I'll bunk on the sofa for the night. That's the good thing about a studio layout; you can see the entire place at a glance. I can ensure you are safe and you can make certain that I am".

"Are you sure you don't mind me hitting the hay? I can stay up with you if you need me too. I'll have to chug some coffee though".

"Don't be silly. You shouldn't lose sleep because I have insomnia".

"Ok, but if you see or hear anything, you wake me up. Ok?"

"Trust me; you would definitely not be able to sleep if that happens".

I attempted to distract myself by reading my book but couldn't seem to concentrate. After reading the same paragraph four times, I decided to put the book down.

"I'd do some sewing but I'd wake Ali if I attempted to drag out my crafting supplies now. I'd better try and get some sleep" I mumbled to myself.

I must have fluffed and punched those pillows half a dozen times every few minutes. I just couldn't seem to get comfortable or in that sweet spot that allows me to drift off to sleep. I finally tossed all the pillows except my large squishy pillow off the sofa. I laid back down and tried to see if I could get comfy enough to relax. Although I thought it would take a long while for me to doze off, I fell asleep rather quickly once I snuggled into the soft, warm covers and the squishy pillow.

Uncertain if it was because she was sleeping in a strange bed or if something had made a sound, Ali slowly opened her eyes. The clock on my night stand announced the time as 5:30 am. Ali glanced across the bedroom area. She brought her hand up to her mouth to prevent herself from screaming. Across the room, I lay sleeping on the sofa. Sitting nearby and watching me was a man. The same man that I had been describing day after day to Ali. He was right there, just a foot away from me. The man did not seem threatening, but it was queer that he just sat there watching me as I slept.

Thoughts ran through Ali's mind. What could she do if the man attempted to harm me? Before Ali could come up with a valid plan, the sun began to flood through the windows. Ali could barely stand the brightness. When Ali looked again, she was even more frightened as it seemed the man had just disappeared. Ali strained her ears to hear if the man was somewhere within the apartment that could not be seen from where she lay. Ali could barely hear anything because her heart was beating so loudly and fast she thought it would burst through her chest... Fear took over and Ali ran to my side.

"Em, wake up, he's in here. I saw him. I have no idea where he is now, but I did see him".

I shook my head. The cobwebs would not seem to clear.

"You saw him?"

"Yes, he was sitting here for the longest time, just watching you sleep. It was eerie. I don't think I'd be more frightened if he were a ghost", admitted Ali.

After checking all the locks on the windows and doors, Ali and I sat down. I tried to stay busy to prevent Ali from seeing my tremoring hands.

"I'll make some coffee". Soon, we sat at the table sipping coffee. Ali couldn't stop shaking.

"I did see him. I did! How did he get in? How did he get out? I didn't hear a door open or close. The windows are all locked. I don't understand".

I tried to assure Ali that she had probably had a bad dream. All the excitement and stress of the day before surely could have played havoc in her mind. Nothing happened. The doors and windows were still locked. Ali must have had a bad dream.

"Maybe you should come stay at my place for a few days", suggested Ali.

"Don't be silly", I replied, "I think your nerves are playing tricks on you. Maybe mine too. There is no one here. The doors and windows are locked. No one could get in here unless they had a key or broke a window. We both would have heard if someone tried to unlock the door. If he broke the window, we surely would have heard that and we would see glass on the floor. I feel badly that I have pulled you into my hysteria".

"I know I saw him" said Ali, "didn't I'?

"Honestly, I think our nerves are on edge and we are making ourselves see thing", I tried to sound logical. My heart was beating hard. I didn't know what to do but I did know that I didn't want to cause Ali any distress or worry.

"But he was so real"! Stated Ali.

"I know. I have dreamed about him so much, and spoken to you about him, and now I think we are both imagining him", I confessed.

Although I encouraged Ali to go home, Ali felt apprehensive for leaving and yet I could see on her face that she was totally grateful for me insisting she leave.

"We are feeding off each other's fears. We can only make each other more nervous and crazy if we keep this up. I think the best thing for us is to try and figure out what to do about that ring. Once we have a plan, and implement that plan, the better off the two of us will be. Right"? I Questioned. Ali just nodded.

Chapter 9

The seedy hotel smelled of body odor, cigarette smoke, and cheap alcohol and yet the three men didn't seem to notice. The wall paper was peeling. The curtains had layers of dried dust and filth. Small holes could be seen at the floor boards where mice had been gnawing.

"Hey, Bill, what's our next plan?" Asked the short, grossly over-weight man named Keith. Keith wore a super large shirt that always seemed to house food stains. His pants were large and did not seem to fit on his hips. The drooping pants often gave his comrades a view of his back side.

"I'm working on it"! Exclaimed Bill as he tilted his head back and swallowed the shot of cheap rum. Bill was the lead man. Bill was of average height and weight but felt he was given jobs that was below his station in life. Bill felt he should be in an office and directing staff members to do jobs instead of being sent out on locations to retrieve selective items.

Bill had been hired to find a ring. The man that hired Bill seemed financially well off but seemed almost desperate to find the ring. A ring that somehow made its way into an estate sell. "An estate sell from England, no less", thought Bill. The man had paid an auctioneer in New York to reveal who had purchased the bulk of the estate from England. It had been Charlie. Charlie who claimed he never found any jewelry, let alone a ring among the things he had purchased. Most of the things had been sterling silver dinner ware, tapestries, and a few coins that amounted to 23 dollars. There were pictures in the crates, but even the frames were not worth much. The pictures were in Charlie's shed. The man didn't want the pictures, only the ring. The man didn't even know what the ring looked like. There was no picture or written description of the ring. To Bill, this was a useless trip and a waste of his time.

Bill knew Charlie would have told him where the ring was if Charlie knew. Bill's method of extracting information from people always worked. Bill prided himself on that. Bill would take a lamp and remove the electrical cord from it. The open wires would be placed on the person's ankle. All Bill had to do was ask a question. If the person didn't give the right answer, Bill would plug the cord in for a few seconds. No one had ever resisted Bill's method. No one. Charlie had admitted to all the junk in his shed, but no ring. Too bad

Charlie died during the questioning. Bill knew Charlie didn't have the ring but maybe it was in something Charlie had sold.

Charlie didn't keep any ledgers on who he sold any of his items to. People that didn't keep accurate books often skimmed money and didn't record their true earnings to the government. Less taxes to pay if the earned income amount was lower. But this method also made it more difficult for Bill and his crew to complete their job.

"Jeff, when is that guy supposed to call back? "Asked Bill.

"He just said later", answered Jeff. Jeff was a mousy little guy with glasses. His dark brown hair was neatly trimmed and he had an arrogant personality. Although he wore a blue striped suit, he hadn't had it cleaned in years. The strong scent of stale cologne permeated from the jacket. His shoes didn't match the suit as they were brown and scuffed.

"You couldn't think to ask for a time? How stupid can you be?" replied Bill. "Now we have to sit around this dump waiting all night for a phone call!" Jeff knew not to respond to Bill when he was drinking.

Keith rubbed his double-chins and yawned. "Can we at least order some pizzas? I'm starved".

"I don't care what you do", replied Bill as he emptied his fifth shot glass. Just as Keith was about to reach the phone, Bill yelled, "Just don't use the phone, I'm waiting for that call".

"Crap", responded Keith as he grabbed the door knob and headed out the door. "You guys want anything special on the pie?" Jeff shook his head. Bill didn't respond. "Ok then".

The telephone rang. "Yeah, we were thorough," replied Bill. "He didn't have it. We looked through everything. You sure it was with this shipment?" Bill listened to whatever was said on the other end of the connection.

"He didn't keep records. He just sold whatever crap he had on his tables at that hick market place". Bill listened. "What do you suggest we do"? Bill listened again. "No one at that place knows who Charlie's customers were, or what he sold. Are you absolutely sure it was with this shipment"? Yelling could be heard coming from the handset. Bill pulled the handset away from his ear.

"We can keep watching the place, but I think you are wasting your money and our time", slurred Bill. Bill hung up the phone. The man must have hung up on him as there were no further words heard from Bill or the handset.

Bill was asleep when Keith came back carrying two extra-large pizzas. Jeff grabbed two slices and whispered to Keith, "We are stuck babysitting that market until we can find whoever bought that ring from Charlie".

"Sounds like I'm gonna get paid to eat a lot of pizza and sit. That's my kind of work", smiled Keith.

"We don't even know if that ring was in the estate stuff that Charlie bought. We may be here for a long time", stated Jeff.

Chapter 10

I was glad that Ali had gone home. I hated to think that I was causing her distress. I held the ring in my hand.

"What should I do with you?" Of course, no answer came. I sat and thought. Charlie is dead. We have no idea where he lived or where he bought the jar of buttons. I wasn't even certain if those men were after the ring. They did want to know what I bought from Charlie. It seemed odd that they were searching for something and were using force to get it. That wasn't a good sign. I held the ring tightly. I wish I knew what to do. I have so many questions and no one to get answers from.

It wasn't long before I noticed the day had slipped away and the evening was making way for night time. It didn't take me long to get into my nightgown and crawl under the covers. I don't know if it was the stress of the situation or my body was trying to catch up on the lack of sleep it had experienced, but I felt tired.

The ring was placed safely on my night stand. I read a few pages of a book I had been attempting to finish but fatigue had become over-powering. I switched off the light and snuggled into my soft feather pillow. The glow of green began to spread around the room as I slept. Daniel found himself standing beside my bed as he had done night after night for months.

"Dear lady, I wish I could give you the answers you have been seeking. Like you, I am at a loss as to what is going on. I have no idea what has brought me to your home or why I cannot leave your presence. The last thing I can recall is leaving my aunt's home. I woke up in the bowels of a ship unable to move about. I next found myself in a huge metal shed, again tethered to the spot. Lastly, I was in a wooden shed until I found myself in your home. I don't understand the situation any more than you", said Daniel out loud.

I slept on. Daniel laid down beside me as I later discovered months later, he had come to do each night. He could feel my skin against his chest. He slide his arm around me and moved so close he could feel the movement of my body with each breath. I slept on unaware of Daniel.

Night after night, as I slept, Daniel would watch over me. He didn't know why he felt compelled to do so. He thought I was so beautiful. I wish I had known her before.

"Before?" he questioned himself, "before what?"

He strained to recall what brought him to me. He remembered his grieving aunt and him leaving her mourning and upset. He couldn't seem to remember what happened afterward. He had no idea why I was so afraid of him when he did try to talk to me. So many questions and very few answers.

"What are we going to do, my 'lady?" asked Daniel, "What are we going to do, indeed".

Ali called me each day. On the weekends, we would get together and drive to the library. We actually enjoyed the drive to the library. The road was lined with beautiful multi-colored trees. The traffic flow was low and the area quiet.

The librarian explained to us, that we could use the computer to access the internet for one hour only each day, however; if no one was waiting to use the computer, we were allowed to use it until someone else requested computer time. We spent as much time as possible on the computer looking for fabric to buy. I was surprised how quickly time could pass when we were on the computer.

We purchased our materials, whether it be fabric, padding, or thread from online sellers. Ali and I continued our quests to challenge each other for the best quilt. As much as we loved picking out fabric and deals at the flea market in person, we were not taking any chances on running into those men again.

Ali suggested she go to the flea market to see if the men were still there.

"No, the one man that attacked me might recognize you" I warned, "It's better to be safe than sorry. Besides, we are getting better deals on line".

Ali nodded in agreement, "I know, but sometimes it's nice to go shopping".

Chapter 11

"It's been three months", growled Bill into the phone. The man on the other end must have been saying something harshly because Bill's ears and cheeks turned beet red. "How long are you going to keep us bottled up here looking for needles in a haystack?" Again Bill listened intently then hung up the phone.

Jeff gave Bill a look of disgust. Bill growled, "He says he knows it was with the last shipment and wants up to keep looking".

"Looking for what and where? That junkman didn't keep records. The item could have been purchased by someone passing through town. Doesn't that jerk have any brains?" Complained Jeff.

"He's paying the bills. I guess he's entitled to call the shots", said Keith as he stuffed another donut into his mouth.

Chapter 12

The slender blonde woman quietly strolled behind the man on the phone. When he slammed the phone down, she began to massage his shoulders.

"How can you be so certain there was a ring in the estate items? Hasn't all that stuff been in storage for decades?" she quietly whispered.

"It's here in this diary. That old broad wouldn't have written something that wasn't true. People didn't do things like that way back then", validated the man.

"Yeah", thought the blonde to herself, like people didn't know how to lie, right.

The blonde slid the diary from the man's hands and began to read the diary.

It is a Solomon day today, my beloved husband is dead. My nephew has come only to leave again. I feel so alone. All I can do is cry. My friend from the church has arrived. She speaks to me but my mind cannot comprehend her words. I can only think of my poor husband.

Daniel returned home briefly. He gave me his ring. Daniel told me the ring is a key to a treasure and instructed me to keep this a secret from everyone. I am to hide the ring until he returns or when the battle in which he is choosing to fight is over. I am not certain the area will be safe any time soon. I fear for my dear nephew. I promised and must protect this secret. I have a plan to make others believe I no longer have Daniel's ring. I didn't wish to let Daniel know that the gardener had been eavesdropping on our conversation. The gardener has always been a devious soul. The gardener didn't realize I could see him in the wall mirror as he stood outside the window. I will discharge him immediately upon my return, after I take care of this ring matter.

I discharged the gardener. I feel unsafe in my own home. The servants are wandering around. I see them watching me. The gardener must have said something to the other servants. I trust no one.

My husband is buried. I think only of how he lies in the cold ground. My thoughts wander from the loss of my husband to my fear for Daniel. I wish Daniel would send word of where he is or when he shall return home.

It has been months and I have had no word on the battle or where Daniel may be. I pray he is safe. My heart aches. I have written a letter to my niece in Ireland, Daniel's sister. I request she travel to me. I ask only for companionship. I will pay her passage to travel here. I hope to receive a response from her soon.

I received a letter from my niece, Elizabeth. She informs me she is making arrangements to come as soon as she can attain passage to England. She will come. I feel my spirits lift as I will not be alone.

It has been over six months since Daniel has left. Elizabeth has not yet arrived. I am in such a state. I cannot eat, I cannot sleep.

My heart pains so and I can barely move without becoming short of breath. I have asked the maid to collect the doctor. Oh, but my heart pains. I wish the doctor would arrive.

I could see the look of finality on the doctor's face. Although the doctor has assured me I will recover, I believe I will soon be with my beloved husband again. My heart.

"That's it?" questioned the blonde woman," just four pages of goofy notes".

"You aren't getting the whole picture", stated the man, "She was protecting the ring. There was something about the ring that hides a treasure. Something of great value. A secret. I need to find that ring".

"Then what?"

"It depends on the ring".

"Surely someone must have found the treasure by now?"

"Not if the secret is hidden. That is all I can figure. It must be of great value or the two of them wouldn't have gone to such lengths".

"You don't know that someone didn't find the ring and the treasure after that last entry".

"The woman must have died before she could pass on the message of the ring and the treasure. The ring must have been in the estate sale that was with this diary. The only reason the diary is with me is because my sorters know I salvage old books".

The blonde woman could only nod her head and smile.

Chapter 13

"Give me some idea on what you want us to do. It's been six months and we still haven't found anything. Whoever may have bought the ring you are looking for, may have been passing through the area. Do you expect us to sit here and collect money from you forever, looking for something that may have been melted down for scrap?" asked Bill.

The man on the other end spoke but Bill only looked more agitated. "Look, we are stuck in this state with no leads, and no way of knowing if the ring even came over. Who knows if it was packed with the other estate items you bought?"

The man on the phone seemed desperate. "Ok, we'll look through Charlie's things one more time. If nothing pans out, then we'll come back home".

The other men heard Bill and they moaned in unison. Another go over at Charlie's place. They have been through his stuff so much they almost have it memorized.

"What if Charlie's place has been sold?" asked Jeff.

"Then we say we went through it again and didn't find anything", answered Bill.

"Why don't we say we went through it and don't", stated Jeff.

Bill smiled and said, "Smart man".

Chapter 14

When I awoke, my breath caught in my throat. Lying in bed next to me was the man I had been dreaming of. The man I had come to know as Daniel. I quietly tip-toed to the telephone and dialed 9-1-1. It seems like hours but only minutes had passed when the familiar red and blue lights flashed through my windows. I slowly and quietly opened the door. The same police woman that had arrived before, was once again responding to my distress call. I could only point in Daniel's direction.

The police woman and her partner neared the bed. The female office went to nudge Daniel but he opened his eyes before she had a chance to. Daniel suddenly disappeared. The female officer was startled and uncertain what had happened stated,

"What the hell just happened?" Her partner looked at her and then looked at me. I stood frightfully still with a slacked jaw.

I didn't know what to do or say. The police had no idea what to put in their report.

"Miss, we aren't certain what is going on here. Obviously, we all saw something. I'm not certain if there was a reflection or if there is something in the air that causes hallucinations. There is nothing we can really do."

All I could do was whisper, "I understand".

As the officers climbed into their squad car, the female office commented, "I have no idea how to write this one up"!

Chapter 15

"You bought a dog?" asked Ali. "Yes, he is the cutest thing. I thought it would make me feel safer if I had a watchdog around when I was sleeping or in the shower. He is a roly poly little guy. His fur is so soft. He has short brown fur and the largest brown eyes you've ever seen in a dog".

"What did you name him?"

"I haven't named him yet. I thought maybe you could help me pick out a name".

"A dog should be named by different criteria. Location, personality, looks, etc. "

"Hmm, maybe you are right. He looks like a little bruiser. Maybe I should name him Dempsey, like the boxer. "I laughed.

"I can't wait to see him. How about we get together next Sunday?" suggested Ali.

"That sounds great. I can make lunch over here and we can work on a quilt while you're here", I replied excitedly. Ali confirmed and mentioned how she had recently purchased more bulk material.

"I'll bring over a few bolts so we can use it for the next quilt".

I could hear Ali was speaking to me, but all I could do was focus on the dog. The dog was looking as if he was watching someone walk across the room. Then the dog began to wag his tail and sit up as if to beg. Goosebumps began to form on my arms.

"Dempsey, come here boy", I called.

The dog continued to wag his tail. The dog rolled to his back and seemed to be enjoying a belly rub by an invisible entity.

"Ali, I'll have to call you back".

I gathered up all the courage I could and spoke aloud, "I know you are here. I am a bit nervous about you being here and I can't see you".

Daniel materialized before my eyes. I slightly choked as he appeared and with shaky legs, I found a chair to sit down on.

"I am sorry Ma'am. It appears I keep causing you distress".

"It's not so much you are causing me distress, it's the whole situation".

"Situation?"

"I have no idea who you are, why you are here, and it kind of creeps me out that my dog can see you and I can't and yet you are clearly here".

"My name is Daniel".

"Why are you here?"

"May I first learn what your name may be?"

"Oh, sorry. I didn't think. My name is Emily".

"I'm not certain as to where I am and have even less knowledge of why I am here".

"You are in Michigan".

"Is that a city?"

"No" clarified Emily, "it's a state in the United States".

"Is the United States one of England's boroughs?"

"England. No. Michigan is a state in North America. Are you from England?"

"Yes, I am from England. You say, I am in the Americas? How did I get here?"

"I have no idea. Maybe you are a kindred spirit. Maybe your remains were accidently brought to our shores. Honestly, I have no idea how you got here or why you are here. I only know you have been appearing in my home for the last several months" I admitted.

"My remains?" Daniel stood solemnly as the news of his own death impacted him.

"Oh, I am sorry. I guess I thought you must have known you were a spirit or ghost. How else can you be appearing and disappearing as you have been?"

"I apologize Ma'am if I have caused you to be put out. I am uncertain why I am here or how I came to be this way. I must confess, I have been here for months. I have been observing you and monitoring you to ensure your safety".

"My safety? Then you know about those men?" I questioned.

"I remember a man behaving unjustly. I did intervene to prevent him from causing you further harm. Why did he attempt to assault you?"

I hadn't noticed that I had grown less afraid of Daniel and now sat facing him.

"I'm not sure. I do have my suspicions, but I could be way off base".

"Off what?"

I smiled, "I am sorry. I didn't think about the language barrier between our countries. It means I was in error. What is the last thing you remember?"

Daniel stopped. "There was a battle. I was attempting to join our town folk to protect our people from the invading forces".

"What else do you remember?" I asked.

"I remember the moon was a mere sliver. I was riding in the dark of night. That is all I can recall". I could see Daniel was straining to pull information from his memory.

I walked over to my bedside table. I picked up the ring and returned to the couch.

"Does this look familiar"? I was surprised when Daniel picked up the ring.

"Oh!"

Daniel looked at me with a puzzled look, then looked toward the door.

"What has frightened you, Ma'am?"

"H...H…How can you pick up the ring, if you are a...a…a spirit?" As I was asking him questions, I could feel the blood drain from my face.

"Ma'am, I am as confused about this entire dilemma as are you. I can only say to you, that I daily discover things I can and cannot do", confessed Daniel.

I stood. "I need to make some tea. I think it may calm my nerves. Can YOU drink tea?"

"I haven't tried to eat or drink", stated Daniel, as he stopped to contemplate that he hadn't noticed he hadn't eaten or had a beverage in days, months, years, or decades.

"I am sorry," I stated," I seem to be causing you some distress too".

"It is not you, Ma'am, it is the situation. I am at a loss as to why this is happening. I am uncertain for what purpose I am here".

I gulped down a cup of tea and realized the tea was not helping.

"I think I need something a little stronger to settle my nerves". I went to the refrigerator. The bottle of whiskey was empty and sat chilling on the shelf of the refrigerator door. I sighed as I turned the empty bottle upside down to ensure it was truly empty.

"I need to go to the store. This entire situation has me totally unnerved". I grabbed my purse and keys. I looked at Daniel. "Do you want to ride to the store with me"?

"Ride? You have a carriage"?

"Well, a carriage of sorts".

Daniel followed me out of the house. I locked the door then showed Daniel the car.

"It's small, but it gets great gas mileage".

Daniel looked more puzzled as he stood outside the car. I leaned over and opened up Daniels car door from inside. Daniel looked hesitant but climbed inside.

"You'll need to close the door so I can drive", I instructed.

Daniel pulled on the door handle and the door slammed shut. Daniel pushed on the door. It held fast. Daniel pushed again with more force. Again the door held fast.

"It's ok. I will show you how to open the door when it is time to get out".

Daniel was getting nervous. I put the keys in the ignition and started the car. Immediately the radio blared a wild and loud song. Daniel dove over me.

"It's only the radio" I stated.

"I apologize, Ma'am, I thought you were in danger" exclaimed Daniel as he moved back into the passenger seat.

I turned the radio off. "That sound is music".

"THAT sound is music"? Questioned Daniel with a discussed look on his face.

"Yes, it's modern music. Could I ask a favor"?

"Ask Ma'am, I am at your service".

"Stop calling me Ma'am. My name is Emily".

"I am not use to using the familiar for someone I barely know". Replied Daniel.

"Barely know. You have slept in my bed. You have been staying in my home for months".

"True. I do see you have foundation to your words, Emily".

"Thank-you, Daniel".

As I drove down toward the main street, I began to explain how cars were invented and how Henry Ford started producing a fleet of cars annually. Other car manufacturers built factories and now there are cars or automobiles as they are properly called everywhere. I began to point out the different modern inventions when Daniel suddenly disappeared. I was freaked. I slammed on the brakes.

"What just happened"? It took me a few minutes, but I managed to gather my wits and continued onward to the store. At the mini-mart, I purchased some vodka, orange juice, Jim Beam, and some cola. I didn't realize it until afterward, just how much alcohol I was purchasing.

When I returned home, Daniel was there.

"Why did you disappear on me"?

"It happened without warning. I had no control over what happened, or why I found myself suddenly back here".

"It doesn't make sense. You were at the flea market when that man tried to attack me. That is further away than the mini-mart".

"Ma'am, pardon me...Emily, I am at a loss. I know not why I am here, why I cannot leave when I choose, and why I can appear when you seem to need me".

"Do you think you are somehow assigned to me? Sort of like a guardian angel or a body guard"? "If that were true, why did I suddenly disappear when I was with you"?

"That's right. What was different when I was at the flea market"? Daniel and I were both stumped. I knew how I felt and that was totally confused. I certainly could see how frustrated he was over this crazy situation. He somehow managed to keep all his frustrations inside. That in itself made me annoyed. I felt as if I had to always ask question after question or make random guesses making me look like the idiot at times.

I don't recall when it was that I finally became so accustomed to Daniel being around that I was no longer skittish or had the strong urge to down a pint of alcohol in any form available. He came to be a much cherished part of my life. A part that I could not share with Ali or anyone else for that matter for they might think me eccentric or plain old crazy. I only know I felt safe knowing he was there.

I had no clue where Daniel went when Ali would visit. I did stop asking Daniel to go places with me. I did however decide to put the ring on a chain and wear it as a necklace, for fear it would become lost or stolen. Daniel and I at this point had not deduced he and the ring were somehow connected. He and I had come up with some strange theories.

One theory was that he appeared to me when I was in trouble. He was like my guardian angel. He rationalized that since he had only appeared recently and not throughout my childhood, that the guardian angel theory was invalid. I suppose he was right in that respect. As a child I was a tomboy and seemed to get into a ton of trouble. Daniel had never showed.

A second theory was Daniel was somehow connected to Charlie. With Charlie dead, he was passed on to the last person

Charlie had interacted with. This theory was full of holes. If Daniel could defend me, why then could he not defend Charlie.

It wasn't until months later that Daniel made a comment that triggered the connection between him and the ring. He and I were again discussing theories. Theories that were lame at best. He finally showed some emotion and loudly shouted, "God, tell me why I am anchored here". The word anchor made me realize, Daniel did have an anchor. We only needed to discover what it might be.

He and I set out one day. Yes, in the car. He didn't disappear. I was dumb founded. I had not brought anything with me and yet he continued to sit in the passenger seat well past the mini-mart and on. This situation was more confusing than ever. I arrived at Ali's place. Daniel, of course, disappeared. Ali and I spent hours working on the next quilt. When Ali went to get up from the floor, she used the coffee table as leverage and accidently tipped the entire tray of beverages, sandwiches, and the large jar of honey right into my lap.

Ali quickly grabbed a towel and rushed with me to the bathroom.
"I'll grab a pair of my sweat pants and a top for you to get into. By this time the honey, tea, and mayonnaise had soaked my pants, underwear, and shirt. I needed to take a shower. Whispering so Ali would not hear, "Daniel, I am going to take a shower, I will meet you in the car".
I had to assume Daniel heard me. Everything came off. I was in the shower for what seemed hours. Honey is not an easy substance to remove once it gets into crevices and hair.

I dressed rather quickly after my shower. Ali had grabbed my clothes while I was showering and tossed them into her washing machine. I had not realized that my necklace with the ring was among the gathered items. I finally finished the shower and told Ali, I needed to get home. Although her loan of clothes was generous, I felt uncomfortable going "commando". Ali and I laughed. She totally understood.

Daniel was in the car, but did not appear until we had turned off of Ali's road. We were half way home when he disappeared again. I assumed he would be back in my house when I arrived. Dempsey was so happy to see me. I asked Dempsey, where is Daniel. Dempsey looked past me as if to wonder the same thing.

It wasn't until Ali phoned to tell me she had found my necklace among my clothes in the washing machine that I put the pieces together. I told Ali I would come over and pick up my clothes and the ring. Although Ali attempted to insist I wait until another day, I was concerned Daniel would appear before Ali and frighten her to death. As I approached Ali's place, I found her crying hysterically and well on her way down her front steps.

"What happened?" I asked.

"That man that was at your place is here. He must have followed you. What are we going to do?" cried Ali. I attempted to get Ali to go back into her house. She refused. I had to spill the entire situation to her outside on her front lawn. She looked at me as if I were crazy. I told her, that I finally discovered Daniel's anchor. It must be the ring. It seemed Daniel would belong to whomever was the ring bearer.

Ali told me where my belongings were. I went inside and brought out everything, including the necklace and ring. I called Daniel. He appeared. Ali shunned away.

"It's ok, Ali. He isn't going to harm anyone. He is somehow stuck here until I can figure out what is going on. If that is even possible". Daniel seemed as distressed as Ali. I knew it was because he didn't expect to be traded off. I realized I needed to control what I said about Daniel's situation around him. I think he felt like a prisoner. He was unable to do much of anything. He was limited on where he could go. He refrained himself as to whom could see him.

His life, if I may call it that was out of his control. Yes, Daniel was a prisoner. The question was, for how long? I began to think of how long Daniel may have been waiting for someone to find out a release for this prison of his. Could it have been centuries? I began to feel for Daniel. I don't think I could keep my sanity, what little I do have, if I had been a prisoner.

I decided to find answers for Daniel. I purchased a laptop and contacted a locale internet server. I was soon, up and running with the internet at my home. I spent a lot of waking hours researching. I did find it was rather difficult to explore the history of other countries on the internet unless you knew what to look for. If you knew what to look for, why would I need to look? It was frustrating at best, but I continued on my newly appointed quest.

I found Daniel was just as interested in learning as I. We found ourselves sitting side by side in front of the computer for hours at a time. Elation could be heard in his voice when we discovered something close to home. His home, which I had to assume existed decades ago. I can recall the night we discovered the battle in which he must have been killed. Although we did not uncover a list of those who participated or those killed, Daniel was so excited he placed his arms around me and hugged me dearly.

I had long since stopped thinking of Daniel as a spirit but thought him as a friend. However; this closeness brought unexpected stirrings within me. I didn't know what to do. It was Daniel that took the initiative. Slowly we drew apart. We may have been only inches apart when Daniel placed his lips upon mine and pulled me closer yet. Some may think me crazy, but it never entered my mind that I was kissing a ghost. I had the same feelings as any other girl may have when a man she was attracted too, took her in his arms.

I hadn't realized I had felt these feelings toward Daniel until that day. To be honest, I hadn't thought about much before that day. We didn't think about the research any longer, we had our minds on other things. I didn't think twice when Daniel rose and led me to my bed.

Again, I had stopped thinking of Daniel as an entity but instead a full blooded man. He proved how tender and loving he was that day. We made love passionately and only with the desire to please each other.

Memories of that night still burn within me. When I close my eyes, I can still feel his lips trailing down my neck. A strong shiver ran through me as he touched me in ways I had never been touched before. I could feel an ache building deep inside. Daniel slowly undressed me as he continued to explore my body. My breathing increased and I could feel myself gulp for air as Daniel explored regions slowly yet attentively. I groaned in ecstasy when Daniel's body laid on mine. He looked so deeply into my eyes with each motion.

Although I have had other boyfriends in my life, none could compare with Daniel. When I think back on that day, I feel as if I am still lying within his arms.

He insisted my long hair be taken down and free when we made love. He thought a woman should be free to do what pleases her when in bed with her lover. I know it sounds vain but I think Daniel was pleased with me too. I could only imagine that women of his day were so prim and proper. I am not certain you could say that of me when we made love. He took hours ensuring I was totally aroused before he would allow himself fulfillment. I truly enjoyed the hours lying in each other's arms after making love. Feeling totally loved and safe must be the best feeling in the world.

Chapter 16

Daniel and I slept until Ali called. We must have been awake for most of the night. My head was very groggy when the phone rang. It took me a while to realize the noise was actually the telephone. Ali was wondering if we could go to the flea market. I thought her crazy.

"What do you mean, do I want to go to the flea market?" I asked. I know she must have heard the doubt in my voice.

"Since we know Daniel will be there to protect us, why can't we go?"

Apparently Ali had been thinking of Daniel as a powerful force. She admitted later that when she had finally calmed down enough to think straight, her first thoughts were of Daniel having the ability to ward off those men who had pursued me. I asked Ali to come over to discuss the idea.

Daniel voiced he felt it was a reckless idea to place ourselves in danger for a piece of cloth. Ali sighed. I know how she felt. I missed being able to do what we had done for so many years. She and I enjoyed shopping and finding deals. We bought what others no longer needed but still held great value. I tried to make Ali understand.

"Just because Daniel helped me the last time, does not mean he can take on three thugs at the same time. It doesn't mean we wouldn't be hurt in the process. I feel the same as you. I miss spending time walking through the flea market. I miss our adventures of finding a stash of material. I miss having lunch at that little café we found last time when we were finished with our shopping".

Ali sighed. "Why can't we at least have lunch at the café? Do you think they are the kind that would sit and eat in a place like that? It is more for college kids".

"What do you think Daniel? Would you mind accompanying Ali and I if we have lunch at this little out-of-the-way café?" I could see Daniel wasn't pleased. It must have been the gentleman in him.

"I shall be near in the event of any trouble. I, however; will not be able to physically join you."

Ali was so happy. "At last, we can actually go out. I have been getting so cabin crazy!"

Ali offered to drive. Daniel sat in the back seat. I think he felt safer there. He was still quite skeptical of the radio after his first encounter in a car.

Ali ordered a tuna sandwich which presented with a home-made roll, coleslaw on top of the tuna, and raisins. There was a side of cottage cheese with fruit sprinkled on top. Ali had a glass of pink lemonade which was made with sparkling water. I could tell she was really enjoying our outing.

I ordered a white chicken sandwich. I was pleasantly surprised to find the chicken breast had been deep fried, de-skinned, and thinly sliced. Fresh crisp lettuce had been placed on top. A layer of homemade mayonnaise was added. There were carrot slivers added to the mix. It was great. I was so glad that Ali and I had come. As I sipped on my ice tea, I told Ali how we should come here weekly since we could not venture out to the flea market. Her eyes lit up and a huge smile crossed her lips.

As we climbed into the car, Daniel appeared. He said he had been exploring the area and found America to be unlike England. Homes and gardens were abundantly scattered about. In England, estates allowed the land to be worked but without being seen. The estate homes had a beautiful entrance way and the gardens were more for leisurely walks. Vegetable gardens were planted quite far from the main estate. In American, it seemed the gardens were mere steps from the back of the home.

"He's an English ghost? How did he get here?" questioned Ali.

It was as if Daniel and I had the same thought strike at the same time.

"We need to find out who brought the things over from England."

Ali pulled into a gas station. Ali and I always got out together. I paid for half the gas and usually picked up some snacks at the mini-store that was attached to the gas station. It wasn't long before Ali and I climbed back into the car. Neither Ali nor I had noticed the beat-up old clunker of a car pulling into the gas station as we began to drive away.

"Hey Bill, isn't that the girl from the flea market?" asked Jeff pointing to Ali's car.

Bill continued to drive through the gas station and followed Ali's small red civic. Ali wanted to stop by her place to pick up a sweater in case she stayed too late at my home. Although the days were quite warm the temperatures were beginning to drop lower in the evening. The beat-up old clunker drove by the red civic.

"We'll come back when it gets dark" stated Bill.

Ali and I had begun working on new quilts. Ali loved to watch me work. I didn't think myself any great sewer, but Ali thought my stitching was outstanding.   As my clock chimed ten, Ali yawned. "I need to get home. I have a lot of paperwork to do tomorrow at work. If I'm too tired, I know I won't be able to read well."

I knew that was true. Ali worked as a paralegal and had to do a lot of reading.

I worked as a secretary of sorts. My little cubical sat in a room full of other little cubicles. I barely knew any of the other secretaries. Lunch was assigned by a stoic matriarch named Josephine, and she didn't like employees socializing. She had a list of rules and no one, I mean absolutely no one liked her. I called her the evil one. She had made comments how two girls had gotten sociable and discussed salaries. That was on the list of rules. The two girls were fired. That incident was enough to make the rest of realize we would not be socializing.

For the most part, I enjoyed my job. I typed a lot of interesting things. I worked for a book publisher. It was wonderful that I was able to read the books before they were published. Of course, I couldn't discuss any of the material with anyone outside of work. I also had time to myself when my projects were completed. I usually packed my lunch and ate at my desk. Others raced to the cafeteria for lunch. I had omitted the travel time and was able to enjoy my lunch instead of trying to consume it within minutes. It must have taken at least five minutes to get to the cafeteria. Stand in line, get the food, pay, and then sit down to eat. There was another five minutes to get back to the cubicle. Not a lot of time to enjoy a lunch when there was only thirty minutes allotted for a lunch break.

I made decent money and was able to afford my house payment and bills. It provided me enough to save for retirement and yet have enough to order material and notions for my passion, quilting. I may not have been the best quilter, but my donations had made me somewhat of a local hero. The money had brought in enough annually to help the church provide for hungry children. That alone made my heart sing.

I had put my quilt away and was lying out my outfit for work tomorrow when Ali called. She was hysterical. Someone had broken into her house. The back door had been shattered and all her belongings scattered about. The odd thing was none of her valuables were taken. I told Ali I would come get her. I didn't want her driving in her present state of mind.

When Daniel and I arrived, I could see that Ali had gathered up some personally items. "Did you call the insurance company?" I asked.

Ali could only nod as tears flowed from her eyes.

"Ok. What should we do about the back door?" I asked.

Ali managed to squeak out that the neighbor was going to nail up some plywood for her. The neighbor also told Ali he would keep an eye on her place until she returned tomorrow morning. The police had shown up and voiced they thought it may have been a young teenager looking for cash or an initiation task assigned in order to join a gang. They had given Ali a business card, similar to the one I had received, and told her to call if anything was known to be missing. A police cruiser would also make regular rounds through the area to keep an eye out.

After we drove to my place, I told Ali that I had decided to take tomorrow off and help her through this crisis. Ali was grateful. It took a while to get Ali calm enough to rest. Daniel was the one who helped calm her.

"I promise Ma'am, that I will keep vigil over you and Emily all night. No harm shall come to either of you." I have to admit, I felt better knowing that Daniel was here. Our sleeping arrangements were switched. Daniel would have to take the couch. Ali and I would sleep in my queen size bed. Dempsey snuggled up to Ali. I know that made her feel better.

Chapter 17

"Yeah, I think we found her," stated Bill to the man on the phone. "We saw them at the gas station. We searched the home of the blonde girl. Her house wasn't too big. We took everything out of the cabinets and drawers. The closets were emptied out too. It wasn't there. We are going to watch her house. I think her little friend may have the ring. It seems where one girl is the other is close by. The boys and I will check in with you in a couple days."
The man on the other end must have been pleased. No yelling could be heard.

Jeff and Keith were not happy. They had to sit in the parked car and watch Ali's house. It was a lucky thing Ali's home was near the corner. Jeff and Keith were on the adjunct street and down the block. They could watch the house without any suspicion. It was a rough assignment for Jeff. Keith loved to eat. Keith was grossly overweight and the sounds that came out of his body were disgusting. Jeff hated to sit in the car with him. The windows could not be lowered much and Jeff was obligated to endure the stench that radiated throughout the car.

Keith didn't seem to mind the odors. He did have trouble peeing in a bottle. They didn't have a bathroom nearby and couldn't leave their assigned post. Jeff was disgusted at Keith and everything he did. He belched, choked on food, and farted. Every few minutes there came a sound of some sort. If the blonde girl did not come home soon, Jeff would be forced to kill Keith just for the peace of mind it would bring.

Chapter 18

Ali called her neighbor from Emily's house. The neighbor had placed the plywood over the broken door and informed her the insurance adjuster had been by. The adjuster had left forms for Ali to complete and return via snail mail. The adjuster had mentioned a two hundred and fifty dollar deductible but wasn't specific on the whole situation. Ali thanked the neighbor profusely. "Well, the insurance man came by. I guess I should call someone to replace the door. It will take me all day and night to get that house in order. I am so afraid to go back there." Confessed Ali.

"You aren't going back there alone," I stated," Daniel and I are going with you. Aren't we Daniel?" Daniel smiled and nodded yes. I could see Ali take a deep breath.

"You truly are my best friend Emily!" I thought Ali was going to cry again so I walked over and gave her a huge hug. Daniel came over as well. When he hugged us both, I could see the look of surprise in Ali's face.

"I could feel him. I could actually feel him hug me." Ali stammered. Daniel and I laughed. Soon Ali was laughing along with us.

I packed some trash bags, empty boxes I had collected, and some cleaning supplies to take with us. It wasn't long before the three of us had arrived at Ali's house. The place was a total wreck. Pictures were tossed off the wall and broken. The dresser drawers were askew and all the former belongings randomly cluttering some part of the floor. Even dishes taken out of the kitchen cabinets were dumped onto the floor. The kitchen drawers had been removed and dumped onto the table. The clutter was too much for the table top and spilled over onto the floor. Ali's clothes from the closet had been ripped out, hangers and all. The clothes were tossed into random piles without any rhyme or reason. The clothes she had in her bedside dressers were also tossed onto the floor. Anything personal, like photos or jewelry was tossed into the mix. It was one huge mess.

"I'll be doing laundry for weeks", claimed Ali. I could see the look of frustration and disappointment on her face.

"We can take anything that needs washing to the Laundromat down the street and wash and dry them all at once".

Ali seemed to brighten up when she realized half the work would be completed in a few hours. We bagged up anything washable and loaded it in my car. It took us a while to get the place in order. Ali would need to buy new picture frames and glass wares. Whoever broke in was certainly handy at breaking glass items. We ran the vacuum to get rid of the obvious glass slivers. Ali emptied the vacuum bag once and reran the vacuum over the areas with the broken glass just to ensure it was all collected.

The door was replaced by two construction type workers who finished the job in under three hours. A dead-bolt lock was placed on the door with the matching lock placed on the front door. An additional security door replaced the front door as well. Ali asked the men to ensure the windows would be safe.

The men stated, "The windows are triple pane. It is very difficult to break in with those type of windows if the window locks are secured".

I could see the stress leaving Ali's face as the knowledge that her home would be safe was confirmed. The men left when Ali and I had just about completed most of the cleaning and organizing. I suggested we go down the street to the pizza place and get a pie and a couple sodas. We could put all the clothes in the washing machines at the nearby Laundromat and then return to put the clothes in the dryer when we were finished with dinner.

So off we headed. The car was packed with garbage bags full of Ali's clothes, linens, and other washable items. Poor Daniel had to sit in the back seat half smothered with bags. We were lucky that only one other patron was at the Laundromat. We filled eight regular washers and one over-sized washer. Ali told the matron that we would be back after getting some dinner. It should be before the clothes were in the rinse cycle.

Ali and I took a booth in the back of the pizza joint. The booths had high backs and this allowed for Daniel to join us.

"So, when did you two become an item?" asked Ali.

Daniel and I looked at each other. I had just taken a huge bite of pizza and almost choked.

"What are you talking about?" I questioned.

"Oh, come on," replied Ali," I keep seeing Daniel hold your hand, you two are always sitting so close to each other, and even now, his arm is around you."

I gulped. It was true. I hadn't realized we were acting just like a regular couple in love. I was at a loss for words.

Suddenly I blurted out, "for God's sake, Ali, you are talking about a ghost." I regretted those words the minute they crossed my lips. I could feel Daniel remove his arm from my shoulders. Daniel looked at Ali and spoke very calmly, "there has been no discussion of any involvement between Emily and I. It is true, I have grown close to you both. I hope I did not offend anyone by my actions. I shall refrain from becoming so familiar again." Then Daniel disappeared.

Ali was stunned. I was in shock. I knew I had screwed up and had inadvertently hurt Daniel's feelings. After Daniel left, I didn't feel much like eating. Ali just nibbled a bit but like me, she really wasn't eating. We decided to pay and leave. We flagged the waitress over and paid the bill. Ali and I made a quick pit stop in the ladies room and then opened the exit door to leave.

Ali and I began walking back towards the Laundromat. As we passed the alley, one of the men grabbed Ali's arms and pulled her into the darkness of the alley way. I screamed for Daniel as I ran toward the spot I had last seen Ali. The alley was extremely dark. The street lamp did not face toward the alley. The stores that made up the alley did not have their back lights on or had not had back lights installed. I moved slowly hoping to get adjusted to the darkness.

The huge man named Keith grabbed my hair and began pulling me further into the darkness. I could see Ali kicking and swinging her arms at the man named Jeff. Daniel was at my side. I am not certain what Daniel did but I found Keith had released my hair. I ran to help Ali. Jeff was still afraid to get too close to her. I saw an old floor lamp near the dumpster just a few feet away from Ali. I grabbed the lamp and began swinging it at Jeff. I know I smacked him rather hard in the face. I knew this because I heard an awful crack and blood began to flow. Jeff grabbed his handkerchief and placed it to his nose. Although injured, Jeff did not stop trying to get near Ali.

I swung the lamp again, this time, the lamp made contact with the right side of Jeff's face. Jeff fell to his knees. Ali and I both smiled. I hit him on the top of his head and he went down. Daniel was still trying to maneuver Keith. Keith had so much weight he couldn't move well, but the extra weight gave him more ump when he went to punch. I kept hold of the lamp and swung the pole high and it landed hard on Keith's head. Keith stopped. He staggered a bit, then fell forward, landing onto his face.

We ran to the Laundromat and asked the matron to call the police. Soon there were four police cars. Ali gave her account of what happened. I gave mine. As far as I could tell, Keith and Jeff weren't talking. The police seemed to know who they were. The police asked Ali and me to come to the station. Ali and I told the police officers we had bought all of Ali's things to the Laundromat after the break-in. We still needed to finish drying the items. The matron said she would take care of it for us. Ali gave the woman enough money to cover the drying charges and we headed to the police station.

"Should we tell them about the ring?" asked Ali.
"We have too. If we don't, it won't make sense why those men came after us." I replied.
Daniel agreed. I could see in his face the worry of what would happen to him if I did not get the ring back. He was sacrificing himself for us. I can't tell you the emotions that I felt that day. I only knew that I had stronger feelings for Daniel than I truly would admit to Ali.

Ali and I gave our names and addresses. We explained the entire story to the police about our weekly trips to the flea market, finding the ring, and how the men had begun to harass me when I went back to the flea market. Somehow they had found us and that is when the altercation in the alley occurred. Somewhere in between all that, someone, I had to assume it was them that had broken into Ali's house looking for the ring.

I slid the ring off my necklace and handed it to the police officer.
"It looks pretty old," was all the officer would say. He placed the ring in a funny looking grey bag with my name and address on a slip that went inside but was showing through a clear plastic square in the bag. No one could tell what was inside the envelope but it was now considered evidence in the burglary case. The ring was not only evidence to the burglary case but also to the altercation in the alley.

When Ali and I walked out of the police station, I stopped and called to Daniel. He didn't come. My heart was so heavy. Ali kept trying to apologize to me. If they hadn't found her, they wouldn't have found me. I had no idea how they had found Ali. I was more worried about her safety at this point then that of how they found us.

"Ali, those men may be locked up, but that doesn't mean they don't have friends. You should stay at my house for a while".

Ali said she was going to go stay with her folks. I couldn't blame her. I wished I could get away and not have to worry either. I drove Ali to her home so she could pick up her car. She and I both kept an eye out to ensure no one was following us. When I got home, Dempsey was so happy to see me. He kept jumping and wagging his tail. I walked him and then fed him. He bedded down early and I was alone. I don't think I have ever felt this alone before. I could only describe it as feeling loneliness and sadness to the core of my sole. Even my home didn't feel like home without Daniel. I'm usually not a crier, but I have to admit, I laid on my bed and tears ran most of the night.

Ali called me the next morning to check in. She could tell I had a late night.

"You sound awful. Do you want me to come by?"

"No, I am just worried about Daniel", I admitted.

"He must have been a great guy in his day. I hope he gets to find his way home, wherever that may be", replied Ali. To be honest, I hadn't thought about what would happen if we discovered Daniel's history.

I had just gotten off the phone and taken Dempsey for his walk when I heard something odd. "Daniel?" Nothing. I knew I must be losing it. Little sleep and being a nervous wreck doesn't make good cognitive ability. I jumped in the shower. When I stepped out, I was almost floored. Lying on my couch was some woman. She looked like a hooker. I walked slowly into the room, glancing around at what I could use for a weapon, you know, just in case.

"About time you turned off that water. I thought I'd have to wait here all day", stated the hooker.

"Who...oo, are you?" I asked.

"I'm Sondra".

"How did you get in and why are you here?"

"Don't go to pieces on me, I have a message from Daniel". I must have blanched, because Sondra said I should either sit down or get something strong to drink.

"How do you know Daniel?" was all I could mutter.

"I ran into him at the jail. He wants you to keep searching the computer for clues. He said he is keeping an eye on those guys to make certain you are safe".

"He spoke to you and you weren't afraid?"

"Why would I be afraid?"

I wasn't sure if I should tell Sondra that Daniel was a ghost or not. "Daniel doesn't speak to a lot of people." That comment should be safe, I thought to myself.

"Geez, you don't know Daniel", then she laughed. She laughed really loud and hard. I was getting a bit ticked.

"Did Daniel say if he wanted me to come to the jail and talk to him?"

"He didn't say. I'll find out next time I see him".

Now I had to sit. She was seeing Daniel. Was I just another one of his girls?

"Where do you live? " I asked, hoping to get more information on Sondra.

"Good one", she said and laughed. She must have thought me crazy but I could only stare. "Well, it's been real. I'll ask Daniel about you visiting. If he wants you to come see him, I'll come tell you". Then she got up and walked through the wall.

I kept hearing the ringing but it didn't occur to me that it was the telephone. I found myself on the floor. I don't know how I had gotten there but here I was, flat on the floor. My right ear hurt. When I lifted up my head, it felt like it was splitting. I felt my ear and it felt moist. I looked at my hand and saw blood. It was then I realized I must have fainted. Then memories of Sondra and our conversation flooded my mind. That was how she knew Daniel, she was a spirit too.

I don't know about other women, but I was angry. Had Daniel been nuzzling up to a female ghost and sent her to talk to me? Giving me instructions to keep searching for his past. I felt my blood boil. I wanted to drop kick the computer into the back yard and let Daniel know he would have to find his own past. Then I thought back at how I had spoken at the pizza place then I realized, I was being stupid and emotional. If I was in Daniel's place, I would use every ounce of help I could get. But did he have to make friends with another woman? Men!

Ok, Emily, what did we learn? I know I talk to myself. I do it all the time. It's an odd habit, but tossing ideas around out loud helps me think. New York. I discovered the auction houses that purchased items from overseas was in New York. I need to start researching auction houses.

Chapter 19

"Hello. I know this is going to sound a bit crazy. I am calling from Michigan. I am attempting to find the auction house that a friend of mine has been purchasing items from. His first name is Charlie."

"You'll need to contact the business office, this is the warehouse."

"Ok, can you give me the number to the business office?" After receiving the number, I was surprised to hear a person on the other end of the telephone.

"Second chance auctions, may I help you?"

"I hope so. I am attempting to find the auction house a friend of mine has been using. I am calling from Michigan. His first name is Charlie. Is there any way you can find out if he purchased items from you?"

"I am not sure if I would be allowed to give out that information. I will need to check with my boss first. Can I call you back?" stated the woman receptionist.

"I am going to be in and out today. I will need to call you back if you tell me what would be a good time".

"I'm not sure when the boss will be in today."

"I see, well, I will call back first thing tomorrow morning then."

"Ok, suit yourself. The office opens at 0900", stated the receptionist as she hung up.

I had to be smart and stay safe. I realized at that moment, fear had taken over my life and I was paranoid that someone may find me. I wasn't going to take any chances. It's odd that one experience in life can turn your whole world around. I hated the way things had changed. I missed shopping in the flea market. I missed finding bargains of material and notions. What do I have now? Paranoia, fear, anger, and loneliness. Not much of a trade.

Chapter 20

"Guess who just called us? Asked the blonde to the boss.

"You know I hate those stupid guessing games of yours. Just spill it" he said.

"Alright, honey, don't get your tighty whiteys twisted. That girl. The one with the ring. She wanted to find out if we sold anything to her friend Charlie."

"What did you tell her?"

"I said I'd have to find out from the boss if it was alright to give her that information", the blonde smiled a huge toothy smile.

"You did ok, kid. Did you get her telephone number and address?"

"She wouldn't leave it, but she is calling you back tomorrow."

"We need to find out some way to track her."

Chapter 21

I continued to call auction houses that were listed in New York until 5 pm. I didn't give up, but I kept getting voice mail after voice mail. I figured I wouldn't find out anything from a machine, so I'd have to call back. I honestly was at my breaking point. I hated not having information about Daniel, and knew he was communicating with other women, well you know what I mean. I don't know if it was my hormones or what, but I made a decision to wait until after court to start the search regarding the ring again.

That evening, Ali stopped by.

"I know you said you were ok, but I had a feeling you are hiding something. You miss him, don't you?" I wasn't sure if I should tell Ali that Daniel was making friends or sending old friends my way. She might freak knowing there were ghosts everywhere.

"I admit it was quiet here without him", that was truthful without revealing too much.

"I wish we could find out how long it will take before this case is going to go before the judge. I hate the waiting and not knowing", stated Ali.

"I know what you mean. Do you think we need to get a lawyer? Those men went after us but what if they lie about us?"

"The officer I spoke to, told me those guys had a record. I don't think we have to worry about that. I am just concerned about the ring and Daniel".

"Then we just have to sit and wait", stated Ali.

Two days later, Ali and I received the notification of the court date waiting for us in our mail boxes. Four weeks later, Ali and I entered the court house. I was nervous. Ali and I sat near the front so we could see and hear better. It seemed like it took all day before those goons were escorted into the courtroom. As the first guy sat in the questioning chair, I saw him look and nod at someone in the court audience. I glanced to my left. Shivers ran up my spine. A middle-aged man was staring at me. I tried to act as though I was simply looking around, but the man never took his eyes off me.

I whispered to Ali that I felt this man had something to do with the goons attacking us. Ali was great. She didn't look immediately, but slowly turned to appear as though she were looking at me. She said the man was saying something to another man sitting in the row ahead of him. Ali also said the staring old man had a young woman with him. The woman seemed brainless as she kept messing with her nails and looking at herself in a compact mirror. The woman was dressed like a wealthy prostitute and chewed gum like a cow chewing its cud.

I don't know if it was because I was distracted by Ali or freaked out at the old guy, but I didn't hear the judge's decision about the goons. The goons didn't look happy and their lawyer seemed a bit niffed. The old guy was shaking his head as he looked at the goons. I turned to say something to Ali, but she had moved to the end of the aisle and was speaking to a young police officer.

The officer seemed pleased to be speaking to Ali. Ali had a bit of a flushed face but turned back and pointed to me. The police officer nodded to Ali. Ali wiggled her way back to me and said, "That police officer said he would walk us to our car. I told him how you and I were a bit nervous about this whole court issue".
All I could think of was, "God bless you, Ali".

It turned out the young police officer's name was Paul. He stayed with us and guided us through the process of retrieving the ring. He then walked us to our car. I pointed out that I was worried that someone would follow us once we left. Paul offered to get into his vehicle and follow us home. I can't tell you the elation I felt with that offer. I nodded yes, and Ali, thanked Paul for his generous offer. Ali explained that she would need to drop me off at my home before going to her house.

Paul said he didn't mind. I think Ali was happy. She couldn't seem to get the smile off her face. Ali and I piled into her car. Daniel appeared as soon as both car doors were closed and locked.
"Ladies, it is a happy day that I am finally, once again in your company". Ali just about jumped out of her skin.
"Daniel, you could have warned us you were going to appear".
Daniel and I laughed. I had to secretly wonder, how Daniel could have possibly warned us without surprising us, but I didn't want to make Ali angry.   Ali pulled out of the court parking lot onto the street and we noticed a small blue car was also pulling out. Ali was in the right lane of a four lane road and going slower than the posted speed limit. The little blue car stayed behind us.
"Do you think that blue car is Paul?" asked Ali.
"I can't tell", I replied. I asked Daniel if he could see who was in the car. He could only reply a man. Since Daniel hadn't met Paul, it was

difficult to determine if the driver was the police officer or not.   I told Ali, to try and get stopped by a red light. Once stopped we could see who was in the car behind us. It wasn't until we drove several miles that the opportunity arose. Ali stopped at the red light. The little blue car did not approach but lagged behind quite a distance.

Ali was getting a bit nervous and so was I. I told Ali we needed to go to some place public. Ali turned right and headed for the strip mall. Traffic was mild. I didn't see the usual number of pedestrians walking on the side walk either.

I recognized a restaurant and told Ali, "I think stopping for coffee would be a great idea. We can make certain it's Paul in the car, or we can call the police and let them know someone is stalking us".

Either way, we are all safe. I didn't think how Daniel would handle this situation. He suggested he stay in the car and see who was in the blue car. Ali and I entered the restaurant, but kept looking back to see if we could spot who was in the blue car. Ali was pale and I could feel her trembling as we walked inside. We managed to attain a table. I ordered three coffees and told the waitress we would be having a friend join us shortly. The waitress turned our cups over and said she would make a fresh pot.

The blue car soon pulled into the parking lot. It parked further away. It seemed like hours went by before the driver's door opened. I could tell it was a police officer. I told Ali, it must be Paul. She sighed with relief. We were both surprised when the man entering the restaurant was not Paul. The man approached us and said he was following us for our own protection.

"Where is the other officer?" I asked.

"He was still on duty", replied the unknown officer.

Ali smiled but then suddenly grew pale.

"Emily, I think I'm going to be sick". I jumped up and took Ali by the waist and made our quick excuses to the officer. Ali surprised me as we entered the women's bathroom.

"Emily, that officer is a fake. He is wearing Paul's name tag".

Now it was my turn to turn pale.

"We need to get to the car. Daniel can help us", I blurted out.

"How can we get to the car? There are no windows in this bathroom", whispered Ali as we both looked around the small room in vain.

"I'll go out and tell that man you have some medicine in the car. I will see what Daniel wants to do".

"What if that man comes in here after me?" cried Ali.

"He won't. He wants the ring. I have the ring". Ali looked as if she were truly going to be sick.

"That man doesn't know that", stated Ali.

"I'll make sure he does before I go to the car". I wasn't certain how I would accomplish that feat but I was going to give it my best shot.

The fake officer was sitting in our booth sipping on a cup of steaming hot coffee. I walked up to him. I prayed he wouldn't notice I was shaking. I told him I needed to get Ali's medication from the car. I told him, I shouldn't have left her medication or my ring in the car.

"You never know what people will do if they think there are valuables in a car", I said. I must have sounded believable because the fake officer offered to go to the car for me.

"No, I know where Ali keeps the medication. Plus you need to keep an eye out for anyone who may be following us". I could see he was trying to come up with another idea on how he could accompany me to the car.

"It would be wise to bring in any of your valuables", the fake officer said.

"Good idea, I think I will", I replied as I walked toward the door.

I could feel the fake officer's eyes on me as I slowly walked toward the car. I opened the door, and suddenly found myself being shoved into the car.

"Hello, my dear". I turned and it was the old man from the court house. Daniel had not appeared and I was getting worried.

"Who are you and what gives you the right to put your hands on me?"

I looked straight into the old man's eyes. He smiled.

"It's not funny" I said, "I suggest you get out of my way. I have a police officer that I am having lunch with and he won't be happy that his friend is being assaulted".

The old man laughed. It wasn't one of those little polite laughs. It was a huge belly laugh.

"What is so funny?" I asked. The old man simply pointed to the restaurant door. The fake officer was escorting Ali out of the door and to the car. His arm was around her waist. I could see that Ali was having trouble standing on her own. Fear had gripped her and she couldn't seem to focus.

"You see, my dear, that officer is actually MY friend. Now, where is the ring?"

I sighed. I felt the battle was lost.

"What ring?" I stammered.

"We both know from your recent court date that you have the ring. Let's not play games now".

"Why do you want the ring so badly? It isn't your family heirloom".

"It holds a secret to a great treasure. That treasure will soon be mine. You, my dear have held me up long enough. Now hand over the ring".

I leaned across the driver's seat and opened up the glove box. A small brown bag was sitting inside. I placed my hand in the bag. The old man yelled, "Hurry it up, we haven't got all day".

As I stood up, I sprayed the pepper spray into the old man's face and then aimed at the fake officer. Although he was a few feet away, it hit its mark. Ali shoved the fake officer away from her and ran to the passenger side of the car. I jumped into the driver's side as Ali climbed into the passenger side. Ali and I both slammed the doors shut and hit the lock button. Ali shoved the keys in the ignition and I started the car.

"I am so glad you bought that pepper spray".

"I was so scared after my house was broken into. I was worried someone would attack me in my car too", admitted Ali.

"It sure came in handy".

The old man and the fake officer were wiping their eyes and coughing up their lungs as I hurriedly backed the car out of the parking space. Daniel appeared and told me to stop.

I said, "No way", as I shoved the gas pedal to the floor. Daniel said he could have secured those two men. "And then what Daniel?"

"I don't understand what you mean".

"It would be our word against theirs. These goons have friends and more friends. Do you think this situation will ever end? You stopping these two will not stop the problem".

"The elderly man is the one guiding the others. If we stop him, it ends", exclaimed Daniel.

"How do you know that?" I asked.

"He said you were holding him up long enough. He is the one that was trying to get the ring. We need to discover why he has such an interest in the ring and how he came to know so much about it."

I hate to admit it, but Daniel was right but at this point, I just wanted to get away and be safe. I had dragged Ali into this mess and now I had to worry she would get hurt. Her home was already broken into and trashed. The fake officer had grabbed her from the lady's bathroom in a public place. These guys don't play by the rules. If Daniel had secured those men, then what? What if they got a hold of the ring? They would have control over Daniel too. I couldn't risk that.

I turned right at the next block then left at the block after that. I turned right at the block after that and then left at the block after that one. I turned left at the following block then right at the next one. I zigzagged through the area. I would stay off the main road, but would make certain no one was following us by not staying on one street. I would only be one or two blocks from the main street just in case someone did manage to follow us.

We finally made it to my house. I told Ali, that we couldn't get her things because the goons knew where she lived. She would have to wear some of my things.

"What are you talking about?" asked Ali.

"We are going away for a while. We need to come up with a plan. A plan that will stop those goons and keep us safe in the process".

Ali helped me pack enough clothes for the both of us. I packed some snacks, water, and dog food. Dempsey is coming with us.

"He can be our ears when we are sleeping," I announced to Ali.

I opened up my cookie jar and removed the cash I had stashed in case of an emergency. It was only 832 dollars but it would pay for a roof over our heads for a while. Ali grabbed my bag of quilting supplies as we started loading up the car.

"Why are you bringing that?" I asked.

"What else will we be able to do while we are hiding out?"

I hadn't thought about the long hours we would be spending sitting inside but Ali had. I nodded my approval.

I should have thought to bring a map. We drove and drove and drove. We started out on regular roads, then we entered into small highways. We took an exit off the highway and drove on main roads for a while. Then we would get back on a highway for a half hour or so and then take another random exit. I had no clue which area we ended up in. We were totally lost.

We finally saw a huge sign illuminating the sky above the trees: motel. I know I was exhausted. We checked in and paid cash for one room. Daniel suggested using his name to sign in. The room wasn't much to look at, but it had two queen size beds, a television, a microwave, a bathroom (which at the moment was the best amenity), a small refrigerator, and a coffee pot with two cups sitting nearby.

It didn't take Ali and I long to jump into our pajamas and scoot under the covers. Daniel stood nearby as Ali and I settled in. It wasn't until she and I both were on the verge of sleep that Ali sat up suddenly and said, "Where does Daniel sleep?"

In the rush to get to bed, Ali had taken one queen size bed and I the other. I didn't want to tell Ali the many nights that Daniel and I had shared a bed. Of course, that was before he began sending his spiritual girlfriend to my house. I was still niffed at him and I know he knew I was angry.

"Daniel, would you mind sleeping in the car?" I suggested. I could see the shock on his face.

"That is a sound idea, Emily. I can guard against intruders" he said, and suddenly disappeared.

Ali yawned and quietly said," He is kind of handy to have a round".

Although I had once thought that same thought that Ali had, I realized Daniel and his ring were the cause of all our current problems. My heart still tugged at how Daniel had blatantly sent another woman to my home. A woman who could have been spending every day and night with him.

Daniel never attempted to clarify that woman or his relationship to her. He had ample opportunity while Ali and I were packing as well as the long tedious drive to the motel.

I couldn't sleep. Ever have one of those nights where you just can't seem to shut off your mind. Your mind keeps running through all the events or tasks you did that day or still need to do? I kept thinking about Daniel. I don't know what time it was when I finally fell asleep. I didn't hear Ali wake up six hours later, or her saying she was going to find a local store to pick up some groceries. Daniel went with her. I had left the necklace with the ring on the bedside table and Ali put it in her pocket.

I woke up to a very quiet room. I saw the car and my necklace was gone. I assumed Ali was going for food. I made a nasty cup of coffee from the supplies offered in the room. The coffee hit the spot though and my brain woke up. I saw a newspaper outside the door of the room. A free paper for the occupants I assumed. I sat and read the paper. I enjoyed the quiet time alone. Then I saw it. The article that was on page eight.

Police officer, Paul Miller was assaulted in the parking lot of the county court house on Friday. Officer Miller was brutally struck in the back of the head by an unknown assailant. The blow caused what the doctors are calling, "an intracranial hemorrhage". Citizens are asked to contact the local police department with any information.

I had to tell Ali about the kind officer. I knew she would feel badly about asking the officer to escort us out to our car. It did explain how those thugs had managed to follow us and why the officer was nowhere to be seen. I gave Dempsey some dog food and used one of the disposable cups for some water. I was lost in thought when Ali came in.

"Oh, you are awake. I was wondering how long you were going to sleep. It sure isn't like the old days when you couldn't sleep at all," Smiled Ali.

She sat my necklace back down and began rattling off the items in the grocery bags.

I heard Ali say something about cold sandwiches, a few frozen TV dinners, and juice. I decided to wait until we had eaten. I would hate to have Ali get even thinner because I told her about the officer. Upsetting news always makes Ali anorexic.

I picked at one of the cold sandwiches and sipped on a small juice.

"What's with you guys?" asked Ali. I must have given her a dumbfounded look.

"You and Daniel have been waltzing around the room. When you are sitting down eating and he sits near you, you rise up and move elsewhere. You've done this several times now. What is going on?" I looked at Daniel. He had the same question in his eyes.

"Look, I'll take the paper and go sit in the car and read. You two can iron out whatever this is that is happening between you".

Ali grabbed the newspaper and left. Daniel sat on Ali's bed facing me. I felt angry and wasn't certain that lump in my throat would allow me to speak.

"Emily, what has happened to make you push me away?"

"Well, I didn't appreciate you sending one of your girlfriends to my house".

Daniel looked puzzled, then realized I was speaking about Sondra. "Sondra was a free spirit who offered to help me. She is not my girlfriend".

"And I should believe you because????"

"I don't know what character of men you are used to, but I can assure you, I do not toy with the affections of the woman I love."

"What did you say?" I was stunned. Did Daniel just confess his love for me?

"I am a man of character. I do not lie. I will not toy with your affections".

"Did you say, you loved me?"

Daniel seemed intensely frustrated. "Yes, I said I love you. I have loved you for a very long time. How could you not know?"

"You never said anything to me before".

"Woman, you can be so infuriating. We have made love. A man does not make love to a woman unless he loves her".

"That may be how things were in your day, but things have changed since then", I replied.

The door opened. Ali came in slowly holding the paper in her hands. "He's been hurt. It's all my fault".

I had forgotten to tell Ali about the officer at the courthouse. I raced to Ali's side.

"We need to decide what we need to do", I said.

"We have to let the police know about those goons that hurt him", stated Ali. Ali was looking more distraught by the minute. I looked at Daniel for answers.

"I suggest contacting the constable by messenger. Write down the specifics of the situation and explain about those men who injured the fellow who was going to escort Ali and you home".

"By messenger?" questioned Ali.

"We could drive an hour away and make a phone call to the police. We could give them the facts then return here", Ali injected.

"And then what? Wait and hope to find some bit of news in the paper?" I asked.

We needed to let the police know about those men, but Ali and I had to worry that we might be discovered by those thugs.

"We could write everything down and drive to the next town. We could hire a car to drop off the information", I suggested.

"That would work!" smiled Ali. I could see the relief on her face. She truly felt badly about that young officer.

"We need paper", I said as I began pulling open the drawers of the desks and dressers of the motel room.

"Hey, here is some motel stationery. We can trim off the address", stated Ali.

Ali and I had our plan, then Daniel spoke.

"After further consideration, I need to ask, if you went to the constable, would he and his fellow members not protect you?"

Ali and I looked at each other.

"Could we get to the police in our area without running into those thugs?" I questioned.

Daniel added, "Can you seek out a constable nearby?"

Ali and I hadn't thought of that. We had figured we would have to risk going closer to home, and in turn, place ourselves in close proximity of the criminals that had been stalking us.

Ali, Daniel, and I sat down to discuss what we would say to the local police. After we finally decided we had our facts together, we gathered our belongings and packed them in the trunk of Ali's car. We asked the motel clerk where the nearest police station was located. After convincing the motel clerk that nothing was wrong with the motel, he gave us the address and directions to a nearby police station.

Chapter 22

It wasn't long before Ali and I was escorted into the office of a Detective Powers. Ali and I took turns explaining the purchase of the ring, the stalking at the flea market, Ali's home invasion, the assault in the alley, the request to the police office named Paul, the pepper spray usage to get free from the goons, our escape, and our current dilemma on what to do. By the time Detective Powers had heard our story and asked all the questions he needed to ask, the entire day had gone by.

I could hear Ali's stomach growling. My stomach was chewing at my back bone too. "Would it be possible to order some dinner?" I asked the Detective.

Detective Powers stopped writing and leaned back in his chair. You could hear the mechanisms of the chair moan and creak as the grossly obese detective navigated his girth to the other side of the desk. He pushed a button on his desk phone and ordered someone named Beamer to come in.

The door slowly opened. A tall lean officer came in.

"Beamer, we need some dinners from the diner". Detective Powers turned to Ali and me, "You girls like anything special to eat or drink, or have any allergies?"

"Would it be alright if we ordered ice tea and chicken Caesar salads?" I asked "and a can of dog food for Dempsey?"

"Sure, sure", replied Detective Powers. Beamer wrote everything down then asked Detective Powers, "You're usual?" Detective Powers nodded yes.

The food soon arrived and everyone ate. I had to wonder if the detective needed to count his own fingers after he finished eating. He dove into his food so quickly and with such force. Then Detective Powers shocked me.

"You won't mind staying in town while we get this situation clarified?" He didn't really ask a question, it was more like an order with a confirmation of our agreement without us really given the option of agreeing.

I wasn't certain why the detective felt we needed to stay in town. I had no idea where we would stay for that matter. Then the detective spouted off to Beamer.

"Beamer, make arrangements at the B & B for these gals".

Detective Powers had Beamer escort us to Main Street. There in the middle of the block was a beautiful old Victorian home that had been converted into a bed and breakfast. Beamer signed Ali and me in, using some special client code. We then climbed the stairs to the second floor.

"Oh, and Detective Powers wanted me to let you know, he'll take your dog home with him. They don't allow dogs here. He'll return the dog to you in the morning", said Beamer.

Ali and I were given separate rooms. Ali's room had a huge antique bed with huge pillars attached to the ceiling. A lace bed ruffle was topped with what looked like an antique quilt with matching pillow shams. The furniture in the room was all antique. It was like stepping back in time. The pictures on the walls demonstrated scenes of yesteryear. Women in long dresses, hair up on top of their heads, and parasols were the main subject of the paintings. It was such a peaceful room.

My room was more masculine in décor. It had a sturdy bed with an old sea chest at the foot of the bed. Two portholes were on one wall. One of the portholes was a window but the other porthole was a mirror. The dressers were made of hard wood and varnished with dark brown shellac. The rugs that were placed randomly across the wood floors were earth tones.

I wanted to explore more of the bed and breakfast, but I was exhausted. Beamer mumbled something about Ali and I staying inside the B & B until Powers or himself came to retrieve us. It wasn't until after Beamer left that the questions began to fill my mind. Why did we need to stay in town? Why were we ordered to stay inside? Lastly, why did we need to be retrieved? Ali and I had explained the circumstances regarding the police officer at the courthouse. We had given that Detective Powers all the information about those goons that we knew. The court house knew two of the goons. Surely the police had ways to find who was associated with one criminal with another. I began to yarn. I needed sleep.

I had just slid into the tub of hot, soapy water when Daniel appeared. I just about jumped out of my skin.

"You scared me". I shouted as I sunk further beneath the bubbles.

"I am sorry" Daniel replied," I shall wait for you in the other room."

I felt badly but I couldn't help but still feel angry at Daniel.

When I finished my bath, I found Daniel sitting in a chair near the porthole window.

Daniel stood when I entered the room. "May I please explain why I sent Sondra?"

Sondra, I thought. I could feel my anger grow.

"Sure", I said, "why not". I knew inside he couldn't explain Sondra away, but I wasn't going to let him think I was one of those emotional women who never gave a guy a chance.

"Emily, with the ring locked up at the police station, I was limited as to how far I could go. Sondra was a spirit who was without limitations".

"I bet she was!" I barked back.

I could see the frustration in Daniels face. "I could have sent Mark, but I was afraid if a man you didn't know showed up at your house, it would frighten you more than if I sent Sondra".

"Who is Mark?"

"Mark is a man that hung himself to prevent incarceration. He offered to take you my message, but I was not sure I could trust him".

"What does that mean?"

"I was a bit jealous, I have to admit." Replied Daniel, "but I was locked away. I didn't know if you were safe or not. I didn't know if you may have recognized that I was the source of all your troubles and you may have been glad to be shed of me".

Now I felt totally ashamed of myself. I had been jealous and the whole time he and I were apart, Daniel had thought only about me and my safety.

"Daniel, I'm ashamed of myself. I missed you terribly when we weren't together. When that free spirit as you called her, showed up, I didn't know what to think. I felt you were making friends while I was home alone and worrying about you. I guess we both were in the same situation".

Daniel walked to my side and pulled me into his arms. "Am I forgiven?"

I started to smile but a yawn over powered my mouth. So I nodded yes. Daniel and I climbed into bed. I would like to say we made love, but Daniel and I just snuggled and slept.

I woke up to the aroma of fresh brewed coffee. I had no idea what time it was and it took me a while to focus my eyes. At first I was disoriented, then remembered the B & B on Main Street. Daniel was still sleeping. I turned and watched him as he lay in slumber. He truly was a handsome man.

Chapter 23

I finally decided to get out of bed. I woke Daniel and we dressed. Daniel could not stay "present" in the event people saw us. I told Daniel I was going to breakfast with Ali. Daniel said he would check the outside parameter of the house and meet me back in my room in an hour.

I walked briskly to Ali's room. Smelling the aroma of coffee had my stomach churning for food. I knocked on Ali's door. No response. I knocked again.

Ali meekly said, "Come in".

When I entered the room, I was totally caught off guard as someone grabbed my arm and swung me forcefully into Ali's room.

Ali began apologizing. "I am so sorry Emily. He threatened to shoot you if I didn't tell you to come in".

All I could think of, was how had he found us?

"I can tell you are surprised that I found you", the boss man said," I have a friend in your local police station. It's good to have connections".

Ali and I looked at each other in disbelief.

"Come on. We're all going out together. My boys are waiting for you two in my car. We've been waiting a long time to have a long talk with you two. I also want to reciprocate for your little pepper spray gift you gave me".

I kept looking around for something to grab. I wanted to yell for Daniel, but I wasn't certain where Daniel was or if he could hear me. Ali looked really scared. I knew she was worried. I was the one with the ring and knew it held secrets. Ali knew once these goons found out she was of no use; she was of no value. I was scared too.

We exited Ali's room. Ali led the way, I followed Ali and the man was behind us. He made certain to let us know he had a gun in his pocket and he had used it before. As Ali and I slowly descended the stairs, I heard something behind me. I turned to see Daniel grab and toss the goon down the hallway. "Run Ali", I yelled.

We scurried down the stairs and raced to the front door. Ali's car was parked just a few hundred feet away. Ali and I jumped in and locked the doors. I thought that was kind of instinct because a gun could easily have hit us through a window. Ali pulled out quickly and I could feel myself breath again.

"Where should I drive to?" asked Ali.

"Just drive fast and we'll figure it out as we go", I replied.

Soon Daniel was in the car with us. Ali smiled when she saw him. "I never thought I'd be happy to see a ghost", she exclaimed.

Our joy was short lived as Ali soon told us she saw in the rearview mirror, a black colored car heading our way. The car was traveling quickly and Ali was certain the car would catch up to us.

I looked around, hoping to find a road to turn onto. There was none. We had to stay on the main street heading out of town. I told Ali to forget about the speed limit. We want a police officer to notice us. She pushed her foot down firmly on the gas pedal. The little car lunged and we sped up. At least we were keeping the black car from catching up to us.

I kept looking around for some way to escape the car that would soon catch up to us. Then I saw it. It wasn't a road, per say, but a drive-through for a tractor. I told Ali to turn right onto the make-shift road. It was bumpy, but we at least bought us some time. The rows of corn weren't fully grown, but they were high enough to hide Ali's small car. I kept an eye out to see how far this dirt road went. It seemed to go on for at least a mile or two. To our dismay, the corn field stopped and was replaced by soy beans.

I could see the black colored car about a quarter mile down the main road. It had kept on going straight, but was now stopping.

Apparently someone had been watching and had seen Ali's car emerge from the rows of corn. I saw the brake lights and then the car made a U-turn.

"Ali, they've seen us. We need to find a way to get back to town and to the police station". I could see Ali was trembling. Then I noticed a creek up ahead. The creek ran through the farm. To the left the farmer was using the water from the creek to water his crops. I didn't see the farmer, but I could see fences and animals a few hundred feet down to our right.

"Daniel, I know you don't know how to drive a car, but could you hold that wheel that Ali is holding right now? Keep that wheel straight and push on the pedal her right foot is on?" "For what purpose" was his reply?

"Daniel, if Ali and I get out and hide in the creek, you can drive down the road and then meet us later. You can't get too far from me and the ring, but I estimate you can lure those guys at least ½ mile or so from us". Daniel agreed to try.

Ali stopped the car and she and I ran to the creek. Daniel pushed on the gas pedal. I could see the fright on his face as he manipulated the car to go straight and fast. I didn't have time to watch Daniel and his first time behind the wheel. Ali and I ran, then half crawled toward the fences. The water was cool and the bottom of the creek was muddy. It wasn't really deep, but the ditch that surrounded the creek water was deep enough to hide us if we bent over and ran in a squatted position.

Ali and I ducked low when we heard the black colored car coming closer. They had passed by us without looking in the creek. I could see the driver and two other men in the car. Ali and I kept going. We reached the fences. Pigs. We had no choice but to climb in with the pigs to hide ourselves. Ali was the first to slip on the slimy mud filled ground. Her blonde hair was soon dripping with muddy water. We kept running, then I slipped. I know it wasn't appropriate to laugh, but I couldn't help it. The pigs would run towards us when we fell. Pigs of all sizes. Huge grunting pigs and what must have been their offspring.   The little pigs were really cute and had the situation not been so serious, it would have been fun to stop and pet them.

"Emily, look," declared Ali as she pointed ahead, "a house". We both ran in the direction of the house. The back door was open but a screen door blocked the way. I didn't knock. I ran inside and scouted around for the telephone.

 "I'll stay out here and keep watch for those goons", said Ali. She hid behind the small porch that led to the house. I found the telephone in the kitchen and dialed "911".

"What's the emergency?" came a voice on the other end.

"My friend and I are being hunted by murders. Please contact Detective Powers. We need protection now". I heard Ali urgently call me. I hung up. I didn't have a chance to let the dispatcher know where we were or what town Detective Powers was in.

I ran out. I realized I had muddied up the house with mud. The farmer would not be very happy that we helped ourselves into their home. I would have to make a point to write them and apologize later. I raced to Ali's side.

"Do you see the goons?" I asked.

"No, but I think someone is in that building over there". I strained to look. The building was a barn. Maybe the owner was there. I told Ali we needed to see if it was the farmer. He may be able to help us hide. The farmer may even have a shotgun too. She and I headed for the barn.

When we reached the barn, we saw Daniel.

"Daniel, are you ok?"

"I didn't know where you and Ali would be, so I began looking here in the barn. I knew you had to be close", he replied. Daniel said that Ali's car slowed down and stopped when he popped out of it. The men in the black car got out and looked around and under the car. Daniel said they seemed really puzzled because they couldn't figure out how the car managed to get so far without a driver. Daniel said he overheard the men say that Ali and I must be hiding in the corn field and drove back there to look.

The corn field was huge, but it ended up only a few feet away from the farm house. That meant that the goons would soon be nearby. We had to find a place to hide or we would be caught. We quickly searched the barn for some place to hide that we would never be found. Nothing. The few bales of hay would not hide anyone. We opened the back door and Daniel smiled. Horses. We can ride away. Ali and I looked at each other.

"Have you ever ridden a horse", I asked Ali. She shook her head no. Daniel grabbed a saddle from the barn and hoisted it onto the nearest horses back. He put a bit in the horse's mouth and instructed Ali to climb on. She shook her head, "Not me".

I knew this was our only way out. I quickly climbed into the saddle with Daniels help. Daniel then saddled another horse for Ali. Ali gingerly climbed into the saddle. The horses were very tame, thank goodness, and Ali and I felt better knowing that Daniel was beside us.

"I will ride with Ali for a bit", he said. I knew I had to be brave. Ali was relieved. Daniel climbed up behind Ali and soon the horse was trotting to the end of the fence. I was a bit confused. There were no gaits on that side of the fence. Then Ali's horse jumped over the fence. My mouth must have dropped. Daniel waved his hand, instructing me to join them.

I knew if I stayed behind I would surely be killed. If given the choice, I may as well die trying to escape. I started the horse trotting by mildly kicking the horse with my feet. The horse soon leaped across the fence and joined Ali's horse.

"We need to make haste", Daniel said. We took off and headed back toward town. I looked back but did not see the goons. I didn't know what to think. We rode for what seemed a long time. I could tell the horses must have felt they too had run a long time, as their hair had become drenched and matted down. My thighs needed a break. I felt as though I was being ripped in two. I wouldn't admit this to anyone, but I also felt as though I may have developed blisters on my butt from the saddle rubbing against my skin. Now I know why people have special clothes to ride in.

Then I heard it. It was faint at first, but the sound grew steadily louder. It was a police siren. Ali must have heard it too. I could see the look of relief on her face. Daniel made himself scarce. Detective Powers, and Beamer were soon flagging us over to the area of the field they had driven the police cruiser. Beamer was assigned to return the horses to the Gorman farm and detective Powers would escort us into town. Detective Powers told us to refrain from saying anything until we reached the station. He wanted to ensure our stories were the same.

Chapter 24

Once we arrived at the station, Detective Powers spoke quietly to two other officers. One of the officers took Ali into a different room. Detective Powers motioned for me to join him in his office. The other officer began making phone calls.

"Please don't let anyone know we are here. Don't even contact our local police department. Those goons said they had a friend there and that is how they found us".

Detective Powers called out, "Morgan, hold those calls for now". The officer acknowledged the order and hung up the phone.

"It seems you've had a busy day", said Detective Powers.

"Detective Powers, Ali and I were almost abducted at the bed and breakfast. Someone must have seen what the boss man was doing and attempted to stop him. In the struggle, Ali and I raced to her car and took off in hopes of getting away".

"Why didn't you come here?" asked Detective Powers.

It was true. The thought had never occurred to Ali or myself.

"In all the excitement", I said, "we didn't' think."

So for the next few hours, I explained to Detective Powers what had occurred. Of course I had to leave out Daniels role in the escape from the bed and breakfast and how he drove the car to lure the goons away from our direction. I could only hope that Ali had done the same.

Detective Powers ordered everyone lunch. Ali and I ate while Detective Powers read what I could only believe was Ali's side of the story. It seemed Ali's and my story were almost identical. The only exception was how the car managed to drive away. Ali had the forethought to say she had put her purse on the gas pedal to ensure it would continue to move. I had said the car seemed to drive on its own when we jumped free.

Beamer returned and told Detective Powers that the Gorman's were not happy about having their horses stolen. However; given the circumstances, they agreed not to press charges against Ali and I. Beamer said that the Gorman's were going to bill the police department for horse rental and the cost to clean the mud from the kitchen. Detective Powers nodded his head in agreement and told Beamer to obtain a blank invoice from accounting. Beamer disappeared.

"The Gorman's recovered your car, but we are going to impound the car." Ali and I looked at each other. "Those men, whoever they are, recognize your car. We need to move you to safe house and we'll put guards on you this time".

"How are we going to find out who is this goon's friend in my local police station?" I asked.

"Right now, that isn't the problem. All of that will be resolved when we find out what is at the bottom of all this mess", declared Detective Powers.

Beamer was assigned to drive Ali and me to the safe house. We drove for about an hour and 45 minutes. We exited off the main road onto a gravel road, then shortly thereafter, onto a dirt road that led into a thick section of woods. We crossed over a log bridge and finally arrived at an old log cabin. I could hear crickets and frogs. The scent of earth and plants filled my nose. Ali sneezed. We were pleasantly surprised when we entered the cabin. It was beautifully decorated. The walls were varnished light colored wood. The windows had shutters inside and out. The ceilings were very high. Each door was made to look like logs standing on end and put together with rope.

The lamps looked rustic as if they were the old oil lamps. The sofa and chairs were also made of wood with specialized cushions sewn to compliment the size. Rugs sporadically were placed around the room. The rugs looked like Indian's had hand woven them. A huge fireplace was made to separate the living room from the dining room. It was magnificent.

Beamer suggested Ali and I pick a room that housed two beds and stay in the same room together for safety reasons. I could see Ali look at me as if to say, do you mind? We chose a huge room in the back of the cabin. The room had two queen beds and an attached bathroom. The bathroom had a large sunken tub with water jets. After that horse ride, I knew my body would enjoy a nice long bath.

There was a large window that overlooked the back yard. The yard led to a small pond that was fed by a tiny stream. In the far distance you could see a river that winded around and through the woods. Ali said she was going to raid the kitchen for something to drink. I told Ali I was going to take a long, hot bath. Ali pulled the shade closed on the window. I read her mind. She wanted to make certain no one saw us.

Beamer knocked on the door. "I stopped and picked up your belongings from the bed and breakfast before we left town. Where do you want your belongings?" I opened the door and Beamer lugged in our mess of scrambled things. He left without a word. I sorted the jumbled mess into Ali's pile and my pile. I then found my pajamas and undies. I went into the bathroom and started the bath water. Ali brought in a large glass of ice-cold cola. I thanked her and sipped the cool beverage feeling it slowly travel down my throat. I told Ali was I was going to soak for a while and then take a long nap. Ali said she was going to catch up on some missed television shows while I was soaking. Ali left our room. I stepped into the bathroom. It felt good to get out of those smelly clothes. I felt ashamed I hadn't asked Ali if she wanted to bath first but I needed some time to think. I needed to contact my job. Ali needed to contact her parents and her employer. I couldn't fathom how this situation would ever end? We had no idea why those men wanted the ring or how they even knew about it.

I don't know how long I had been in the tub when a quiet knock was heard on the bathroom door.

"Emily, I need to bath too", whispered Ali. I stepped out of the tub and began drying myself. "I'll be out in just a few minutes". I cleaned the tub with a cleanser I found under the sink and rinsed the tub. It no longer shown the ring of mud that had washed off my body. I made certain there were towels and a washcloth for Ali, then unlocked the door.

Ali looked a bit distressed when I opened the door. "What?" I asked. "

"Paul is coming here!" exclaimed Ali.

"Ok," I said, "and?" I could see Ali was getting nervous. Then it dawned on me, Ali liked the officer. Ali had always been very shy. She wanted to make a good impression on this officer.

"Well, you'd better get in the tub so we'll have time to do your hair and make-up", I said.

Ali smiled and ran into the bathroom. I sighed. "Ali, you'll need some clothes to put on when you're done".

Ali came out of the bathroom with a pink hue on her face. She sheepishly smiled and rummaged through her things. It wasn't long before Ali and I were both sitting in the living room and Officer Paul, Detective Powers, and Detective Triplett had arrived.

Although I had wanted to remain in my pajamas, Ali convinced me to put on street clothes. It seemed appropriate when speaking to detectives. I threw on a pair of jeans and a tee shirt and grabbed a pair of flip-flops. I had told Daniel about the meeting so he wouldn't feel left out of the loop.

I don't recall when I fell asleep. I was sitting on the couch. I had given Detective Triplett the same information that was given to Detective Powers. I mentioned how I was very unnerved that the lead crook had admitted he had someone inside the police station that was providing him with information. Detective Triplett had deduced that if that information were true, the person was not a police person but ancillary help. The next thing Detective Triplett said was that it was possible to use that information to set a trap for those men who had attempted to kidnap Ali and me.

When I woke up, I was on the couch and someone had placed a blanket over me. I could see Officer Beamer in the kitchen making a pot of coffee. I stretched and slowly walked to the bedroom that Ali and I would be sharing. I barely started to open the door when Daniel stopped me. He must have seen the puzzled look on my face. He motioned me to close the door and follow him down the hallway.

"What is so important that we couldn't talk in the bedroom?" I asked.

"Ali and Officer Paul are in there", Daniel replied. My jaw must have dropped.

"Are you sure?"

"Yes, Ali was talking to the officer and like you, fell asleep. The officer kept staring at Ali while she slept. He covered her up and laid down next to her. He must have fallen asleep too. I felt it would be only proper to prevent them embarrassment".

I nodded in agreement but where would I sleep now. "I guess it is back to the couch. Do you plan on getting any sleep, Daniel?"

"I will keep awake and watch the house. Detective Powers and Detective Triplett left Officer Paul and Officer Beamer here. Since Officer Paul is asleep, I believe I will replace him in his sentry duties".

"Daniel, I feel so badly about how things have turned out".

"It is I who should apologize. If it were not for my ring, you would not be in danger".

I had to admit it were true, but I was not going to let Daniel feel guilty. It was then that I realized I loved him.

It didn't take me long to fall back to sleep once I laid back down on the couch. I fell asleep to the aroma of fresh brewed coffee and soft music playing. I had assumed Officer Beamer had turned on a radio. The next morning, I awoke to Officer Paul chatting with Officer Beamer. Officer Paul had said he had stayed with Ali as she was afraid to be alone. Beamer shrugged and sipped on his coffee. "Powers and Detective Triplett will be here soon. They are bringing breakfast for everyone", mentioned Beamer.

Ali emerged from the bedroom dressed and looking more rested than she had in days. I sat up and rubbed my eyes. "Why didn't you wake me?"

"You were sleeping so well, I didn't have the heart to disturb you", replied Ali.

I stretched and told Ali I needed to take a shower. I wasn't certain where Daniel was, but I hoped he would meet me in the bedroom. Ali joined the officers in the kitchen. Officer Paul stood up and offered Ali a cup of coffee. Ali blushed and nodded yes. He sat next to her and they began to chat.

I had just stepped into the shower when Daniel appeared. "Geez, you have to learn to announce yourself or something. You startle me every time you just appear like that", I scolded. Daniel climbed into the shower with me. It felt wonderful to have him wash my back. He seemed to enjoy shampooing my hair. Of course, we kissed and touched while cleaning ourselves. When Ali knocked on the bathroom door to make sure I was alright, Daniel and I knew it was time to get dressed.

Just as I was joining Ali, Officer Paul, and Beamer in the kitchen, Detective Powers and Detective Triplett entered the cabin. Dempsey came running to me. I had missed that little guy. I scratched his ears. He rolled to his back and whined until I scratched his belly.

Everyone ate breakfast, even Dempsey, then sat down to discuss the situation.

"Officer Triplett believes we can funnel false information to the snitch in his department to catch those crooks". Ali and I smiled. I could feel the tension begin to ease in my shoulders.

"That is the good news. The bad news is, we would need bait to lure them".

Ali and I looked at each other. "Bait?" I asked.

Detective Triplett spoke, "We can put in a call from Detective Powers, announcing you will be returning to your home tomorrow or the next day. We will assume the snitch will pass this information on to those men who attempted to kidnap you two".

"So you don't need us to get involved, right?" asked Ali.

"We were thinking it would be nice to place your car in the driveway, but I am not certain that will convince those criminals that you are there. They may need to see you enter the house".

"I'll do it, but Ali stays with Officer Paul. I don't want her mixed up in this anymore. It's my fault all this happened. I bought the ring and she has been put through enough", I exclaimed.

"Em, you can't do this alone. I wouldn't feel right letting you do that. Plus, won't those goons be looking for both of us?" questioned Ali.

Detective Powers and Detective Triplett said they would need to work out the details and we girls would need to stay put until a plan was gelled. Whatever that meant.

"Couldn't you get a few police women to ride in Ali's car so it appears to be Ali and me?" I asked.

"The problem with that idea is someone in the department may tip off whoever is funneling information." Said Detective Triplett.

I hadn't thought of that. Detective Triplett had handled more cases than Ali and I. I had to assume he knew how to handle these types of cases.

"What do we do next?" Ali asked.

We need to get a hold of a few chosen police officers to set up a perimeter around your home. Once all that is in place, we will have you head home. We can contact Detective Powers to notify you when to leave," instructed Detective Triplett.

Ali and I didn't know what to say. I know I was nervous. Ali and I went into our bedroom and Daniel appeared. "Do you think it will turn out ok?" Ali asked.

"I will be with you during the entire trip. I will protect you in every way possible", exclaimed Daniel.

I could see the tension ease in Ali's shoulders when she heard Daniel would be with us. I had to admit, it made me feel a whole lot better too. The only thing that bothered me was, what if someone shoots at Ali or I while we are driving. Daniel couldn't protect us from that. I simply looked at Ali and gave a half smile.

"Do you think we'll be safe?" asked Ali.

"I sure hope so. The police are doing everything they can. Daniel is offering to be with us throughout this ordeal. I guess we are better off than others that may have been in a situation like this." I replied.

"What do you mean?" Ali asked even more puzzled now.

"Daniel is here to help us. How many others can say a spirit has protected them in the past and has offered to continue as a body guard?" I smiled.

Ali nodded. I knew she was still frightened, but at least she was feeling a little more confident knowing Daniel was on our side.

Chapter 25

Ali and I kept our minds busy by working on the quilt that Ali had brought along with us. We were nearly completed with the top of the quilt when Beamer said Detective Powers was going to be arriving soon. It had taken Detective Powers and Detective Triplett two days to get a plan orchestrated. Ali and I sat listening carefully. Detective Powers sat at the dining room table. He spread out a map that covered 2/3 of the table.

"If you take these side roads that I have marked, you should not encounter much traffic. The less you are seen the better," he said. I looked at the map. We had to cross over that river that flowed in the back of the property several times. The river, it seemed, snaked around through the immediate and distant area until it divided into smaller streams that led out of the state.

"When do we leave?" I asked.

"Tomorrow morning, really early. Taking into account that many of the roads are gravel and have speed limits of 25 to 30 miles an hour, I suggest you leave at 0430,"instructed Detective Powers.

"Will one of the officers follow us? You know, to make sure we are ok on the road," ask Ali.

"I'm afraid that isn't possible. If by chance anyone does recognize your car, we don't want them to know you have the police involved."

I could see Ali was thinking of all the potential problems she and I could run into.

"Ali, if we are taking back roads, there is little chance that anyone that is looking for us will see us. We should be ok on the drive. It's the approach to my house that I am more concerned with", I stated.

"We have a group of men, plain clothes and in unmarked cars that have been strategically placed around the area near your home. They are watching for anyone that is, shall we say, of a suspicious nature. My men are instructed to run all plates that contain one or more men. We are making certain to keep you gals as safe as humanly possible", declared Detective Powers."

"I know I am asking for the impossible, but have we found out why these men want my ring so badly?"

"Detective Triplett has a man investigating the records of your friend Charlie. Charlie, it seems had purchased a lot of different items from the internet. That kind of search takes time. Charlie bought estate items in bulk. Weeding through all the invoices to find a ring, is going to take time", sighed Detective Powers.

"The ring would not be listed on any invoice. The ring was inside a jar of buttons. I purchased two jars of buttons and the ring was hidden inside one of the jars," I sighed. Geez, how many times can a person explain something?

"I'll give Detective Triplett a call and let him know the specifics. You have no idea why that ring is so important to those men?" Detective Powers asked.

"I wish I knew" I said.

Chapter 26

I know I was having a difficult time falling asleep. I could see Ali was tossing and turning as well. The last time I looked at my watch it was 1:30 a.m. When Officer Beamer knocked on the door, I just wanted to sleep. My head felt foggy and I had trouble getting my eyes to focus. I know Beamer was saying something, but I couldn't comprehend what it was he was trying to say.

Ali slowly climbed out of bed. "Did you want to shower first or do you want me to go first?" she asked.

"You go first, I can't focus yet".

I heard the water running and just wanted to lie my head back down. Daniel grasped my hands and began pulling me from the bed. "Let me sleep five more minutes", I begged.

"Emily, you need to wake up. You have a long drive a head and the longer you delay, the darker it will be when you reach your residence".

"Ok", I replied. I guess I hadn't really thought about the time we would reach home.

"The darker it is, the more easily it will be for someone to hide", Daniel explained.

Suddenly my mind jolted awake. Now I understood what Detective Powers was trying to explain to Ali and me. We needed to get an early start to ensure we didn't lose daylight.

Soon Ali and I were sitting at the breakfast table, sipping hot coffee and stuffing toast and bagels into our mouth. Beamer loaded our suitcases and other random belongings into Ali's car. Ali and I both decided to use the facilities. While Ali went first, I coyly opened the door to the cabin. It was still dark out, but we were safe here. At least that is what Ali and I thought. No one should know we had stayed here or were leaving from this area. I still felt unsafe. While I had waited to use the bathroom, Daniel had said he would be in the car waiting for us. I knew Daniel would keep an eye on the outside while we were inside. So when we ran to the car, it was pure adrenalin that had kicked in. Ali immediately locked her door and that of the back door behind her seat. She then reached over to lock the driver's door and the back seat behind the driver's seat. Although the windows thoroughly exposed her and me, it did make us both feel a little better. Paul said he would care for Dempsey so we wouldn't have to worry about making pit stops for the dog.

Beamer handed me the map and told us not to stray from the pre-planned route.

"What if we need to stop for gas?" I asked.

"Detective Powers made a notation on the map, regarding stations you can stop at safely. He will have surveillance people in place at those sites only. Do not stop anywhere else", instructed Beamer. This was it. Ali and I were heading into the unknown. We had no clue as to why this ring was so important and why it warranted the harming of others to possess it. Ali and I had looked under a magnifying glass looking for clues that may give us an idea of the rings secret worth. No luck. It didn't even have the usual karat markings. Ali asked me if I would drive because she said her hands were too tremulous. I agreed.

The sun finally began to show a bit of light around 6: 20 a.m. I turned off the headlights once the sunlight was so bright, they were no longer needed. If Ali and I didn't have this heavy, dark cloud over us, this drive would have been a pleasurable trip. The country was beautiful. A rabbit was sighted shortly after we crossed the first bridge crossing that same river that was seen from the cabin. A white and brown colored horse grazing in the field was the next sign of life.

I could see we were beginning a slow descent. A small forest was divided by the road on which Ali and I were currently driving upon. A bridge could be seen but it was difficult to tell if it crossed that same river. Ali was the navigator while I continued to drive.

Daniel was lying down in the back seat to ensure no one could see him. I told him I had read about cameras that could see for miles. The paparazzi could get pictures of celebrities without their knowledge because of the capability of those cameras. Daniel said he didn't mind lying down, but I could tell even his nerves were strained because he couldn't keep an eye on the area from where he lay. It wasn't until we were about to cross the bridge that trouble showed itself. A car pulled out of the wooded area. It was a black car and I immediately went on the defense. Ali turned and saw the car. Her eyes were as big as saucers and I could see her hands begin to visibly shake.

"Daniel, we have a car that just pulled out from the woods. I don't know if it's something to worry about or if it's just a local going to town. Can you keep an eye on it?"

Daniel disappeared. I knew that meant he was watching without being watched. I told Ali to keep her head straight ahead. She could pull down the visor and look in the mirror that was housed in the visor if she wanted to monitor the car. Under no circumstances should we let them know we were aware of them behind us.

As I drove onto the bridge, I realized I had entrapped us. We had no way to exit except by the road ahead. If the black car was the goons, they could easily catch us. I had just come to that realization when the black car sped up quickly.

Soon the black car was nearing the back of Ali's car. I sped up, but the black car went into the oncoming lane.

"They're trying to catch up to us" yelled Ali.

I heard Daniel ask, "How do you put down this glass?"

I pushed the power button for the back window. It was after that moment that Daniel appeared and leaped through the back open window onto the black cars front windshield. The driver couldn't see past Daniel and the black car struck the rail on the bridge. Unfortunately, it bounced off and headed for Ali and me. I pushed the gas pedal down to the floor and the little car sped up as quickly as possible. The black car just missed us. Ali turned to watch what was happening. I could only glance through the rear-view mirror while driving. The driver of the black car turned on the wipers, but Daniel hung on. Instead of stopping, which would have been the safest and more logical choice, the black car seemed to be picking up speed. The black car swerved left, than right, left and then right again. Daniel held on tight although the driver made every maneuver possible to unlatch Daniel from the car. The driver was paying more attention to Daniel than to where the car was aiming. The black car suddenly broke through the bridge rail and plummeted downward. I screamed. I was so afraid for Daniel.

The bridge it seemed did not cross over the river but a ravine. The bridge was about 50 feet or so above the ravine. The car landed on its right front side and then rolled several times. I was afraid to stop, so I kept driving. I know tears were streaming down my face. Ali was quiet and very pale. I was afraid she was in shock.

"Ali, where is the next gas station we can stop at? "She didn't answer.

"Ali?" I said, mustering up all the energy I could to remain calm. "I need to know where the next safe gas station is. I need you to look at the map and tell me. Can you do that for me?"

I could see Ali's head slowly move. "I am so sorry Em. I was so scared. It was like my body and mind just shut off."

We crossed the bridge and drove rather quickly down the road to the next cross road and made a right turn. It wasn't until we were a few hundred feet on the new road that Daniel suddenly appeared. Ali and I both screamed, then tears ran down both our faces. I wasn't expecting Daniel to reappear in the car. I guess I hadn't thought things though. My foot hit the brake and Ali's car came to an immediate halt throwing Ali and me forward. The seatbelts strained against our shoulders and our hip bones. The motor stalled and made a few clinking sounds. At that moment Ali and I didn't care, we were so happy to see Daniel.

"I didn't think I'd see you again", I said to Daniel.

Daniel looked a bit confused. Then I realized why. He was already dead. How could he die again? "Just to see you go off that bridge made my heart stop".

"Mine too", whispered Ali.

Daniel smiled. "I love you both too".

"Em", Ali said, "How did those guys find us on this route? I thought we didn't have to worry until we were closer to home."

"I don't know Ali", I responded," Someone told them where we would be". Now we had to worry about the entire trip. After I had calmed down a bit, I turned the key but the engine would not start. I looked at Ali.

"Maybe it flooded when we stopped", said Ali.

I waited a few minutes before trying the key again, but no luck. A strange clicking sound could be heard but the motor remained silent. Ali and I looked at each other with the same questions in our minds. Should we stay with the car? We may be sitting ducks if the men in the black car survived or if they had friends that would come looking for them. If we walked, would we get anywhere safe? How long would it take us to find a telephone and get a hold of the police? Neither Ali nor I had a cell phone. We never found the need to get one. We worked, went shopping together, or were at home. Now I wished I had joined the 21st century and purchased one. It sure would have made me feel safer than I did right now.

Daniel suggested we leave a note in the car that the police could understand and start walking towards the nearest town. Ali agreed. She felt sitting in a disabled car was like waiting in a cage. So we packed what we thought we would need. I left a note saying we would head for a safe place. I didn't say where we were walking, what direction we were going in, when, or how we were going to get there. Ali had the foresight to bring along some bottled water. I took our quilt out of the oversized bag and put the water, the map, and a jacket for Ali and me inside. We headed down the road away from the road leading to the bridge.

Unfortunately, Ali and I had not worn walking shoes. Ali was wearing flip flops and I had on pumps. It seemed that every few feet, a rock collected between Ali's foot and her flip flop. We had to stop for her to remove the small pebble or stone that had made its way between the flip flop and Ali's foot. Daniel suggested we leave the road and walk in the fields that nestled up against the road. Rows and rows of corn, soy beans, and other unknown vegetable plants that were growing in soft dirt. Ali and I agreed. After leaving the road, Ali and I both acknowledged our feet were very grateful.

The day was nice. A bit over cast with a slight breeze. It was warm enough for us to walk without our jackets. The corn rows weren't totally grown, so Daniel, Ali, and I all walked in separate rows but in unison of each other. We must have walked for at least an hour when we came to a creek.
"It must be one of the branches of the river behind the cabin we stayed in", deduced Ali. I didn't care. I took off my shoes and put my feet in the cool water. Ali followed suit.
"My feet were hurting so badly from all those rocks", admitted Ali. Daniel sat between Ali and me and studied the map.
"The next town is kilometers away. Maybe we should try and find a farm house and call Constable Powers", Daniel suggested. Ali and I looked at each other. Kilometers?
"It must be far", I thought to myself, wishing I had learned the metric system.
"I agree", said Ali, "It's nice out now, but if we are still stuck when it gets dark we will be in some serious trouble". I hadn't thought that far ahead. I thought for sure we would see houses along the way, but then we left the road.

We agreed to keep an eye out for farm houses, electric lines or poles, or telephone lines and poles. The rows of vegetables had to belong to someone, right? So we took our feet out of the creek and began walking barefooted down the rows. We sipped on water and kept trying to trouble shoot how the goons could have found out where we were. Someone had to have told them. Only two police officers from Ali's and my area knew. Detective Triplett and Paul. I could see the worry on Ali's face that maybe she had trusted the wrong man.

Soon we came to the end of the vegetable field. A thick wire was strung with metal poles three feet apart holding the wire. The wire was humming.

"Where there is electricity, there are people", I stated. Ali and I ducked under the wire. Daniel jumped over. He landed in soft pile of dirt and fell face down. Ali and I laughed. It was the first time we had laughed in a while. I have to admit, it felt good to laugh. The trouble and tensions Ali and I had been facing the last several months had made us cautious and tense. Even Daniel laughed.

We began walking through the field when Ali suddenly stopped dead in her tracks. "Em, there are bulls in this field". I followed her line of sight. There was one bull and several cows. "If we ignore them, then maybe we won't frighten them", I said. "Frighten them?" questioned Ali, "What about us being frightened?" I didn't get the chance to answer that. The bull began to charge at us. Ali ran to her right. I ran several feet behind her. Daniel stood in the middle of the field attempting to get the bull's attention. He was having no luck. The bull had Ali and me in his sights and he didn't want to stop until he met up with us.

Ali reached the end of the wire and hurdled over it, just as Daniel had done when we first reached the field. I didn't realize the wire was there and ran right into the wire. The shock was unbelievable. I felt it encase my entire body. My heart felt as though it had been hit by a huge unseen force. Daniel lifted me over the wire and placed me on the grass. It took me a long while to catch my breath. I had been stunned. I wasn't sure how long I had stopped breathing. It was as if all of my control over my body had ceased. I was still shaking from the jolt when suddenly, a man with a shot-gun ran towards us. "What are you doing on my property? Are you cattle thieves?"

Ali began crying and explaining with mumbled words broken up by huge bouts of sobs. The man looked more confused than he initially had. I tried to stand. The man could see Ali and I were not dressed for cattle rustling and asked, "What goes on here?"
After explaining in the most rational way I could, I think the man finally understood why we had taken the route across his fields. He told us to follow him and he would take us to his farm house and we

could contact the police from there. He had us ride in the back of his pick-up truck.

I wasn't entirely certain the farmer believed us, but how often do you see two women stealing cows in the movies? NEVER! I noticed my shirt was burned slightly where the wire had touched it. The farmer had carried his shot-gun like a baby. I'd seen people carry guns like that in movies. It was so they could quickly shoot if needed. Ali and I were not going to give him any reasons to. The farmer sat his shot-gun on the front seat of the truck and started the engine. We drove for about a half hour before turning into a dirt driveway.

Daniel had disappeared but I knew he wouldn't be too far away. The old farm house looked battered and worn down. It needed a new coat of paint and new shutters. The roof looked sound, but it did look old. We followed the farmer inside. To my amazement, the inside was clean and homey. I could smell coffee and fresh baked bread. An older woman appeared in the room in which we were standing.

"Who are these young girls, Fred?"
Fred told the older woman he had found us in the cow yard. The older woman looked at us and could see we had gone through a rough time of it.

"Come inside, you two. Let's get you cleaned up a bit and give you some food." Fred stood there shaking his head. Ali and I took turns using the facilities. The older woman set out a wash cloth and towel for each of us. We cleaned up as best we could and then joined the older woman in the kitchen.

We explained the situation to the older woman, Martha. She was Fred's wife. Martha fed Fred in the kitchen but had us eat in the living room. Martha was a great cook. I hadn't realized it was almost dinner time when Fred found us. We had been walking for hours and hadn't noticed how the sun had crossed the sky. Fred was about to milk the cows when he found Ali and I. Thank goodness the cows needed milking. Ali and I discovered that Fred owned land that spread out for miles. His farm house was miles away. We may have wandered for hours or days before finding anyone.

Martha called the local sheriff. She didn't say on the telephone why she needed him, but told him not to interrupt anything important. Ali suddenly squealed. I jumped.

"What is wrong child?" asked Martha. Ali pointed to a pile of quilts that Martha had sitting in a corner.

"Did you see a mouse?" asked Martha.

"No", responded Ali, "You sew quilts!"

Martha laughed. "I have never had anyone scream because of that", she said.

Ali asked Martha if she could look at her quilts. Martha explained they were years old. Martha rarely worked on quilts these days as the farm kept her busy. She did pick up the needle in the winter time when activities were limited to the indoors.

"Em, look how beautifully done they are. The patterns are so detailed". I had to admit, if Ali and I were competing against Martha's quilts, Martha would have won hands down. Ali began explaining how she and I make quilts and donate them to the church. Martha commended us for our efforts and offered to allow us to take a few of hers with us to add to the donation. I thanked Martha, but suggested she donate to her own church. I didn't want to take something so beautiful away from her own community. Martha said she would take Ali's and my suggestion and begin donating her quilts to her church. Martha also said she would get a group of her friends to do the same. Martha said she remembered that as a young girl, her mother would have sewing bees and all the women in the church would take turns going to each other's homes to sew quilts for the church or the needy. Martha didn't know why that tradition ended.

"It seems all good things do come to an end no matter how much we don't want them to", said Martha.

Our conversation was interrupted by the door opening. Ali's eyes grew large. The sheriff, called out, "Martha, Fred".

"Come in Jim". Jim was a lanky looking guy. He was dressed in a police uniform but wore boots. He had a gun and badge. "What's up Martha?"

Martha explained our situation. Jim scratched his head and said, "Don't that beat all?"

The question now was what to do with us and how would we be kept safe?

I suggested calling Detective Powers. We were safe while in his care. It was when we attempted communication with our own police force that the situation went awry.

I explained to Jim that he could not use any police equipment to contact Detective Powers. He would need to use Martha's telephone or a public telephone. I explained how there was a leak in the police force in our area. We didn't think it was police personnel, but someone who frequented the police station that was passing on information to the goons.

"Goons?" Jim asked.

"Well, that is what Ali and I call those men that keep following and attacking us".

"Oh", Jim kind of smiled. "I guess they are goons", he said, "but we call them criminals".

Martha called information and retrieved Detective Powers telephone number. Jim called Detective Powers. He wasn't in. Jim said he would call back every hour to reach Detective Powers. Jim mentioned it was very important. Jim didn't mention where he was calling from or what the topic of discussion was about. Jim was trying in every way he knew how, to protect Ali and me.

Martha made more coffee. The night drew close and then arrived. Martha yawned. Jim said he would need to check in at his station, but would let no one know of Ali and me. He said he would take Detective Power's telephone number with him and call him each hour from a public telephone. Once he reached Detective Power he would return back to Martha and Fred's house. I could see Martha was weary. When I asked her what time she and Fred got up, she replied, "I get up at 4:00 a.m. and I wake Fred up at 5:00 a.m. when breakfast is ready. I looked at the clock. It was 10:15 p.m. I felt badly.

"Martha, Ali and I can wait outside for Jim. I hate keeping you awake".

"I tell you what. I will make a pallet on the floor for you two girls. You can get a little shut eye too. Jim said he would keep trying that Detective. When Jim comes back, we would have had a little nap". Ali smiled at Martha's kindness. I thanked Martha. Soon, Ali and I were snuggling under the warmth of Martha's quilts. I don't know if it was the long walk, the excitement of the day, or the softness of the quilts, but I fell asleep as soon as my head hit the feather pillow.

I had expected to be groggy and only get a few hours of sleep but I woke when I heard the rooster crow. I blinked and rubbed my eyes. It was just beginning to get light out. Did Martha over sleep? Did we keep her and Fred up too late? I climbed out of the quilts and shivered. I didn't realize how warm I had gotten under those wonderfully sewn quilts. I shook off the chill and walked into the kitchen. Sitting at the table was Martha. She had a worried look on her face and a half cup of cold coffee sitting in front of her.

"Martha, I thought you were going to wake us up?"

"Jim never came back. Fred said that Jim was too reliable to not come back. We've known Jim for a long time and his word is as good as gold. Fred said he would go down to the police station in town and see what may have caused the delay. That was three hours ago. Fred hasn't come back yet. It only takes about 45 minutes to drive there".

"Maybe Fred had a flat tire", I tried to rationalize.

"Nope, Fred put new ones on that truck just a month ago".

"Why don't we call the station and see what the holdup is", I suggested.

"I already did. There is no answer. There are two officers that are in the station at night while two are out on patrol. Someone should have answered".

I could see Martha's lip quiver as she spoke.

"Let me call Detective Powers and see if he can give us some idea on the situation".

Martha's face brightened. I dialed the number for Detective Powers. It went to voicemail. I left a message for Detective Powers to call me. Martha gave me her telephone number so he could reach us directly.

I asked Martha if I could warm up the coffee. Martha jumped up and apologized for not offering me something sooner. I was soon sitting in front of a cup of piping hot coffee and a plate full of fried eggs, farm fresh bacon, and toast with home-made butter. Ali smelled the coffee and shuffled into the kitchen. Martha and I explained the absence of Jim and Fred.

Ali added that sometimes an accident can put down a telephone line. That made Martha feel better. Jim may be at the station with Fred waiting for the phone lines to be repaired.

"Nope, Fred would have come home if he met up with Jim. We just wanted to make sure Jim was alright".

We all jumped when the telephone rang. Martha answered it. It was Detective Powers. I took the telephone and explained the situation about the car coming out of the woods and now our current situation of the police officer, Jim and Fred not returning. The police station not answering their telephone. Detective Powers said he would take care of the matter and for us to hunker down and wait for him and several of his officers to come to us. I sighed. I hate this waiting game. I still couldn't figure out what was so special about this ring that those goons were after so badly. The only person besides Daniel that knew about the ring was his aunt. His aunt would never have told anyone. This situation was getting out of hand.

      I told Martha I needed some air and walked outside. The grass was wet from the dew that hadn't yet dried from the sun. I walked behind the barn and called Daniel. Daniel appeared.

"I heard", announced Daniel.

"Daniel, this situation has to end".

"I know", he said. I could tell he was thinking what would happen to him and me if the goons were given the ring.

"People are getting involved in this that may get hurt. It's all my fault. I have no idea what to do about it. I don't want to lose you, but I can't bear the thought of someone getting hurt because I was selfish".

"I will leave the decision in your hands", replied Daniel. Great! Just what I wanted to be the cause of his unhappiness and mine as well.

"Daniel, if you can come up with some way to fix all this, I'm all ears".

"Let me think", said Daniel.

Suddenly a thought occurred to me. What if we had another ring made to look like this one. We could give the new version of the ring to Detective Triplett to hold in evidence. Hopefully, whoever is the contact within the police force will pass the word and goons will leave Ali and me alone.

Hours passed before Detective Powers car pulled up into Martha's and Fred's driveway. We were surprised to see Fred in the passenger's seat. When Fred climbed out of the car, a bandage could be seen on his forehead. Martha raced to his side.

Everyone gathered in the living room to hear Fred tell the tale of how he had stopped by the station to see Jim, only to find the two desk officers locked up in one of their own cells in the back of the building. Fred had been looking for the keys when someone struck him from behind. He must have been knocked out for quite a while. He didn't hear the telephones ringing or the caged officers calling his name.

Jim was found in his cruiser. He had been tied and gagged. Jim reported that three men had approached him. When he was stopped to make a phone call to Detective Powers. The men attempted to extract information from Jim on Ali and me but Jim played dumb. Jim told the men he had no clue what the men were talking about. Jim even asked what jurisdiction the men were from. The men never responded with words but struck Jim from behind.

Jim too had been unconscious for a while. He had no choice but to wait and hope someone would find him and release him. He was now at the local hospital getting checked out. After talking to me, Detective Powers had sent several of his men to the police station to find out why no one was answering the telephones. Detective Powers came across Jim's cruiser on his way to us.

The EMS were called for Jim and Fred. The two desk officers were embarrassed that they had been overtaken by the three men and locked up in their own precinct. Martha made Fred lay down and then she called several of her neighbors to help do Fred's daily chores. I felt guilty that my situation was affecting so many and causing harm to others. Detective Powers collected Ali and me and took us back to his police department.

Chapter 27

Detective Triplett was contacted and he was soon expected to arrive. It was determined that his estimated time of arrival would be approximately two hours or so. Detective Powers wanted to hear what happened to our previous made plan. Ali and I explained about the car coming out of the wooded area and the attempt by those inside the black car to stop us on the bridge. Ali and I explained how the black car had attempted to strike us but we sped up and the black car went through the rail. Ali and I had kept driving out of pure fear but the car stalled after we turned at the next turn. We were afraid to stay in the car so we went looking for a house so we could call.

Ali and I told our story of the bull and Fred finding us, Jim stopping by and his role in attempting to contact Detective Powers.

"So, we still have a leak", stated Detective Powers. Detective Powers called Beamer. "Contact Detective Triplett and tell him to meet me at the station, then I need you to drive the girls to the safe house. You girls will be safe there. I won't let anyone go there without me personally giving them the ok". Ali and I looked at each other. I could read the puzzled thoughts going through Ali's mind.

After Detective Powers saw Beamer, Ali and I off, Ali asked me, "Do you think Paul is the leak?" I put my finger to my mouth and said "Shhh, we'll discuss this in private". I knew we could trust Beamer, but I wanted Daniel in the conversation too. We arrived at the new safe house and Beamer explained how he would be waiting outside. He expected two officers to come and stand guard. Once the two officers arrived, Beamer would go and purchase some clothes for Ali and me to wear for the next several days.

Ali and I gingerly entered the house. It smelled earthy. Plants were randomly scattered about. I secretly wondered who kept the plants thriving. "Ali, to answer your question now, I don't think we can rule anyone out, that includes Detective Triplett as well. They all seem nice, but maybe that is just a ploy". Daniel appeared and startled us both.

"I made a check around the area. I didn't see anyone. I will continue to monitor the perimeter until the local constables arrive".

"Daniel, you have no idea how much you being here is appreciated," stated Ali.

I could see the worry on Daniel's face but he gave Ali a small smile and then disappeared. Daniel made another check of the area and came back to check on Ali and me before Beamer knocked lightly then entered.

"Detective Powers had me stop and pick up dinner for everyone before heading out to get you some supplies. Detective Powers asked me to see if you had any needs that we may not have on our lists".

Ali turned beet red. I guess I had to take the ball and run, so I said, "Would you mind picking up some feminine products, tooth paste, tooth brushes, hair brushes and deodorant?"

Beamer wrote the list of items in a small notebook and nodded his head to affirm he would. He left just as suddenly as he had arrived.

Ali and I dug into the meal that Beamer was good enough to bring. We hadn't realized how ravenous we were. I think Beamer was starting to warm up to us. Dinner consisted of burgers and fries along with ice cold colas. As Ali and I sat in the living room and ate, I realized I had lost track of the days. I had no idea what day of the week it was. Time had also eluded me. I should have mentioned to Beamer I needed a wrist watch.

Beamer returned several hours later. He walked the bags of belongings into the bedroom that Ali and I would soon be sleeping in.

"I wonder who is the leak?" mentioned Ali.

"Or what" injected Beamer.

Ali and I turned to see Beamer standing in the doorway.

"What do you mean?" I asked.

"Detective Powers is having the cars searched. He believes there may have been a tracking device placed on someone's car".

I hadn't thought of that. I wondered if that was how those goons had managed to track Ali and me to the bed and breakfast. But, if they had a tracking device placed on Ali's car, they surely would have found us at the motel unless it was placed there when we stayed at the bed and breakfast place. There had to be someone else that was leading them to us.

"When will Detective Powers know?" I asked Beamer. Beamer just shrugged his shoulders as if to say, who knows when.

"Everyone's car has been to this area. Doesn't that mean that they may find us here too?" Ali questioned. I could see the gears rotating in Beamer's head. I was counting off too. Ali's car, Detective Powers, the one police cruiser, Detective Triplett and Paul. Beamer had his cruiser and no goons had shown up. I was beginning to realize just how smart a detective had to be. Beamer retreated to the kitchen and put on a fresh pot of coffee.

Ali and I decided to retire to our bedroom. Once the door was closed, Daniel appeared. We updated Daniel on the latest information regarding trackers. Although Daniel understood what we were saying, he admitted he could not grasp the concept of how it was done. Poor Daniel, so out of his element but trying so desperately to understand.

"Do you think we'll be safe here?" asked Ali.

"I will stay up all night and guard the area", replied Daniel. Then Daniel disappeared. Ali and I eventually went to bed. I know Daniel would check in on Ali and me so I purposefully stayed awake. Ali tossed and turned for quite a while but finally settled down into a quiet slumber.

Daniel came to check on us as I had expected. I waved him over. He kneeled down beside my bed and held my hand.

"I miss our alone time together, "I confessed.

Daniel smiled and replied, "I do as well". I yawned and Daniel stood.

"I'll be making regular rounds. You need to sleep". He stood, planted a kiss gently on my lips and then disappeared again. I pulled the covers over me, thinking how comfortable Martha's quilts had been compared to the store bought blankets that were on the beds that Ali and I were in. After a few minutes, I must have fallen asleep.

I woke up to Ali closing the bathroom door. I stretched and looked at the clock. It read 5:00 am. I wondered where Daniel was. I walked to the kitchen. Beamer was sleeping in the chair. His feet rested in another chair and a cold cup of coffee in front of him. Poor Beamer. He had been on duty without any breaks to speak of since Ali and I had stumbled into his life. I quietly returned to the bedroom. Daniel was sitting on the bed. He looked tired. I wrapped my arms around him.

"Will this ever end?" I whispered.

"I surely hope so", he whispered back.

Then I heard a shot. Beamer yelled something through the door.

"Lock the door and don't come out until I tell you it is safe!" Daniel disappeared again. Ali was in the bathroom and I had no idea if she had heard the shot or Beaming yelling through the door. There was no sense in making her worry unnecessarily. So I waited for her to come out. When Daniel appeared, it startled me and I nearly jumped off the bed.

"There are two men in the woods with guns. There is no way to tell if they are friend or foe. I will keep you abreast of my findings". Daniel then disappeared.

"Ali", I said as I tapped lightly on the bathroom door.

"Out in a minute" was Ali's reply. When Ali came out, I told her what had happened. It seemed as though time was moving as a snail's pace. Soon Beamer knocked on the door and announced, "All clear".

Just as I was reaching for the door handle of the bedroom, Daniel appeared and grabbed my hand. He shook his head "No". Now I was confused. He took Ali and me by the hand and led us into the bathroom. Daniel told me to lock the bathroom door as he looked through the window to assess the outside.

"Those two men are holding the officer prisoner. I need to get you two out of harm's way".

I could see the panic in Ali's eyes.

"We can't just leave Beamer", Ali whispered.

Daniel helped us out of the window and told us to run toward the river. He took one of my flip flops and threw it toward the driveway. "I'll help Beamer as much as I possibly can", he said as he urged us to run.

Ali and I ran through the barbs and thorn infested weeds toward the river. A small dock that had been hidden from view when Ali and I had looked out of the cabin windows, was now our life-saving grace. A canoe was secured to the dock. Ali climbed in the canoe first. I untied the rope and somehow managed to get inside the canoe without tipping me, Ali, or the canoe into the water. Ali handed me a paddle that had been resting in the bottom of the canoe.

"We need to stay near shore so we won't be seen", I said.

The current chose our direction and Ali and I paddled as hard as two out of shape people could. The river snaked around the land. The canoe followed the river downward. Ali and I discovered it didn't take long before we were not only safely hidden by the curvature of the river but we barely needed to paddle because of the power of the current. Soon, Daniel joined us.

"Were you able to help Beamer?" Ali asked with worry in her voice.

"I had to wait until the two men rendered Beamer unconscious, then I was able to subdue the two of them. I put Constable Beamer on the davenport and tied the two armed men up. I had to use a grey colored rope that was so sticky, I doubt the men will be able to break free".

I had to laugh. Daniel and Ali looked at me as if I had lost my marbles.

"Daniel", I said, trying to tone down my laughter, "that's what we call duct tape". Now Ali was laughing too. The laughter actually helped relieve some of my tension. I think it helped Ali too.

The canoe continued onward. We passed a lot of desolated areas, then bridges that crossed over the river began to appear. As we approached the second bridge, I could see cars crossing the bridges. People within the cars smiled or waved at us as they watched us go under the bridge they were now crossing.

"Daniel, when do you suggest we stop and get back on dry land?" I asked.

"When we see another dock", he replied. So now the search was on. I wish I had worn a watch. Ali had forgotten to wear her watch. By the position of the sun, it had to be close to nine or ten in the morning. I silently wondered what Beamer would think when he woke up. More curious to me was how he would explain the situation.

"Ali yelled, "there's one" as she pointed to a pier. Ali and I began paddling toward the dock. It took very little effort with the current flowing in the direction in which we were heading.

My legs didn't want to work when I stepped out of the canoe. I think Ali had the same problem. We tied the canoe to the pier and began walking toward the building closest to us. It looked like a club of some sort. Maybe a boating club, I thought to myself. Ali and I must have looked like escapees from a looney bin. We approached the door. The man inside looked stunned as he gazed at Ali and me standing before the doors in our pajamas.

Ali managed to explain the situation well enough, that the man called Detective Powers for us. The man even gave Ali and me a tee-shirt to wear over our pajamas and jogging pants too. It took Detective Powers a good hour to get to us. We explained about the gun shots that we had heard and how Beamer had sounded stress when he returned. So Ali and I were afraid to take any chances and bailed. I tossed a flip flop toward the drive way to throw anyone who may be looking for us off track and then Ali and I went in the opposite direction.

Detective Powers dialed his telephone. "Send a couple officers to the safe house and check on Beamer. Ali and I once again found ourselves in the protective custody of Detective Powers. While we were driving, I posed a question I had been wanting to ask Detective Powers.

"Detective Powers, this may seem a little far-fetched, but what if we purchased another antique ring and had it made to look like mine. We could have you give it to Detective Triplett to put in the evidence room. Do you think if we did that, it would stop all of this cops and robbers stuff?"

All Detective Powers said was, "Interesting notion".

Chapter 28

Detective Powers waited until Ali and I had been able to shower and dress in our clothes before he had us meet him in his office. I guess Detective Powers felt we would be safer if we showered and dressed at the precinct. When we entered Detective Powers's office, breakfast was waiting for both Ali and I. As we ate, Detective Powers spoke. "I have been giving your idea about making a copy of your ring some thought. I believe it has merit. We will have to plan everything out to the letter for this to work". I could only nod yes as I sipped on warm coffee. After the morning incident, I needed some comfort food. Coffee was my beverage of choice in the morning and I sure did need lots of it.

The Detective asked me for the ring so he could take it to a jeweler who could make a copy. I refused. I told the Detective that I had been through enough and was not going to let my ring out of my sight. He acknowledged that he understood. So Detective Powers and I drove for an hour and a half to an out of the way jewelry store. The Detective rang the buzzer and we waited on the stoop. Soon an elderly gentleman opened the door, after looking us over for a few minutes first.

Once inside, Detective Powers spoke to the man about making the duplicate ring. The man seemed pleased to announce he was skilled enough to do the job. He asked to see the ring. I made certain to explain that I would not leave the ring. The duplicate would have to be made with me in view of my ring or not at all. "That's preposterous", said the elderly man.
I just glared at him. Detective Powers went on to explain the situation.
"Well, I will examine the ring, take pictures, and measurement while you are here. You can then take your ring with you. I should be able to have your duplicate in several days, if that is satisfactory", stated the man.

So I sat there watching closely as the elderly man whose name I soon discovered, was Nigel, measured and examined my ring. When Nigel removed the stone, he blinked several times. I could see his eyes clearly puzzled by something. Those enormous magnifying glasses he wore made his eyes look a hundred times larger than they really were.

"Did you want the numbers on the duplicate ring as well"? Asked Nigel. Detective Powers and I looked at each other with what must have been utter confusion.

"Numbers?" I asked.

We all crammed around the ring to look at this new development. The ring had numbers and what may have been letters written in the space behind where the stone had been. Detective Powers suggested to me, we should make the ring as authentic as the original. I agreed. The jeweler took a picture of the numbers and letters. Measured the diameter of the ring, the sword, the stone, etc. Nigel put my ring back together and handed it back to me.

"If you ever decide to sell that ring, please, come to me first".

I explained the ring would never be an item that I would consider selling. I could see Nigel nod his understanding but he housed the look of disappointment on his face.

Detective Powers and I headed back to the precinct.

"Do you have any idea what those numbers were"? Detective Powers asked.

"Not a clue", I replied, "I didn't even know they were there until Nigel showed them to us".

"They looked as if they could be coordinates", said Detective Powers.

"For what"? I asked.

"That is what I intend to find out", he replied.

Chapter 29

Nigel came through as he had promised. The ring was ready in two days. Detective Powers had the ring picked up. I wasn't told how much it cost to have a duplicate made, but I can imagine, it had to have cost a pretty penny. Now we needed a plan to make this work.

Detective Powers asked Detective Triplett to meet him. It would be somewhere outside both precincts to ensure no one but the two of them knew what the entire plan was. When Detective Powers returned. He called me into his office.

"I need you to call Detective Triplett and tell him you are at your wits end. Tell him you are sending him the ring and that you don't want to ever see the ring again. Do you think you can make it sound as if that is the way you truly feel?"

"I'll do my best", I replied.

Detective Powers had someone at the telephone company place my call. I later learned the telephone company was routing the call so no one would know where the call actually came from. When Detective Triplett's secretary answered, I asked to speak to Detective Triplett. The secretary informed me he was out of the office. It was then that Detective Powers slide a note in front of me.

Leave a message with the secretary. Tell her you are fed up with all this cops and robbers stuff and you are sending him the ring in the mail.

"Can I leave a message for Detective Triplett?" I asked.

"Of course", replied the secretary.

"Tell him I am tired of all this cops and robbers stuff. I am tired of being hunted like an animal. I want my piece of mind back. I am sending him the ring. He can do with it what he pleases. I am so done with this situation".

"Let me make certain I have taken down your message correctly. You are sending a ring to the Detective?"

"Yes, he will know what I am talking about when he gets the ring". I don't know why, but it sounded as if there was excitement in the secretary's voice when she told me she would give the Detective my message. I later realized the secretary had hung up and hadn't even ask me my name. Detective Powers noticed that too.

Next, the detective asked me to write a letter to Detective Triplett repeating what I had said to the secretary. The duplicate ring and my note was placed in a large secured envelope then placed in the mail. Detective Powers had notified the postal service and no identifying post mark would be placed on the envelope. Now we only needed to wait. I was not privileged to the entire plan. I only knew the ring was being sent to Detective Triplett. I didn't know what the plan would be on his end.

When the envelope arrived at Detective Triplett's precinct, no one noticed the secretary sliding the envelope with the duplicate ring into her bag. The secretary made a call to someone using her cell phone, then asked to be excused the rest of the day. Detective Triplett called Detective Powers who smiled and stated, "The bait has been taken".
I later learned that the ring had a special transmitter hidden inside. Detective Powers and Triplett had discussed putting a transmitter in the envelope but feared the envelope may be tossed. The ring would eventually be with the crooks, so they made the choice to add a small transmitter inside the ring. Nigel had made the ring look exactly like mine even with the transmitter added.   The secretary drove to a seedy looking motel. The secretary was monitored closely as she entered a room at the back of the motel units. She didn't stay very long. After she entered back into her car and left the motel did Detective Triplett have her picked up by several plain clothes policemen.

The secretary admitted she was following police orders. Puzzled, she was asked to explain. Apparently, someone had come up to the secretary when she was leaving the precinct one day. The man stated he was from internal affairs and was concerned about evidence being taken by someone from within the precinct for their own personal gain. This impersonator said he was looking at Detective Triplett and had heard he was attempting to gain access to an antique ring. The imposter instructed the secretary to monitor all communications to Detective Triplett and keep him informed after hours. Recently, the man had learned about the mailing of the ring, and instructed the secretary to bring the ring to him for safe keeping. The man said he would monitor to see if Detective Triplett would reveal his hand. The secretary explained that the man had shown her a badge and everything.

The secretary was escorted back to the precinct to give an official statement. Detective Triplett had a swat team gathered at the motel. They would need to collect the men that had been waiting for the secretary. Several of the swat team went to the manager's office and instructed the manager to call each patron in the motel. The manager was instructed to encourage each patron to come to the manager's office. Patrons were not very happy to get the call, but the patrons followed the instructions as given. Soon the manager's office was packed with patrons wearing various outfits. A swat team officer was informing the patrons of why there was the need to bring all the patrons to an area of safety, while criminals who were hiding out in the motel, were being rousted out.

Soon swat men were everywhere. I have no idea how the swat team managed to get all the men who were in that small motel room gathered up without anyone getting shot or hurt, but they did. And to Ali's and my relief, they had captured the head man and his girlfriend too. Detective Triplett had said that his men were very skilled at retrieving criminals when they were hunkered down. I had to agree.

Detective Powers and Detective Triplett asked Ali and I to do one more thing. We were asked to look at a line up, to see if we knew any of the men. We agreed. The lineup was not what I had expected. Ali and I were in a small dark room looking through a window. We could see the men lined up, but apparently the men could not see us. Ali and I both identified the head man, and a few others who had attempted to run us off the road. Ali thought she recognized one other, but I had not. I wasn't certain what the detectives would do with that information.

Detective Powers informed Ali that he had her car looked at by their local mechanic and was having a man drive it over today. Ali's face glowed when she noticed it was police officer Paul who was bringing the car. It seemed it was a transducer that had burned out on her car. The mechanic had also discovered a locator device on the bottom of her gas tank. It had to have been placed on the car when Ali and I were at the bed and breakfast. I guess our get-away from them at the restaurant made them want to have easy access to us.

"Would it be too much trouble if I were to ask for a ride back to my precinct"? Asked Paul.

"I would feel safer knowing you are with us, right Emily"? Stated Ali looking at Paul.

I could only smile. I was sad knowing Daniel would not be able to appear while Paul was in the car. Dempsey was brought to me by Beamer who was banishing a huge black eye.

"Oh, I am sorry about what happened at the safe house. I feel guilty about leaving you behind with those thugs", I declared.

"It's my job. I will be sorry to see this little fellow go though", stated Beamer.

"Would you like to keep him?" I asked.

Beamer's eyes glistened. "Really?"

"I think he would be happier with you than he would be in my house. I have a small yard and live in the burbs. I know Dempsey would love to live in the country".

Beamer shook my hand and thanked me profusely, then scurried off. I secretly think he was afraid I would change my mind. The truth be told, I had been thinking about poor little Dempsey. I would need to find out more about Daniel. That wouldn't leave me much time for Dempsey. My heart ached that I wouldn't see him again, but I knew Dempsey would be loved and given a great home.

Paul offered to drive and Ali just giggled. I rolled my eyes and climbed into the backseat. I told Ali I was going to nap while they drove. I felt totally exhausted. I didn't know if it was because the situation was almost over or I was so stressed and now the stressor was gone. I only know that once I snuggled into the back seat, I was out. I didn't notice Ali had placed her head on Paul's shoulder while he drove. I hadn't noticed Paul would place a small kiss on her forehead when we stopped at traffic lights. I hadn't noticed anything. I simply slept on.

Paul dropped me off at my home first. He made certain the house was safe and empty before allowing me to enter. I had to promise to wait for him and Ali to come pick me up the next day to do the final paperwork thing. I promised. As soon as they left, Daniel appeared. I ran into his arms. I could tell he was happy the adventure was winding down for me. Then it hit me. We hadn't figured out about the ring for Daniel.

Daniel and I talked for half the night. We finally decided that I would ask Detective Triplett to find out information about the ring. Maybe he would could discover which auction house Charlie had purchased the buttons so we could find a connection to follow. I fell asleep in Daniels arms that night. Part of me was fearful we wouldn't find out Daniel's secret. Part of me was fearful we would. My heart was so scared I would lose him.

Chapter 30

It didn't take long to complete all the forms that Detective Triplett needed completed. It seemed the lead man, had been using an auction house to collect valuable items. Anyone who gave him a problem, his men would eliminate that problem. Detective Triplett was told he was up for an award from the Mayor for bringing this crime ring to justice. I was happy for him. The auction house records would be thoroughly investigated. Detective Triplett informed me that Ali and I would be notified if any information regarding the ring, or jars of buttons were discovered.

I delayed in returning to work for another week. I felt I needed time to get my nerves back in shape and plus, I had an excuse to spend more time with Daniel. It was just Daniel and I for days. Ali was occupied with Officer Paul. Ali called to say she would call me in a few days. I explained I needed some alone time with Daniel. We decided to get together the following Saturday and go to the flea market.

On Friday, I received an envelope in the mail. It was from Detective Triplett.

Dear Ms. Wells,

As promised, through our research, my detectives have discovered the jars of buttons were in a bulk estate sale. The only contact is an attorney. I include the contact information and wish you luck on your endeavor.

Again, accept my gratitude for your participation in assisting my department and myself in our investigation.

Respectfully,

Detective Triplett

The attorney information was an address, with no telephone number included.

Darren Green, 2434 Elkins Ave., Quicken, New York, 21309

Daniel and I discussed what our options were. We could travel and make an appointment to see Mr. Green or we could write a letter and explain our situation. Daniel and I opted for the latter.

Dear Mr. Green,

I recently purchased several jars of buttons at our local flea market. I discovered a ring within one of the jars and believe the family who sold the buttons may not have realized their loss. I am therefore writing you in hopes of contacting the person or persons who you

have represented in the estate sale. Detective Triplett gave me your
contact information and I am in hopes of hearing from you soon.
Sincerely,
Emily Wells

Daniel was nervous. He paced around like a caged lion. I know he was worried that he may leave me and yet I know he felt out of place in this situation he was thrust into. I finally sat him down.

"Daniel, no matter what happens or what we learn, you know I love you very deeply".

"And you, I", replied Daniel.

"I have to admit, I am frightened that I will lose you forever. I don't think I can handle that".

Daniel pulled me into his arms and we held each other. No words could explain the fears we each held in our hearts. I empathized what Daniel must be going through. In a country and time he knew nothing about. He had only one connection, me. Was I worth staying for? Did he even have a choice in the matter of staying or leaving? Time would tell and we didn't know how much time, if any we had.

Chapter 31

I had returned to work and had pushed the thoughts of hearing from the attorney anytime soon out of my mind. I was surprised to see when I checked in my mailbox there was a response. I was terribly fearful to open it. I owed it to Daniel to be brave. I walked into my home and held the envelope up, "We have a response".

I didn't think it possible, but Daniel grew pale. He sat down and had a faraway look in his eyes.

I sat beside him.

"No matter what, I will always love you". Daniel held me tightly. I could feel him tremble. For the first time since I met him, I could tell he was frightened. I kissed him. I thought our kiss would never end. I can still feel that kiss upon my lips.

I opened the envelope. It read:

My Dear Miss. Wells,

I am merely the attorney hired for the estate sale. In lieu of your concerns, I have contacted the owner of the estate, Ezekiel Potter IV. He informs me he has no interest in any jewelry that may have been present in the estate. Mr. Potter is a man of wealth in his own rights and feels that the ring in question was purchased by you and therefore; is your property. The proceeds of the estate are being donated to charity. If you do not wish to keep the ring, you may at your own discretion sell or donate the ring to a charity of your choosing? I hope this clarifies the matter.

Cordially,

Darren Green

Daniel and I could only stare at the letter. Daniel stood up and said he needed to be alone. I nodded to him. He disappeared. I admit, that made me more frightened than I had ever been.

I put on some water for tea and gathered my cup and sweetener, when a thought came to me. The water was soon boiling. I made the tea and sat near the computer. I began looking up genealogy.

I discovered a site that would allow genealogical research in England. I started my search with Ezekiel Potter. His mother was Constance Doyle. Constance Doyle married Franklin Potter. Franklin Potter came to the United States six years before Ezekiel was born. Ezekiel Senior. I continued searching and searching.

When Daniel finally returned, he looked fatigued.

"Daniel, I found a new way to find out where you belong". I explained how the genealogy sites traced families. Daniel seemed tired but hopeful. I hadn't realized the hours had slipped away as I researched. It was almost 2 am. I needed sleep.

"Daniel, I need to rest. Let me get a nap and I will get back into our quest". Daniel held me and kissed me tenderly.

"I know you realize our time is short. I wish things could have been different. I don't know what the future holds, but I can't guarantee I can be here for you", he whispered. I don't think Daniel saw the tears slipping from my eyes. I yawned and wiped my eyes as if I were sleepy. I didn't want Daniel to feel badly. After all, it wasn't his fault my heart was breaking.

Daniel and I spent the entire weekend researching. It wasn't until late Saturday night and early Sunday morning that we found his uncle and aunt amongst our findings. It felt like a huge weight had been lifted off my shoulders. Daniel seemed excited that we knew where he had originally come from. But now what?

I decided I needed to request a vacation. If my vacation request was approved, I would plan a trip to England. I would need to arrange a car or driver to drive me to the various places that Daniel had mentioned. I purchased a stenographers notebook and I wrote all the information down that would be needed on the quest. My boss wasn't too thrilled about me wanting a vacation after being gone for so long on the police stake out, but I did have the available time. Truth be known, she was probably happy to have me gone. I watched her as much as she watched me.

I arranged my flight to Heathrow Airport. I wanted to leave at night so there would be less people on the plane. I wasn't certain how Daniel would handle an airplane flight. After all, Daniel hadn't handled his initial introduction to the automobile very well. I also wanted to make certain Daniel had a place to be during the flight. It was a two hour flight from Metro airport to New York, then we caught a connecting flight to Heathrow. The flight seemed long, but I dozed part of the time. When we arrived, a driver met us at the curb. I admit, I felt a bit like royalty not having to take a bus or cab. My first stop was at the hotel I had booked. Apparently, some of the hotels were renting apartment buildings and using each single apartment as a hotel room. The apartment had a small living room, a kitchen and a bedroom. The kitchen had a combination washer and dryer. I had never seen anything like it. The driver informed me, the trip to Thatcher town was over 12 hours and involved back roads. He suggested we leave early.

"What would be a good time?" I asked.

"Seven thirty would be a good time to start the day. That would give you time to eat a hearty breakfast and we would arrive in before dark". I agreed.

Chapter 32

The driver arrived at seven thirty as agreed. The driver also mentioned a nice place to stop for tea around four in the afternoon. Daniel whispered that tea at four is a normal tradition for the English. I acknowledged my agreement and climbed into the car. The English country side is a beautiful one. I should have had the forethought to bring a camera with me, but my mind wasn't on tourism when I planned this trip. I, therefore would have to be satisfied with remembering the trip in my memories. The drive took less time than originally expected. We arrived in Thatcher town at twenty minutes after six. My bones ached from sitting. The driver pulled up in front of a small hotel.

"You need to stay here tonight. I usually rent a room when the drive is over eight hours". The driver was use to the long drives and had made provisions for me as well as himself within the hotel.

I told the driver I would want to explore the city of Thatcher town tomorrow but would need a ride back to the big city the following day. The driver understood. Daniel and I made our way to our assigned room. I couldn't wait to see Daniel. I knew he was with me, but I needed to see him. Knowing that I could lose him at any given moment had me on edge. He held me all night. I must have fallen asleep, because I awoke within his arms.

After breakfast, Daniel and I walked through the town. Daniel recognized sites here and there. The bridge, the river, and the site where his aunt and uncle had once lived. The house had been left to ruin and had been abandoned for what looked like centuries. The city had demolished what was left standing for fear of children entering the dangerous building. It currently remained a vacant lot. Then Daniel seemed to begin remembering things.

He raced ahead. There around the curve in the road stood a brick and stone building. Daniel pointed and said, "I remember, I remember." I wasn't certain what he was trying to say. He suddenly stopped and stared at me. "We need to get a horse", he said.

"Daniel, we need to get a car".

The hotel could not offer an automobile, but they did offer me a tandem bicycle. It was the only mode of transportation they had available for visiting guest. I thanked them and climbed on the front portion of the tandem bike.

After pedaling for several minutes, Daniel and I were out of sight of the hotel. Daniel appeared and attempted to assist with the pedaling. He and I almost crashed twenty times before Daniel finally got the knack of riding a bike.

I should have had the sense to bring some water with me. After an hour or so, my throat was parched and my lips hurt from me licking them. Daniel suggested we stop and walk to the river to get a drink. I tried to explain how civilization was polluting our waterways, but my legs needed a break. Daniel and I began walking through the woods. He seemed to know where he was going. We spoke softly as we walked. Discussing what he was feeling.

"I am at a loss to explain the situation thoroughly. It is almost as if I am driven to find something, but I am uncertain as to what it may be", he explained.

I simply nodded and walked on. My legs were achy and now the skin showed signs of scratches from the random weeds that crossed our path and prevented a clear walk way. We came to a small stream and Daniel suggested I moisten my lips. The water looked clear. The area seemed void of any people or animals. I took a chance and sipped at the water. It was ice cold and felt like heaven as it slid down my throat.

Daniel and I continued our quest. I followed him as he led me deeper and deeper into the woods. It wasn't until my stomach began to growl loudly that I realized the sun had traveled well across the sky.

"Daniel?"

Daniel stopped and looked at me with the expression of bewilderment.

"I need to eat. We've been walking for hours". Daniel hugged me and apologized for not having the foresight to plan a picnic.

"Hindsight", I said with a grin. "We need to get back to the hotel".

"Yes, of course", replied Daniel, but he stood in place.

"Ok, let's get going", I replied. Daniel looked around. I could see the look on his face he had no idea which way to begin walking back. Then it hit me. We were lost. Neither Daniel nor I had made any effort to mark the trail for our return. Thoughts of me and my body being found appeared in my mind.

"Do you have any idea which way we came from?" I asked Daniel. He shook his head no. And if this situation wasn't bad enough, the sky had grown cloudy and I could feel the moisture in the air. Great!

It looked as if a storm would soon be upon us and I had no coat, no umbrella, or any means of shelter to protect me.

"What if we follow the stream? Wouldn't that lead us to a city or town?" I asked.

"I am uncertain where it would lead. It may coil around upon itself and lead us to the ocean or it may lead us further inland away from any town", explained Daniel.

I wanted to cry. I blinked back the tears that I could feel welling up inside my eyes.

"What should we do?" I questioned. I was asking a ghost who had been dead for who knows how long, to decide my fate. How crazy could I be?

I made the decision to follow the stream. At least if I were going to die, it would be my own fault and by my own choosing. As predicted, it began to rain. Not the little misty type of rain, but the huge rain drops type of rain. It was cold and the clouds made it dark. The woods were dense and permitted me to see only a few feet ahead. I shivered and coughed as the rain came down. I have no idea how Gene Kelly could sing in the rain. I wanted to cry and to cry loudly. The only reason I had not yet ended up a bawl baby was for Daniel's benefit. I didn't want him to feel guilty for leading me so far away from town and getting us lost.

My legs felt like heavy bags of wet sand. I was fatigued and drenched. I was hungry and exhausted. I couldn't help myself. I began to cry. I could see on Daniel's face how sad he was for me. He failed to think of food or water because he didn't need those staples. It didn't matter if he were lost for years in the woods because he would be unchanged when he came out. I however; had limited time to find shelter and food.

The weeds made our trek even wetter as we brushed up against the rain soaked plants in our endeavor to find our way back to civilization. My jeans had absorbed as much water as they could and now felt like heavy weights. Excess rain ran off my jeans and shirt making my shoes slosh with every step. I began to shiver. It was just a chill type of shiver. Then my body trembled so hard I could barely walk. There was no place to take cover. I began to trip and fall. It must have been my third time down that I just felt like staying down.

Daniel kept trying to encourage me to keep going on, but I was exhausted and hypothermia was rapidly setting in. My body shook so hard from the cold, I thought I would chip my teeth. My mind was getting foggy. I told Daniel that no matter what happened, I hoped he would find the answer he needed to pass over. I could tell by the look on his face that he was frightened for me. Then it happened. I just couldn't go on anymore. Not one more step. I slid down the trunk of a large tree and curled up in a fetal position. I knew physically I had reached my limit. I closed my eyes. If I died here, no one would find me. I don't know what would happen to Daniel. I wish I had more endurance but my energy was spent. I closed my eyes and slept.

Chapter 33

When I woke up, I was disoriented. I was in a bed. A warm, dry bed with covers. A woman that I didn't know was wiping my forehead with a cool cloth. She must have seen my eyes flicker open briefly.

"You are safe now. I don't know how you managed to get to our door, but you are safe now".

I drifted back off to sleep. I could hear voices intermittently but I didn't have the strength or the desire to open my eyes.

"I think she has pneumonia. If we don't get her to a doctor, she may die", said a woman's voice.

"The rain has turned all the roads to mush. I don't know if the bridges are passable. We will have to wait until the roads are dry before we seek help", said a man's voice.

I could hear Daniel whispering into my ear. "Emily, you need to try and wake up. You need to eat and drink something. You need nourishment".

I could feel warm fluid being spooned into my mouth. I wasn't hungry any longer. I just wanted to sleep. I wanted to stay in the warm blankets and sleep forever.

"Emily, swallow the warm broth. You need food", said Daniel.

Then it occurred to me. If I died, I could be with Daniel forever. I know a smile must have crossed my face. I tried to tell Daniel that I wanted to be with him forever. I don't think the words came out very well. I could hear the woman say something about me trying to mumble something.

"Just let me die. We can be together forever then", I mumbled to Daniel.

Then I heard Daniel. "Emily, do not allow yourself to die. I cannot be responsible for your death. If you do not survive, I will give up. I shall never be able to face you again if you die. It would be because of me and my anchor that you are in this situation. I cannot nor will I choose to continue on if you die".

I don't know if it was the delirium or my mind was too weak to think straight, but all I could contrive was obviously, Daniel did not love me as he had said he did. He was worried about himself. This would solve our problem. He and I could be together forever. But he didn't want that. He didn't want me. I began to cry. What I didn't count on was when I cried, I had to take deep breaths to sob. Then came the coughing. It seemed as if I coughed morning, noon, and night. The woman gave me a bed bath, and washed my hair. She spoon fed me broth then bread. I could feel my body begin to ache. I needed to move. I began moving my arms and legs. I don't know how long I had been ill, but soon I was sitting in a chair and eating soups and stews.

Then I noticed the sun was out. A man came into the room and spoke to the woman that had been caring for me.
"I think the roads are passable now. We can try and get her to the doctor".
The man carried me to his car. The woman placed a pillow in the back seat and encouraged me to lie down. She covered me with several blankets and closed the door. She climbed in the front passenger seat and waited for the man to start the car.

I fell asleep on the drive. When I woke up, I found myself being lifted out of the car and placed on a gurney. Several people in white uniforms pushed the gurney into an area within a building. The wheel of the gurney squeaked all the way. A nurse came in and introduced herself. She took my temperature, blood pressure, and pulse. She listened to my heart and lungs. Next came the men in uniforms. They wheeled me down several hallways and into another room.
X-rays were taken. Then I was wheeled back to where the nurse had first met me. A doctor came in and told me I had double pneumonia and would need intravenous antibiotics. Without any further notification, an intravenous catheter was inserted into my arm and a bag of fluids was dripping into my veins. I was admitted into a room that smelled of disinfectant. I slept.   Periodically, a nurse would come in, take my temperature and have me swallow some pills. A man would come in and place a mask on my face and suddenly a mist would occur. I would breathe in this mist and I could feel my lungs open up and my heart speed up.
I had lost track of time. I had no idea what day of the week it was, what month it was, or even what year it may be. I did begin to feel better. I was made to sit up daily. Food was placed in front of me. I was encouraged to eat. I was told if I didn't eat, a tube would be inserted into my nose and pushed down into my stomach to give me nourishment. I began to eat. I didn't want to have anything stuck into my nose.

I hadn't seen Daniel since our last conversation. I know I missed him but I didn't think he missed me. After all, it was Daniel that didn't want him and me to be together forever. It took a long time before I could stand or begin taking steps. I finally did get to the point where I could ambulate. It was short distances at first. After practicing twice a day, I finally built my stamina back up to the point of being independent.

"Emily, you are well enough to go home. Take it easy, but keep up the plan of care we have been doing here", said the doctor. I agreed. The nurse brought in my belongings, but they reeked of mildew. "I'll have to get you some clothes from our donated supply", she said.

"Is my wallet in that bag?" I asked.

"The nurse donned some gloves and slowly pulled item after item out of the nasty smelling bag. "Do you mind if I throw these things away?" she asked.

"I don't want them. I need my personal belongings though", I exclaimed.

When she pulled out my necklace, I realized why Daniel had not come to see me. He had been anchored to the bag. The nurse handed me my necklace and found my smelly wallet. I looked at my wallet and realized I needed to throw it away. I removed the money and my identification and then tossed the wallet in the trash can.

The nurse brought in some clothing and some funny looking shoes.

"These are shoe covers that the operating staff wear in the operating theatre. They will do for shoes until you can buy another pair". I dressed. I looked like a person with extremely bad taste but at least I could leave the hospital. The nurse made me sit in a wheel chair. She then pushed me to the front door and even waited until I was safely inside the cab before returning to her floor.

Once at the hotel, I explained the situation and the hotel manager found my things among the held items. I booked a room for the night and the manager arranged for a car and driver for me. I took a very long and very hot shower. It felt good to be in my own clothes. I put on my shoes and called to book a flight home. Then Daniel appeared.

Daniel attempted to put his arms around me. I shrugged him away.

"You don't need to pretend any longer. I will help you figure out what you are seeking because I don't go back on my promises but don't act like you care. You've proven to me, exactly how you feel".

I could see the shock on Daniel's face. I had deeply hurt him. I wanted so badly to be in his arms. For him to hold me, kiss me, and make love to me. He had proven that he didn't want to spend eternity together.

I could see Daniel gathering his thoughts.

"Emily, I know you thought if you died, we would be together forever. But there is no guarantee that if you died, that would happen. I am anchored here for some ungodly reason. You may have passed on and gone where good souls go to when they die. As much as I love you, I couldn't see you giving up your life. At least not for me".

I was still angry. "I need some time to think this through". Daniel just nodded and disappeared. I sat on the bed. My head felt like it would explode. My emotions were all over the place. I loved Daniel and I did want to be with him. Was it possible for us to be in each other's world?

Then there came a knock at the door. I almost jumped out of my skin. When I opened the door, a young woman stood in the hallway.

"Can I help you?" I asked.

"It may be me who can help you", she replied. I could feel my brows furrow at her response.

"I don't understand", I exclaimed.

"May I come in?" she asked.

"Yes, of course. Excuse me, I am still recovering from an illness".

"Yes, I know", she replied.

"You do?"

"Yes", she said as she handed me a newspaper.

I read the article. It was about me. A poor picture of me was included with the article. It spoke of how I had gotten off the bicycle and managed to lose myself in the woods. It also said how I was rescued and cared for by the family in the cabin.

"I made the paper. That is very odd, don't you think?"

"No, a small town prints anything that is news. However, it was your picture that made me come see you", stated the woman.

"Why is that?"

"You'll have to come with me for that answer", replied the woman.

"And just who are you?" I asked.

"Sarah Oliver"

"I don't understand why I should go anywhere with you".

"According to the article, you were looking for something but you couldn't say what. I believe I have something that may guide you in the right direction", exclaimed Sarah.

"What might that be?"

"Let's just say a picture is worth a thousand words, shall we?"

I put on my necklace with the ring. I knew Daniel would be close by.

"Ok. Let me get a jacket".

Sarah had a moderate size car. I slide into the front passenger seat on the left. It was so odd getting in on that side of the car without a steering wheel being in the way.

I actually enjoyed being out and about again. The climate had turned colder. I hadn't considered how long I had been ill.

"What is the date?" I asked.

"The end of September, why?" asked Sarah.

"I didn't realize how long I had been ill. It's a strange feeling knowing weeks have passed and I have no true recollection of it".

Chapter 34

Sarah pulled into a driveway. A very long driveway. It snaked through over hanging tree branches and large shrubs. Soon a small house came into view. Sarah pulled into a small grassy area. After pulling the hand brake, she turned off the motor.

Sarah ushered me into her home. It had an earthy scent and brought back memories of the safe house Ali and I had stayed in. I looked around and could see dozens of house plants. Some plants were hanging from homemade macramé hangers and some were potted and sat in corners of the room. Several large fern like plants gave the room a focal point. Sarah continued to lead me through her dining room, and then into what she called her library.

As I entered, I didn't notice the large picture hanging on the wall to my left. I did notice the wall of book shelves that held copious books of various sizes and shapes.

"You really must like to read", I said in astonishment. Sarah then pointed to the picture. As my eyes crossed the room to the picture, my knees almost buckled. It was as if I had spent hours posing for an artist. For there, hanging on the wall was a portrait of a woman who looked just like me.

"I don't understand. Who is she? Who painted her?" I fired off question after question.

"First, let me put on the kettle and we'll talk" said Sarah calmly.

I couldn't take my eyes off the portrait. It looked just like me down to the loose hairs that tickle my ears. I walked closer. I couldn't make out the signature of the artist.

Sarah came back holding a tray with a plate of biscuits and tea. She sat the tray down and invited me to sit at the small table nearest the portrait.

After the tea was poured and a biscuit placed on a small plate in front of me, Sarah began.

"The woman has long since died. However; the woman's great-great-great granddaughter lives not too far from here. I thought I would show you the picture and then, if you were up to it, take you to see her". I choked on my biscuit.

"Are you serious? Of course, I want to see her. How did you come to attain the portrait?"

"Well, that is a long story. Let's have you meet the artist's granddaughter first and then see if we have time for more stories".

Sarah excused herself and telephoned the artist's granddaughter. When Sarah returned, she told Emily, "I am sorry. Lillian is not up for company today. She suggested we stop by after breakfast tomorrow. If you'd like, I can drive you there or I can give you Lillian's telephone number and address".

"I would feel better, if you were with me. I don't really know the lady".

"Shall I pick you up tomorrow around 9:00 a.m.", Sarah asked.

"That would be great. I hope I'm not inconveniencing you".

"Not at all", replied Sarah, "It's always a treat to see Lillian".

"I'll have to cancel my car and make arrangements for another night at the hotel", I spoke to myself. Sarah grabbed her car keys and we headed for her car.

After Sarah had driven me back to the hotel and I entered my room, Daniel appeared.

"I don't wish to intrude, but I had no recourse but to be with you when you viewed the portrait of yourself. May we discuss this new situation or do you wish me to leave?"

"Daniel, I am still very confused. I have no idea where I need to go or want to go from here. I feel hurt and alone".

"I am here, if only you would see things clearly".

"You mean, your way, don't you Daniel?"

"Emily, there is no certainty into what happens after we pass from this world. I do not want to lose what little time we may have together. I am truly sorry if I have hurt you in any way. I do love you. So, to quote you, the baseball is in your court".

I had to smile. "It's the ball, not baseball is in your court. You have put your sentence together incorrectly".

Daniel saw the smile on my face and drew closer.

"I have been thinking about what you said. I'm still not sure I agree with you or not. I do know that I don't want to spend what little time we may have fighting with each other".

"Nor do I", said Daniel, "Nor do I".

Daniel swept me up in his arms and kissed me so deeply, I wasn't sure I wouldn't suffocate. I had to admit, it felt good, having Daniel's arms around me. As angry as I had been, I sure felt better receiving this bear hug.

"I need to cancel the car and ask for another night here at the hotel", I informed Daniel.

After placing the necessary calls, I realized my stomach was beginning to growl. I told Daniel I needed to get to the restaurant within the hotel before they closed. Daniel suggested he stay close by, just in case I became too tired.

"You are still recovering from your illness", he said.

I agreed with him and we left the room.

I was lucky to arrive a half hour before the restaurant closed. I ordered what is called "toad in the hole" for lunch. Sausages within a bowl surrounded by mashed potatoes with whole cooked peas included on the side. The food was good! I had a cup of hot tea. I realized the tea in England was more flavorful than in the United States.

After lunch, I did feel fatigued. I paid for my lunch and returned to my room. The maid service had been completed by the time I returned. Daniel appeared as soon as the door closed. "The color has gone from your face. You need to rest", exclaimed Daniel.

"I do feel tired", I admitted. I slid my shoes off and laid down on the bed. Daniel sat in a chair nearest the bed. I could see the worry on Daniel's face.

"I'm just tired, Daniel, I just need to take it easy for a few days. The doctor has me on a regime and I have not deviated from that plan". Daniel just nodded.

I closed my eyes. I didn't feel Daniel placing the covers over me or sliding into bed beside me. I didn't notice the sunlight fading into night. I didn't notice I had slept past dinner or that I hadn't set an alarm clock. I hadn't placed a wake-up call. But I slept.

Daniel woke me up at 7:00 a.m. When I looked at the clock, I had to shake my head and rub my eyes to believe I had slept so long. "I can't believe I slept for 17 hours", I said as I slowly slid my achy body from the bed. "I can't believe how achy I can get just from sleeping".

The hot shower helped to alleviate the aches and pains my body felt. I brushed my hair back into a ponytail. I dressed in a plain black blouse and black pants. I had an hour to eat before Sarah would arrive. After slipping on my black loafers and a black sweater, I tucked my money in my pocket along with my identification and left my room. I told Daniel that I would eat and wait outside for Sarah. Daniel understood and agreed he would still remain close by. I could still see the worry in Daniel's face.

Sarah arrived a little early. "Do you mind if I have a quick cup of tea?"

"Of course, I don't mind", I replied. I sat with Sarah as she prepared her tea. She poured milk in her tea. I found that strangely odd. It must have shown on my face as she smiled and said, "It's sort of what you American's do with your coffee. I did want to speak to you before we go to Lillian's".

"Alright", I said, not certain what information Sarah was going to convey.

"Lillian is a bit eccentric. I don't want you to be taken by surprise by some of the things she says. I thought it best to discuss this with you beforehand". I nodded. I wasn't certain what I was getting myself into. Now I was a bit nervous.

Chapter 35

The drive took us into the country side. I did enjoy seeing the beautiful buildings slowly disappear into land that stretched as far as the eye could see. Small mansions dotted the country side. When the scenery began to demonstrate sporadic sections of trees, Sarah informed me that we were very close.

Lillian's home was a very large brown stoned building. Some may even call her home a mansion. A huge brick wall made from the same large brown stones surrounded the home a good portion of her land. Hedges and trees landscaped the area nicely. A small river could be seen flowing well behind the back of the home. Sarah pulled her car through the gate and into the long driveway. When Sarah parked the car, a valet came out and said, "I shall move the car into the garage". Sarah nodded confirmation. We slowly walked up the few stairs to the front door.

The butler held the door as we entered. After the door was closed and latched, the butler led us into the library. Lillian was sitting on a large cushioned sofa. When I entered, the look of shock upon her face made me worry for her health.

"Are you alright?" I asked.

"Forgive me, my dear. Your resemblance to one of my ancestors is quite remarkable".

Sarah sat down to the left of Lillian. I sat to Lillian's right.

"When Sarah called me and told me that you looked like one of the subjects in one of my portraits, I never dared dream you would look exactly like her".

"Her?" I asked.

"Elizabeth, my great-great-grandmother".

"Sarah, would you mind handing me that book from the table?" asked Lillian.

Sarah placed the large worn book onto Lillian's lap.

"This is my family album. Long ago, my great-great-grandmother decided to paint a portrait of each of her ancestors to decorate the walls of this home. Many still hang on the walls. However; my great-great-grandmother never painted a portrait of herself. I decided to continue my great-great-grandmother's work. You see, I am a painter too. Although my family is independently wealthy and able to sustain itself on the family money, I have earned to a small degree, some recognition for my work. My paintings have sold for thousands. I do not believe I have any more talent than any other artist, but somehow, my paintings seem to have a life of their own". Then Lillian opened up the family album.

"This is one of my cousins. I don't remember if he is from my mother's or my father's side of the family. His portrait hangs in one of the guest rooms. He wasn't a very memorable character. He died in his thirty's without ever marrying or traveling.

The next page held a picture of an older woman with three children. This was my great-great aunt. Her children surround her in the picture. Fred, the oldest, then Arthur, and Virgil. Poor Virgil. His hair was so long and he was so cute, at first glance he appears to be a girl.

Next came a picture of Elizabeth. The picture was black and white but it looked as if someone had recently taken my photograph.

My mouth must have dropped open because Lillian looked at the picture and then at me. "It really is uncanny". I could only nod in agreement. I stared at the picture trying to see if there were any differences between the woman in the picture and myself when Lillian said, "I speak to her often". I shivered.

"Excuse me?" I said. Obviously I must have heard wrong.

"I speak to Elizabeth often".

I knew people often speak to their loved ones who have departed this earth.

"My grandmother use to speak to my grandfather after he died. I think it made her feel as if she hadn't lost him".

"You don't understand, my dear, I speak to her and she speaks to me". I hoped Daniel was hearing this.

"Emily, Lillian holds séance's" added Sarah to clarify the situation.

"Yes, I do. I am holding one tonight and I am insisting you stay".

"For what purpose?" I asked.

"My dear, there is a reason you and the portrait have found each other. I believe Elizabeth may be reaching out to you".

"I'm not sure what that is supposed to mean".

"Do you believe that it is a coincidence that you have found a portrait of a woman that looks exactly like you? "Lillian asked.

"Actually, I am really confused. I do think it odd that the events that led me here have resulted in this situation. How did Sarah end up with the portrait?"

"I was at one of Lil's séances when Elizabeth told Lillian it was imperative I have the portrait. At first, I felt it should remain with Lillian but Elizabeth said it was fate".

"Fate?" I said.

"Elizabeth didn't explain, but said the portrait must be given to Sarah", said Lillian.

"To make a long story short, Lillian had a heart attack. I was assigned to care for Lillian during her recovery stage. Lillian refused to go to hospital so Lillian's doctor insisted Lillian have a companion to stay with her. That was several years ago. I am friends with the doctor's wife. She suggested I fill the position. The rest of the story is history", explained Sarah.

"I was very weak after my cardiac episode. I dreamed my great-great-grandmother came to me. She told me I needed to survive because she had a task for me. When I was able to get out of bed. I had strict orders from the doctor not to exert myself. That meant hours and hours of sitting. I picked up my paint brushes again. My first portrait was of Elizabeth".

"Ma'am, would you like tea served in here or the dining room?" asked the Butler. The butler was so stealthy, I hadn't even realized he had entered the room and stood only a few feet away from me.

"In here, please", replied Lillian.

"We always have tea at 4:00 pm", said Sarah.

The tea and biscuits aka cookies were delicious.

"I will arrange to have the medium come tonight. Sarah, will be able to attend?" asked Lillian.

"I'm afraid I have made other plans. I actually need to leave soon or I shall be late" said Sarah.

"Emily, you will come?" said Lillian not in a question but confirmation like statement.

"I don't have a means of transportation. Sarah was kind enough to bring me here today".

"Then you shall stay the night and I can have my driver take you back to the city tomorrow".

I didn't have a clue as to what would happen at the séance'. I had never attended one. Maybe it was my church upbringing, but I was never curious about such things.

"May I use the powder room?" I asked.

"My apologies. I should have offered you the conveniences when you arrived", and with that statement, Lillian called for her maid.

"Julia will show you to your room. You will find everything you require there. I suggest a nap before dinner. The séance will begin at midnight".

Chapter 36

The room was unbelievably beautiful. It was decorated ornately and large enough for a queen. The bed had pillars that hovered close to the ceiling. Paintings hung randomly around the room. I used the facilities adjunct to the room and explored the art. Some portraits were signed "Elizabeth" while others had signatures more difficult to read. I was amazed at the different types of clothing the person within each of the portraits wore.

As I wandered and explored the room, Daniel suddenly appeared. "You startle me every time you do that", I screeched. Daniel just stared at the portraits.

"I know that man", he said.

As I examined the portrait closer, it was one of the portraits painted by Elizabeth.

"Who is he?" I asked.

"That is uncle"

I stared harder at the portrait. I could see the family resemblance.

"I remember seeing the name Elizabeth in our genealogy search but I forget exactly where in the family she actually was".

"Elizabeth was my sister"

"Your sister? Why didn't you tell me you had a sister? Why didn't you tell me she looked exactly like me? This entire situation is getting more bizarre by the day".

"Elizabeth was much older than I. Long before my father met and married my mother, my father was married to Abigail. Abigail had a young daughter from her first marriage. That young daughter was Elizabeth. Abigail was a widow. Her first husband had died at sea. From what little I have heard, it sounds like Abigail's first husband was a merchant of some kind.

My father married Abigail and took Elizabeth as his own daughter. Two years after my father married Abigail, she died in childbirth. I would have had a brother had they lived. When Elizabeth was 13 years old, my father met and married my mother. I was born three years later. By that time, Elizabeth was 16 years old. She was sought after by many young men. Although father had wanted Elizabeth to marry someone local, she had married a man from Ireland when she was 17 years old and relocated outside of England.

"What happened to your mother and father?"

"A carriage accident of sorts. My Mum and father went out of town to see a home they were considering purchasing. Although I was four years old, they decided the trip would be too much for a child of my age. They left me with the nanny. Uncle said the bridge they were crossing gave way. They fell to their deaths". I could hear the change in Daniels voice when he spoke of his parents.

"I am so sorry".

"Uncle was my father's brother. He took me in and raised me as his own son. Elizabeth was sixteen years my senior and always thought of me as a "little" brother, so we rarely wrote to each other. Men don't correspond as much as women do, so Auntie kept in touch with Elizabeth".

"Elizabeth had her own set of troubles. Her husband wasn't good with money and he took heavy to the drink. Elizabeth began painting to bring in extra money. She did have talent. A gallery owner recognized her talent and began placing her works in his gallery".

"The portraits I have seen are very good", I exclaimed.

"Elizabeth's husband became ill. He was bed ridden for several years. By that time, Elizabeth had two or three children to care for".

"It doesn't sound like her life turned out the way she had planned", I speculated.

"When I was older and had taken a position, I sent Elizabeth a few pounds each month. I told Auntie to mail it to her and say the money was for the children".

"That was very kind of you. Did Elizabeth ever thank you?"

"Elizabeth always wrote Auntie back saying the children used the funds for clothing or something of that nature".

"Did Elizabeth know you joined forces the night your uncle died?"

"I left the day after my uncle's death. I don't' know if auntie wrote Elizabeth or not".

"Well, we may just be able to find out", I stated.

"I don't understand", said Daniel.

"You did hear Lillian say she has been talking to Elizabeth, didn't you?"

"Yes, and Lillian is her great-great granddaughter"

"If Elizabeth shows up tonight, we may be able to discover what it is that you are searching for".

Daniel got a faraway look in his eyes and a sadness came over his face.

"Our time maybe short, Emily", he said. I could hear the sadness in his voice.

Yes, our time may be very short, I thought.

I called my hotel and gave my sincere apologies. I asked the clerk if she would be so kind as to cancel my car and driver. I explained that I would be staying the night in the country but would return to the hotel tomorrow. The clerk voiced she was happy to perform the tasks given her and would leave the confirmation in an envelope at the front desk.

Chapter 37

I don't remember falling asleep. I had laid down on the huge bed. It was very soft and comfortable. Daniel and I had been talking. The next thing I knew was I was awakened by a knock on the door. "Yes", I said.

"Ma'am, your presence is requested in the dining room", announced the butler.

"I'll be there shortly", I answered.

I rushed to the bathroom and freshened up. I ran a brush through my hair and then looked for Daniel.

"Daniel, are you here?" I asked.

Daniel appeared. He looked so sullen. "I am here, Emily".

"Daniel, no matter what happens tonight, you know I love you".

"I love you too. It is very difficult for me, knowing I may not see you again".

I wanted to cry. A second knock on the door, jolted us back to reality.

"I'm coming", I replied. I kissed Daniel. "My love will be with you forever", I confessed. To prevent myself from crying, I opened the door and headed for the stairs.

The butler ushered me to the dining room. The table was an antique. The top was polished to a high gloss that it could have been used as a mirror. Lillian sat at the head of the table. She was sipping a glass of wine when she noticed I had entered.

"Please, come sit by me. These tables are much too large for small gatherings but I do enjoy dining at the table my husband and I shared for over 57 years".

I sat to Lillian's right. The minute I sat down, the butler clapped his hands. A maid came in carrying a tray with soup.

"What soup do we have today?" asked Lillian.

"Pumpkin squash soup, madam", replied the maid.

"The pumpkin squash soup is wonderful", exclaimed Lillian.

I placed my napkin on my lap and brought the spoon to my lips. With the first sip of soup and I knew I wanted the recipe.

"This is delicious", I announced.

The bowl emptied too quickly. I had hopes of having more but the maid whisked the bowls away before I could put my spoon down or make the request for seconds. The next course was stuffed mushrooms. The mushrooms were very large. The stuffing used to stuff the mushroom contained crushed walnuts and a strong sage taste. Melted cheese topped the mushroom. A dap of caviar garnished the plate. I was in awe.

"Do you have meals like this every day?" I asked.

"Yes", replied Lillian, "but I usually take my meals in my room. It is nice to have a guest in which to share a meal". I felt badly for Lillian. She was obviously very lonely.

The main course consisted of rack of lamb, boiled potatoes, and turnips. I was getting stuffed. Dessert came. A layered cake with buttery looking icing.

"I don't think I have any room for dessert", I admitted.

"You must try at least a small sliver", encouraged Lillian as she placed a thin piece in front of me, "carrot cake with sour cream icing".

The cake wasn't too sweet and literally melted in my mouth. I smiled and slowly devoured the cake. I was overly full and I noticed my breathing was shallow. I was stuffed to the maximum but it was worth the discomfort. I told Lillian I had never had a meal that was so satisfying. She glowed as she said, "my servants have been with me for years and they have yet to make something that is not well liked".

The butler soon appeared and assisted Lillian out of her chair. Lillian held the butler's arm as he escorted her to the library. "We shall take our coffee in the library". I didn't know if she was speaking to me or the butler, but I acknowledged I had heard and agreed to the plan.

The clock on the mantle sounded eleven thirty. The butler and maid entered the room and began rearranging the room.

"May I help?" I asked.

Lillian shook her head "No" as she continued to sip on her coffee. Lights were dimmed or turned off. The dark wooden walls made the room very dark. Candles were lite and placed randomly around the room. A large round table was soon carried in and placed in the middle of the room. A woman dressed in white chiffon stood in the doorway. The butler walked ahead of her and pulled out the chair at the head of the table. Lillian stood and then sat to the woman's right. An empty seat was on the woman's left. For me, I assumed.

"Emily, I would like you meet Yvonne. Yvonne has been asked to come tonight to speak to Elizabeth. If you would have a seat, we will begin", said Lillian.

Yvonne, didn't say much. She lite a small bunch of plants that had been tied together.

"Yvonne begins by burning sage to cleanse the room and to prevent any evil from entering", explained Lillian.

Next, Yvonne lite some incense and placed it in a small ashtray like platter in front of her.

Yvonne then asked everyone to clear their minds and she closed her eyes. Yvonne began to mumble something. I gave a puzzled look at Lillian, but Lillian just placed her index finger to her lips as to say "hush".

Yvonne continued to mumble something for twenty minutes or so. I did notice the room did feel a little cooler. It's after midnight and it's an old drafty house, I rationalized.

Then I noticed the white fog-like matter forming in the air behind Yvonne's chair. I opened my mouth to speak but Lillian again, shook her head "No".

I could only stare in the direction of the fog. As I stared, the fog began to take form and morphed into a figure.

Yvonne spoke and I jumped.

"Elizabeth, we have a surprise for you".

Before Yvonne could explain my presence, Elizabeth spoke.

"Daniel, where are you? I know you are here but I cannot see you".

Yvonne and Lillian looked at each other with expressions of surprise. I squirmed a bit.

"Daniel, I know you are here. Why do you not come forth?" asked Elizabeth.

Daniel appeared. He stood beside my chair only momentarily. Elizabeth held out her hand, and Daniel walked up to Elizabeth and said, "Hello, sister".

"There is much we need to discuss", informed Elizabeth to Daniel. Daniel took Elizabeth's hand and nodded yes. Then Elizabeth and Daniel walked through the wall and disappeared.

Yvonne and Lillian just stared at the wall. I had no idea how long Daniel would be gone. I didn't know if he and Elizabeth would return here or not. Would I see Daniel again?

"Does this sort of thing happen often?" I asked acting as if I had no clue about ghosts.

"Never", said Lillian.

Yvonne was still in shock.

"Yvonne", called Lillian. Yvonne just kept staring at the wall. "Yvonne, do we need to end this séance", Lillian said.

"What? "Said Yvonne, "Oh, yes, of course". Yvonne began mumbling something again and then stood. The lights were suddenly on. I felt my eyes pain as the bright lights stabbed at them. The candles were snuffed out and Yvonne, asked if I would like to stay an additional day to try another séance. I declined.

"I think I would like to go bed now", I said, faking a stretch.

"Of course, dear". The butler was somehow contacted and appeared. Lillian spoke to the butler, "Please show Emily to her room".

Chapter 38

I slowly climbed the staircase. After closing the door to my room, the fears began to form in my mind. I called for Daniel. No reply came. I didn't know if Daniel was still tethered to the ring or if Elizabeth's presence had changed whatever forces that be, that had first imprisoned Daniel. Then the thought hit, what if Daniel didn't return. I never got the chance to say goodbye. I've never been an out of control emotional person before but I sure turned into one that night.

The last time I looked at the clock, it was 2:30 a.m. Of course, I was looking at the clock through tearing and blurry eyes. At 7:30 a.m. Daniel woke me by softly calling my name. "Emily". I sat up on the bed. I rubbed my eyes to ensure I was truly seeing Daniel. When I realized he was standing there, I climbed out of bed and ran into his arms.

"I thought I'd never see you again".

Daniel lifted up my chin and pressed his lips to mine. I held onto Daniel. I was afraid to let go. "Emily", Daniel said. Here it comes, I thought to myself. I put space between Daniel and myself. "Where did you and Elizabeth go? What did she tell you?"

Daniel looked down. I could feel my legs shaking so I sat on the bed. "Talk to me, Daniel. I'm one raw nerve. I don't like being left behind in the dark".

"Let me tell you Elizabeth's story", Daniel said.

I could only nod. There was a lump in my throat the size of a grapefruit.

"My aunt wrote to Elizabeth after I left. What auntie didn't know was Elizabeth's husband had recently died. Auntie's letter to Elizabeth was a godsend. She packed up her belongings and moved her children and herself to England. Auntie's health was not good. Elizabeth took care of auntie until her death. She died only eight months after my uncle's death. Auntie told Elizabeth about a secret she held. Apparently the secret involves me. Elizabeth wouldn't go into the secret tonight".

"Will this secret about you impact your ability to stay here with me?" I asked.

"I don't know. Elizabeth has been waiting for decades for me to come find her. She and I have much, much more to discuss".

"I don't understand".

"Elizabeth spoke of how auntie had left her estate to Elizabeth and I. Elizabeth said I had been wounded during the battle. She said I was struck above my right eye. I guess I was out of my head for a few days. Elizabeth ensured I was cared for. Elizabeth said I went from hallucinating and wild to deathly calm. I failed to wake up again. The head wound had caused my memory to be lost and ultimately caused my death. Poor Elizabeth. She lost her entire adult family in only a few months. Her only salvation was her children".

"I still don't understand", I said.

"What is it that confuses you?"

"Why is Elizabeth still hanging around?"

"I believe it is the secret she promised to keep", stated Daniel.

"So when is she going to tell you this big secret she knows?"

"Elizabeth said she would reveal the secret later."

"Later? When is later?" I asked.

"Now", said Elizabeth as she appeared.

I jumped. My heart was beating so fast it felt as though it would beat itself through my chest.

Elizabeth stared at me. She must have noticed how much I looked like her.

"Emily, this is my sister, Elizabeth", said Daniel, "Elizabeth, this is Emily".

Elizabeth continued to stare at me.

"Elizabeth is hesitant to reveal the secret", explained Daniel.

"But why?" I asked.

"Because of the consequences that may result from revealing the secret".

"Consequences?" I questioned.

"Just as you and I believe that I may pass over when I find out why I am anchored here, Elizabeth believes if she divulges the secret, she would pass on", explained Daniel.

"Isn't that what you both want? To end whatever it is that is holding you here?"

"To go where?" asked Elizabeth.

"Where ever we all are supposed to go after …." I couldn't finish the sentence. I could see Elizabeth looked uncomfortable.

"Why is she here?" asked Elizabeth as she pointed to me but looked at Daniel.

"Emily owns the ring that I seem to be tethered to", stated Daniel.

"The ring!" exclaimed Elizabeth. Daniel appeared surprised. How did Elizabeth know about the ring?

"You know about the ring? "Asked Daniel.

"Yes, I know", she replied.

"Tell me", insisted Daniel. Elizabeth looked distressed. I have to admit, I was distressed too. If Daniel unlocked the reason he was attached to the ring, would he leave me?

"Elizabeth. Are you afraid to pass over?" Daniel asked.

Elizabeth nodded, "yes".

"You really don't know for certain you will pass over. You are assuming things, aren't you?" I asked.

"Emily, we are not certain what the consequences will be once Elizabeth reveals her secret. She and I may both be affected", said Daniel. I could hear the sadness in his voice.

My face grew pale. I know Daniel and I were searching for why he was tethered to the ring, but I didn't think I could lose him so soon or so suddenly.

"Emily, I need to speak to Elizabeth", stated Daniel. Elizabeth looked up at Daniel. He reached out his hand. She placed her hand in his and they disappeared.

Chapter 39

When Daniel and Elizabeth disappeared, they appeared between environments. There was a misty lite area in which they stood.

"Elizabeth, we were not meant to live forever. We must end this non-existence now".

"Daniel, I am frightened. I have become accustom to being here, around. I can take walks through the garden. I can sit in the library and read books. I can interact with live people if so choose too".

Daniel took Elizabeth's hands in his. "Sister, if you are here because of a secret promise. And I am here because of the secret, we will go together when the secret is revealed. You need not be afraid".

"Death is the one trip we all make alone Daniel. I am still afraid".

"You need not be", proclaimed Daniel.

"Daniel, I have always feared the afterlife. I have sins I cannot be forgiven for".

"You could never do anything that would prevent you from entering the gates of heaven".

"You have no way of knowing that brother".

"You were raised in religion, married, and raised several strong sons. How could you not have earned your place in heaven?"

"I wasn't a good wife. When John took to the drink, I began to hate him. He resented my painting notoriety. He was a very sad man. When he became ill, I avoided him as much as possible".

"You could not have been blamed for wanting to avoid a man who would not or could not work because of his love of the drink".

"He would become angry. He would verbally assault the children and me. He struck me more times than I care to recall. I grew to hate him. The children hated him too".

"Hating someone does not prevent you from entering heaven".

"I let him die. Did you hear me brother? I let him die".

Daniel's face grew pale. "What are you saying? You would never intentionally harm anyone".

"You knew me when I was young and innocent. I was so naive. I should have known that John was only interested in marrying someone with a large dowry. Uncle gave John 500 pounds when we wed".

"Was your life that awful"?

"Not at first. John left the house each morning. Our very tiny house, I tried to make it a home. I cooked and cleaned. We couldn't afford servants. John would attend gatherings in the evening. He always went alone. I believed he was going to these functions to further his business connections. I later discovered he was telling others he was a bachelor".

"Why would John do that? I'm certain you were a great wife. There must have been some misunderstanding".

"John would come home with the scent of wine and perfume on his clothes. Occasionally an invitation would arrive at our home. A perfume scented invitation. I made the error of opening one. A woman, her name was Beatrice, thanking John for the romantic carriage ride and a secret meeting. This Beatrice invited John for a small intimate dinner. I took the liberty of responding for him. I explained to Beatrice that John would no longer be available for carriage rides, secret meetings, or anything else for that matter. I told her since John was married and would soon be a father, I felt it only polite to let her know she was wasting her efforts. When John discovered what I had done, he struck me. It didn't seem to matter to him I was carrying his child".

"Why didn't you come home to us?"

"I wrote uncle. I explained to him what I have just told you".

"And?"

"Uncle explained that John was just young and had manly desires. He told me it was my fault. If I couldn't keep my husband interested, men had the right to seek affection elsewhere. Uncle explained that if men weren't satisfied at home, men had that right to find someone who would make them feel manly".

"Uncle wrote that?"

"How could I come home after he responded to my pleas with that logic?"

"Did you tell auntie?"

"No. How could I explain to her what her own husband had said? I couldn't risk causing them to have troubles".

"Why didn't you contact me? "

"You, baby brother? I couldn't put such a burden on you".

"I wish you had. My blood boils thinking what that man put you through".

"John continued his behaviors. Through the years, John forced himself on me. A husband's right, he would say. After our second son was born, John's health began to decline. I had started painting portraits. I was using the money I earned with my painting skills to pay for our essentials. I was squirreling away a little money here and there. I had plans to leave John when I had enough saved. The doctor told John he had to stop drinking. He told John he had to start eating right and to get rest. My boys and I tried to care for him. But John spoke to us as though we were of no worth".

"What did your sons do when they heard their own father speak to them as though they were of little or no worth?"

"They grew to hate him. They would avoid him. My boys would offer to cook, clean, or do any other task rather than go near their own father".

"I cannot find fault in that".

"I hated John. I hated him for what he did to our marriage. I hated him for what he did to our lives. I hated him for what he did to the lives of our sons".

"Hate is understandable, given the situation you had to endure".

"I began putting spirits into John's water jug".

"You did what?"

"I gave him spirits. I kept him quiet, appeased, and ultimately hastened the end of his life. He didn't deserve to be cared for. He slowly tortured my sons and me when he was healthy. He continued to treat us badly when he needed us. It was almost as if he felt so superior to us that he felt he deserved care and yet could continue his vulgar and demeaning behavior without consequence".

"Would John have lived had he not had the spirits you gave him?"

"The doctor said he would survive, but would continue to be in poor health for years".

"I see", said Daniel. "I also see a woman who did what she felt she needed to do to protect her sons. You may have given him wine or spirits, but nothing more than what he would have given himself had he had the strength to do so".

"Oh Daniel, I feared you'd hate me once you knew the truth about me and my indiscretions. I have prayed for forgiveness from the Lord each and every day".

"Elizabeth, I am most certain the Lord forgives you. Although I don't believe you have done anything wrong".

"Daniel, go say your goodbyes to your friend Emily. By noon, I shall reveal the secret to you. We shall pass over together, hand in hand".

Chapter 40

By the time Daniel appeared, I was a basket case. I had no idea what was happening. Daniel looked distressed which in turn made me more worried.

"Daniel, are you alright?"

"We have precious little time left. Elizabeth is going to share the secret she has protected for decades. She believes, as do I, that the secret she has kept is what is keeping her and I anchored to this existence".

My heart ached as Daniel spoke. He must have realized how I had taken the news.

"I love you, Emily. If this secret does release me from this world, I shall wait for you at heaven's gates".

I ran to Daniel. He kissed me hard. I could tell he wanted this kiss, possibly our last kiss to last a long time. I put my arms around his neck. He hugged me so hard I could barely breathe, but I didn't care. I was still in Daniel's arms when Elizabeth suddenly appeared. Daniel gave me a soft kiss on my forehead then turned toward Elizabeth.

"Your injury prevented you from remembering your past, Daniel", she said.

"Remembering my past?" questioned Daniel.

"Auntie said you had hidden a fortune in coins to prevent our enemies from using the money to pay mercenaries to fight against us"

"I don't remember hiding anything", stated Daniel.

"Auntie also said, you had the coordinates placed on a ring so the money could be retrieved. She said you told her to hold onto the ring until you returned or the battle was over".

"Again", Daniel admitted, "I do not recall any of this".

"The jeweler found numbers behind the stone on your ring", I added. Daniel nodded in agreement.

"Auntie never had the chance to tell me where she hid the ring. I searched everywhere. Auntie died before she could tell me".

"Are you saying the coins are still buried somewhere?" I asked, looking at Daniel.

But Daniel was looking at Elizabeth. Elizabeth had a look of fright. She was slowly fading. It appeared as though she were trying to speak as she had opened her mouth, but no sound was heard. She reached for Daniel. Before he could reach her, Elizabeth disappeared.

I didn't know what had happened exactly. I think Elizabeth had fore-filled her promise and had been released. I believe she had passed over. Daniel just stood and stared at the spot that Elizabeth had up until moments ago, stood.

"What do we do now?" I asked. Before Daniel could reply, a knock was heard. I was startled. It took me a moment to get myself calm enough to answer.

"Yes", I responded.

"Ma'am requests you to join her in the dining room for brunch".

It was after noon. I tried to ignore my growling stomach, but of late, it was more difficult to push the hunger pains away. I washed my face as Daniel continued to stand looking around for Elizabeth. I think he found it difficult to accept that she had been released and yet he still remained.

"Do you think she passed over?" I asked.

"I hope so", he whispered, "She deserves some peace of mind". Daniel had such a sad look on his face.

"Will you be ok, if I go downstairs and have a bite of lunch?" Daniel just nodded. He seemed as though he were in shock, yet I could tell he had something weighing on his mind.

I met Lillian in the dining room. Lillian was seated at the head of the table. A place was set to her right for me.

"Good morning, my dear. I hope you were able to get some sleep after our harrowing experience last night. I must say, Yvonne and I have never encountered two spirits in one night. I hope we hadn't frightened you too much".

"I managed to get a few hours of sleep. I have to admit, the experience did leave me with a lot of questions".

"I looked up my ancestors after we retired last night. The gentleman that appeared to us last night was my great-great-grandmother's brother. Although not exactly a blood relative, but none the less, an uncle by marriage. Elizabeth actually painted a portrait of him".

"Really?" I inquired looking around the room at the pictures that were placed randomly around the room.

"His portrait hangs in the lower level hallway".

"I would love to see it", I announced.

"I will have James show you the portrait after we finish our coffee. I am not up to a lot of stairs today. I have a touch of rheumatism". The coffee was a godsend. I needed some caffeine to jump start my tired brain. When we had completed brunch, James escorted me down the stairs to the lower level. The hallway, just like the rooms upstairs were filled with picture after picture. All were wonderful creations. I was stunned when James stopped in front of Daniel's portrait. Daniel was still just as youthful and handsome as he was the day the portrait was painted. He was wearing an outfit similar to the one he currently wore. What stood out more than anything was the ring he wore in the picture? It was the ring that now hung from a chain around my neck. I could feel the sadness of the situation sneaking up on me. It was only a matter of time until Daniel would be in the same situation that Elizabeth had just experienced. He would pass over and I would be left alone. Alone and broken hearted. I could sympathize for those women, you know the wives and girlfriends of the men they loved but lost due to the necessity of war. Here I was on the verge of losing the man I loved. I wasn't certain if I could handle it.

I don't know how long I stood just staring at Daniel's portrait. James came to inform me that Lillian had arranged for the car and driver to return me to my hotel. I joined Lillian and thanked her for all of her kindness. The meals, the beautiful room, and the company. I gave Lillian my address and voiced I hoped she would stay in touch. I didn't know if Daniel stayed behind at Lillian's home or if he came with me. I didn't have time to speak to him before leaving.

The ride back to the hotel was long. I could no longer enjoy the beautiful scenery that passed quickly by the window. My future with Daniel seemed bleak. I felt tears slip from my eyes. I flicked them away with my fingers hoping that the driver didn't notice. Time flew by. We pulled up in front of my hotel. I thanked the driver, while pulling out a twenty dollar bill from my pocket and handed it to him. I knew it wasn't much due to the currency rate of American money to that of the English pound, but it was all I had on me.

I immediately went to the front desk to arrange two additional days at the hotel, tonight and tomorrow night. I asked the clerk to cancel my car once again and to arrange my pick up on the morning after my last night that I had just booked. I had to make myself breathe as I climbed the stairs to my room. I closed the door and Daniel appeared.

"I can see sadness on your face", he said.

"Daniel. Do we have to find this secret money? We could put it aside and be together for the rest of our lives".

Daniel looked at me with such disappointment. "Emily, you would age, but I would remain as I am. As I have always been. Would you really want us to remain like that? Then what happens when you reach the end of your life? Will you will the ring and me to someone else?"

"Daniel, how can you say such awful things to me?"

"I am only speaking the truth", he said.

I knew in my heart that he was correct. He would remain the same. He looked just as youthful as he did in the picture that hung in Lillian's home. How many decades ago was that portrait painted? How long had Daniel been locked into this world without any choice? How long had he been waiting, hoping, and praying for someone to set him free? Here I was asking him to prolong his wait with no guarantee he would ever be set free. What was I doing to him? What must he think of me? I was ashamed of myself.

What is that saying about loving someone and setting them free? "I'm sorry Daniel. I am being very selfish. I was only thinking of myself. To be honest, I'm afraid I won't be able to survive losing you".

He took me in his arms and hugged me tight. I don't know how long we stayed like that. I only know, I felt safe. I wanted to stay like this forever.

"Well, we have only two days before I head back to America", I said to Daniel. I could feel the empty feeling inside growing stronger. I knew I was losing Daniel. I didn't want too, but if I loved him, I had to give him what he needed. Even if I died inside.

"When we search for the money, we don't want to wander aimlessly. I don't want you to risk your health again".

"We can ask the desk where we can find a map. We need to find out where the numbers or coordinates behind the ring, tell us to go", I said. I could tell Daniel wanted to be free from the ring but he was trying to protect me in the only way he knew how.

I called the front desk. I asked if I could purchase a map of England. The desk clerk said she could have one of the delivery staff pick up a map when he was in town later today. It was already early evening. I readily agreed.

Daniel and I needed to look at the map and find where we needed to go. Once we discovered the area in question, we could determine if we needed a car, a cab, or a bike to get there. I felt drained. Totally and utterly drained. I loved Daniel so much and yet, here I was on the verge of losing him.

"I need some tea", I said. I know Daniel was fighting the same struggles I had been but men tend to hold their emotions inside. I couldn't read Daniel's face. He was quieter than usual but he seemed to stay closer to me. I picked up the telephone and ordered some tea via room service. Daniel and I just seemed to wander around within the room. Like strangers that didn't know how to start up a conversation.

"Daniel, I know you have to do this thing. You've waited so long. Our meeting and falling in love was just bad timing on the part of fate. Before we do anything else that may result in your leaving, I wanted to tell you how much you mean to me".

"Emily, you need not say anything. I feel very deeply for you too".

"Daniel, you have shown me how to have patience. You have shown me love is something that is strong and can endure anything. I have grown more in our time together than I have in my entire life. I realize that I should make certain whoever I love respects me and cares for me and puts nothing else before me. I have learned that I can be strong when I need to be and have the right to be weak too. You have shown me all these things. No matter how this turns out, I will always love you".

Before Daniel could respond, there was a knock on the door and the words, "room service, ma'am" could be heard. Before I opened the door, Daniel of course, disappeared. The waiter pushed in a small cart. The cart was filled with a tea pot with a cozy over the top, a plate with a cover, a single cup and all the condiments. He pushed the cart to the area of my room that had a small comfortable chair. "Shall I pour, ma'am?" he asked.

"No, thank you", I said as I signed the invoice giving the waiter a nice tip.

"Oh, madame is too generous. Thank you. Just call when you want the cart picked up" he said and raced out of the room.

The tea was warm and relaxing. I decided to take a nice long hot shower and get ready for bed. I didn't know what to say to

Daniel. If this was our last night together, I wanted to spend it in his arms. I climbed in bed and pulled the blankets open motioning for Daniel to join me. We laid in each other arms without a word spoken. I closed my eyes. I wanted to memorize this moment. He and I must have fallen asleep. Around 7 pm, the telephone rang. I groggily reached for the phone. "Hello?"

"Mame, we have the map you ordered. Did you wish for us to bring it up to you tonight?" asked the desk clerk.

"No. I will pick it up in the morning when I come down for breakfast".

"Very good", the clerk said and hung up.

Chapter 41

The night passed too quickly. I guess that is always true of time when you want time to stand still. The sunlight wasn't as bright as I thought it would be. I peered out of the window. The sky was overcast. It was almost as if Mother Nature had known my mood. I dressed and told Daniel I was heading down for breakfast but would be back shortly. The coffee was tasty. I didn't feel like eating but the doctor had told me I needed to keep up with my healthcare plan. I opted to eat at least a piece of toast. I chose to cover the toast with the home-made jam that the hotel provided. It would add calories and help to prevent further weight loss. After breakfast, I picked up the map of England that the clerk had so graciously arranged and headed back to my room.

Daniel and I studied over the map.

"I memorized the numbers so I wouldn't have to worry about having the ring taken apart again", I told Daniel. The numbers were 52N0E. We began analyzing the map. We definitely would need a ride. I called the front desk. I think they must have been afraid I'd get lost again because they offered to have one of the staff drive me where I needed to go.

The driver must have thought me a bit eccentric as I gave him the spot on the map that I wanted to see. As we neared the area, I noticed a huge cemetery in the distance. I don't know why I knew that was the spot, but I told the driver to pull into the gates. I asked the driver if he could give me a few hours to walk around and then come back for me. He agreed.

Daniel waited until the car could barely be seen before he appeared. We slowly walked through the cemetery. I suggested we walk toward the older section of the hallowed grounds. At first we both glanced from head stone to head stone. We didn't see anything that Daniel recognized. We didn't see any occupants named Potter either. As we came closer to the rows of mausoleum, Daniel stopped. "I am beginning to remember", he said. He sped up his pace. I was getting short of breath trying to keep up with him.

"Daniel, slow down", I yelled. Daniel did slow down but not because I had asked him too. He stopped in front of a huge old mausoleum. Daniel just kept staring at the building.

"What?" I asked.

"I remember this place", he said. I tried to open the doors and was surprised they opened. They squeaked a lot but they opened. Daniel and I slowly walked inside. It was dark. There were several small windows at the top of the building but they were dirty and didn't let in much light. We left the doors open to aid in lighting our way. Then Daniel looked at one of the tombs.

"This is the one", he said. I looked around to make certain no one else was in the cemetery that could hear us.

"What do you mean?" I asked. But before Daniel answered, he slid one end of the coffin out of its resting place. When he stuck his hand inside the coffin, I thought I'd fall over.

"What are you doing?" I whispered in a higher tone.

When Daniel withdrew his hand, he held an old dirty bag.

"It's still here", he said. I was still standing nearby with my jaw dropping. Daniel held the bag out towards me.

"What am I supposed to do with that?" I asked.

"I need you to give it to the city. This is my anchor", he said, "I was supposed to make certain that the enemy didn't get this money. Now my purpose was clear. I need to return the money back to the city".

"How will I explain how I managed to come in possession of this?" I asked.

"That will take some thought", he said. I waited for Daniel to speak. He seemed to be lost.

"Why don't I just tell the truth? A spirit guided me to the money. If they think I'm crazy, then so be it".

"I am uncertain if that is the best way to handle this situation".

"Well, like it or not, it's going to have to be my story". Although it hadn't been over an hour since the drive had dropped me off, I could see the driver heading back toward us. Daniel looked down and said "I owe you a great debt, Emily".

"I love you Daniel", was all I could say before Daniel disappeared and the car pulled up next to the rows of mausoleum.

I climbed into the back of the car and requested the driver to take me to the city hall or town hall. It was only moments before we stopped.

"This is our city hall, ma'am", said the driver.

I climbed out carrying the dirty old bag. I walked inside the city hall. A desk was directly to the left side of the entrance door.

"May I be of service?" asked the woman at the desk.

"I have something for you. I found this while walking near the cemetery". I placed the bag on the desk and began opening the top of the bag. The material of the bag tore as I attempted to open it and coins spilled out all over the top of the desk.

"Oh my", said the clerk, "Those coins are really quite old. Let me call my superior".

Shortly afterward, a short, balding man appeared. I told him my story. He became very excited and said, "There may be a reward".

"I really don't believe I deserve any reward. It is the property of England and part of your history. I don't deserve anything, however, just for a keepsake, I will keep one coin". With that said, I lifted up a coin, tucked it in my pocket and turned to leave the building. The short man followed me out of the door.

"We need your name. We will need to fill out forms and report this to our government".

I climbed in the car, instructed the drive to head back to the hotel and waved good-bye to the short man as we drove away.

Chapter 42

My heart was beating fast the entire trip back to the hotel. My mind had racing thoughts too. Daniel was gone. His mission was completed. I helped the man I love to leave me. I could feel the lump welling up inside my throat. Once we stopped in front of the hotel, I gave a huge thank you to the drive and ran to my room. The tears were flowing before I managed to unlock the door. Thank goodness the maid had already finished my room. I threw myself on my bed and wept.

"Don't cry, Emily", said Daniel. I just about jumped out of my skin. "I thought you were gone. What happened?" I was worried for Daniel but deep down inside I wanted to shout for joy.

"I don't know. I can't think of why I am still here". He looked distraught.

"Let's go for a walk. I think I need to burn off this crazy nervousness I have inside. You could use the walk to help clear your mind too". Surprisingly, Daniel just nodded in agreement.

I grabbed my jacket and slide it around my waist. As we exited the hotel, we walked the opposite way of where we had ridden the bike. We hadn't walked very far when an idea came to me. If it worked, I would lose Daniel forever.

"Daniel, what will you do if we can't find your anchor?" I asked. "What can I do? I shall be a prisoner of time".

After we had gotten out of view of the hotel, I saw a small park. I motioned to Daniel that I wanted to go and sit on the bench. There was a beautiful bush of blue flowers that made the bench very inviting. To sit and rest while enjoying the view and scent of the flowers. Daniel and I sat down.

"I think I know what we need to do".

Daniel looked as if he had doubt. I pulled the chain with the ring from my shirt. I unclasped the chain. "I believe you need to have your ring".

Daniel looked at me. I could see in his eyes that he knew the sacrifice I was making for him. I was giving him his freedom and pushing my breaking heart to the side for the man I loved.

He kissed me softly and said, "Words can never express my feelings of gratitude for you helping me on this quest. You know I love you dearly. I am sad that we cannot have the relationship we both so desire. I shall love you till the end of time". My hand was shaking as I slid the ring onto his hand.

Daniel stood up slowly. I could now see what could only be described as a glow around his body. I had no idea what was happening to him. I cried out for Daniel, but he didn't respond. I must have looked frantic because a woman came out of a nearby building. She saw me screaming Daniels name. She said she suspected I had lost a dog. She probably thought I had lost my mind. "Miss are you alright?"

The woman didn't see Daniel as he stood there, almost frozen in time, but slowly fading. "I lost my friend. I thought he came this way, but I can't find him".

The woman told me to sit. She disappeared back into her building and then came back a minute later with a glass of water.

"You should probably drink this and rest for a while". I know I was shaking. I didn't know what to think. Did I lose Daniel forever? I could no longer see him.

The woman kept talking. I had no idea what she was saying. I think I may have been in shock. I couldn't seem to get my thoughts together. I felt stunned.

"Are you able to stand?" asked the woman. I must have nodded yes because she helped guide me from the bench and we began to walk down the pathway to her building.

After entering through the door, the woman said, "I usually don't have patrons come to this room, but I am certain you will understand why I am showing you this when we get there". Why did she keep talking? Didn't she realize, I didn't care about anything but Daniel?

As I entered the room, a huge painting caught my eye. It was a picture of Daniel and me. "How is that possible?" I asked.

The woman began to explain. The portrait was of a wounded man being held in the arms of a woman, assisting the man to drink what looked to be a glass of water. The soldier looked like Daniel, and the nurse looked like me. Daniel was in my arms.

I soon learned that the woman who had been so kind to give me the water was the curator of the museum. The museum was the building into which the woman had led me.

"The granddaughter of Elizabeth had painted the portrait from the memories her grandmother had given her. The soldier in the picture, was her grandfather, Daniel Potter. He was injured in a skirmish with some rebels who were robbing small towns. Elizabeth was one of the volunteers who helped in the make shift hospital.

Daniel and Elizabeth were married only hours after his recovery. Although it was said they were related, their marriage was never questioned because Elizabeth and Daniel were not true blood relatives. Unfortunately, his head injury caused him grave memory loss. Daniel's aunt and uncle had owned the land that the museum was built on and currently resides. His wife, Elizabeth and he inherited the wealth from his aunt and uncle. Elizabeth paid to have the museum built for the artist, her granddaughter. That must have been Lillian's grandmother, I deduced.

Daniel died days after he and Elizabeth were married. It was assumed his death was from the head injuries he had sustained during the battle. He never knew Elizabeth was expecting their children.

"Children?" I asked.

"Yes, Elizabeth had twins. A boy and a girl. The boy, Franklin and a daughter, Metta. Franklin left home when he was a young man. I guess he must be like most young men in his day. He left home to make his fortune. His sister, Metta, married and had one daughter. Metta named her daughter after her mother. Elizabeth was a talented artist and her grandmother, the original Elizabeth, built this museum to house her works".

"What happened to Franklin?" I asked.

"He made a decent living. He worked his way up, from working on the docks, into the business end of the shipping business. He married, but I am afraid, there isn't much known about his where about or that of his children. It was rumored that they moved to the United States".

"Is this the only picture Elizabeth's granddaughter painted within the museum? "

"Yes. Her works and the museum was donated to the city of Thatcher town. I'm not certain what happened to her other assets". I sat there looking at Daniel and me in the picture. Daniel had somehow found me twice. Something inside me felt sad. The curator gave me a brochure describing the museum and its founder. The brochure included pictures painted by Elizabeth Potter-Evans, Daniel's granddaughter. One of the pictures was the one I was currently looking at. Daniel in my arms. I thanked the curator for her assistance but felt like I could now ambulate on my own.

I walked slowly back to out of the museum. Daniel was nowhere to be found. I slowly walked toward the hotel. I couldn't stop the sadness that seemed to lay within my chest. My heart ached. I kept looking at the brochure. The hotel clerk saw me walking into the lobby.

"Oh, I see you've seen the museum". I could only nod yes.

I went to my room. I hoped and prayed Daniel would appear but somehow I knew I wouldn't see him again. I laid on the bed and cried. I must have cried most of the night. I woke up to the telephone ringing.

"Your driver is here, ma'am", announced the clerk.

"Tell him to have a cup of tea and I will be down shortly". I dressed quickly and grabbed my suitcase. I decided sometime within the dark hours of the night, I would keep Daniel's story fresh and share it with others. After all my memories were all I had left of Daniel.

I flew home. The trip was long and dull. I didn't know how to act. I felt as though part of me was missing. I felt as though my best friend, the love of my life had just died. I know it seems odd to say that, with Daniel having been dead for years, but to me it was all still so fresh.

When I got home, there was a message from Ali on my answering machine. It seemed that Ali and her relationship with Paul was going strong. I couldn't call her back. I needed time to mourn. I had just lost my love. I didn't think I would ever recover.

It took me some time, but I finally did pull myself together. I filled my days with work and got back into my quilting. It had been quite a while since Ali and I had donated quilts to the church. I kept in touch with Martha and Fred. Martha would mail me patterns for quilts. I couldn't seem to get her to understand that I enjoyed making up my own patterns. Her kindness was so great, I kept the patterns but considered donating them to the local college's sewing program.

It must had been almost six months after returning from England, that I began to have some very vivid dreams. Daniel was in them all. I sadly woke to the disappointment of being alone. Now a year later, the dreams were no longer causing me restless nights. I was beginning to move forward as most women do when they lose a loved one. I never thought it possible but I was beginning to forget what Daniel looked like.

Then one day after work, I arrived home to find a large crate blocking my front door. I couldn't imagine what it could be. I hadn't ordered bolts of material or anything else for that matter, in such a long time. Then I saw the address; the crate was sent to me from Lillian.

I somehow managed to wiggle the crate into my front door. I discovered my hammer amongst the miscellaneous things in the junk drawer. I used the hammer to try and pry the nails loose. After an hour of putting a lot of elbow grease toward those nails, I managed to remove the top of the crate. By then I was sweating bullets but I had achieved my tasks.

On the top of the wrapped packages lay a note from Lillian.

Dear Emily,
Don't think an old woman crazy who has been given instructions by a spirit. Elizabeth visited me in my dreams. She told me to send these to you.

"These?" I thought. Before finishing the letter, I opened up the packages. Inside the crate were the portraits of Elizabeth and Daniel. Tears ran down my face as I gazed onto the face of the man I loved so dearly and missed so terribly. It took me some time to get myself back under control. I then returned to read the rest of Lillian's letter.

Elizabeth said you would need these portraits as a reminder so you could complete the task that lay before you. She also said that fate was causing confusion in your life and having Daniel's portrait would help you to achieve your quest.

I had no idea what this task or quest would or could be. I had helped Daniel attain his freedom. He had been anchored to this world for such a long time without reprieve. I just happen to fall in love with him while he was here. Now that I was finally getting back to my old self, here stood a reminder of my loss. I spent my nights sitting home just staring at Daniel's portrait. I would close my eyes and reminisce about his and my time together. Our very short time together.

Then one day, Ali called to ask if she and I could meet for lunch. I agreed to meet with her at our favorite cafe. When we had finally sat down and placed our meal orders, I told Ali about my dreams. She said I was thinking too much about Daniel before falling asleep. Maybe she was right. I didn't know if I should tell Ali that Lillian had been visited by Elizabeth. Even though Elizabeth was visiting Lillian in her dreams, they were still visits. Before I could decide if I should share that information, Ali said she needed to tell me something.

Ali had some very happy and exciting news. She and Paul were going to be married. Ali wanted me as her maiden of honor. Of course I said yes. We must have giggled and chatted about how it all came to be for hours at that little café. Paul had arranged a very romantic night out on the town. Paul had pre-arranged for a few surprises along the way. First, he rented a limo. He invited Ali to a very fancy restaurant. Ali had purchased a new dress for the date.

Ali said her dress was layers of sheer black with beads sewed randomly about. The layers of sheer black made her blonde hair stand out. Ali had curled her hair and let it hang loose about her shoulders. She put a few sparkling clips in her hair to keep those stray hairs from falling forward. Paul picked her up at 7:00 p.m. Their first stop was at a florist. He went inside and came out with an orchid wrist corsage. They continued onward. They stopped for cocktails at an exclusive club. The orchestra began playing their song, "Just the way you look tonight". Paul and Ali danced to their special song.

The next stop was to visit the police department. Paul said he had to get something. Ali and he walked in to the police station only to find the entire police force waiting for them. Paul kneeled down on one knee and proposed to Ali. He told Ali he had chosen the police station to propose because it should be against the law the way she makes him feel. Paul put the ring on Ali's finger. Ali then received a kiss on the cheek from every male officer and a hug from the female officers before they went back to the limo.

They went to the fancy restaurant for dinner. They shared a bottle of champaign. After desert, Paul escorted her back to the limo. They went down to the Detroit River where a small yacht was waiting.   They boarded the yacht and sailed around Lake Erie for hours. There was a waiter on board who offered cocktails and later that night coffee. When Paul went to drop Ali off at her home, he took her in his arms and thanked her for accepting his proposal.

My heart was so excited for Ali. Our next conversation became the planning stage of the wedding. I got an idea of what Ali liked and wanted. We then went straight to work on the plans. We registered her at a few of her favorite stores, contacted our pastor to get the approval for the use of the church, him to preside, and also booked the hall for the reception.

The next few months were a blur of hurried and scattered organization of the wedding. Getting the minister to determine the time to perform the ceremony, getting an organist for the church for the wedding, getting a DJ for the reception music, invitations to be printed only after determining the invitation list, flowers for the church, decorations for the reception hall, dresses for Ali, me, and the flower girl, shoes, and all the other things that come from planning a wedding were finally completed. The wedding day arrived. I stood in the back of the church with Ali.

Ali made a beautiful bride. Her flowing blonde hair sprinkled with glitter and small baby breath flowers. A headband like vein draped on top. The veil was long and cascaded down her back to her ankles. Her white silk dress with flowing lace was breath-taking. The dress had long sleeves and small antique buttons caressing her wrists. A small blue cameo necklace was the only jewelry she wore. I had loaned her my coin to carry in her purse as "something old". The music began and just as we had rehearsed, I walked slowly down the aisle with Ali following a few feet behind.

As I approached the front of the church, I took my place to the side of where Ali would stand. As Ali reached the front, Paul was wearing the largest smile I had ever seen. Paul took Ali's hand in his. A small tear trickled from my eye. My best friend is getting married. I was so happy for her. Then I began to think how I could have been standing here with Daniel. My heart began to race and I could feel my legs grow weak. I know the minister was saying something to Ali and Paul. They leaned toward each other to kiss and that was all I remember.

I woke up resting on a couch. I had no idea where I was or how I had gotten there. Then Ali came in. She placed a cool wet wash cloth on my forehead.

"Oh, I am so glad you are awake. Are you ok?" Ali asked.

"I was thinking of Daniel", I confessed.

"And?" asked Ali.

"I guess all the excitement got to me", I said.

I could see Ali's concern.

"I am so sorry for disrupting your wedding. Please, let's get back to the festivities".

Ali helped me stand up. I brushed the wrinkles from my dress. The wedding celebration was grand. The music encouraged the feet of young and old to dance or sway. I couldn't stop laughing when they played the chicken dance. Young and old got up on the dance floor and participated in the dance.

The food was outstanding. Porcupine meatballs, baked chicken, and sliced ham were the main dishes. Side dishes included potato salad, macaroni salad, pasta salad, and vegetable salad. Scalloped potatoes, green beans, home-made baked rolls with dairy fresh butter. For the children, hotdogs baked in biscuits, macaroni and cheese, and spaghetti.

The company was enjoyable. Ali had invited her parents, close neighbors, and friends of her and Paul. Ali and Paul even invited Beamer, Detective Power and Detective Triplett and they came.

After the reception, I slowly drove home. After hanging up my dress, I sat down in front of Daniel's portrait. It was then that I realized, I needed to let others know that love is an adventure. You may be like Ali and Paul. Lucky to have found each other and able to plan a life together. You may end up like Elizabeth, and want to distance yourself from someone. Or you could be like me. Love someone who can never be.

Chapter 43

I had settled back into my life without Daniel. Daniel had disappeared on me a little over a year ago. No, he hadn't run off and joined the foreign legion, wasn't kidnapped, nor entered the witness protection program. Daniel was a spirit that had been tethered to an antique ring. He was limited on earthly movements and could not cross-over because of this tie to the ring.

Daniel and I went through a harrowing adventure to get him free. Unfortunately for me, I fell in love with Daniel before he disappeared. It took me a long time to face walking into my home without Daniel waiting for me to arrive. It was lonely at night. I'd gotten use to Daniel being in bed, holding me in his protective way. I could tell you all the little things that constantly reminded me of Daniel but instead, I threw myself into my work and hobby. I made myself get over him.

This morning I went to work as usual. Today was a busy day at work. I work for a publishing company. I am a proof reader. I am stuck in a little cubical all day reading and flagging errors. Today, I sent off my corrections. I sent them directly to my unit manager. The unit manager failed to save my work and her computer locked up. All my work was lost.

The manager was angry. She ranted and raved stating it must have been a virus that had come from my computer. After being unjustly accused of using my work computer for personal web searches, which must have attracted a virus, the IT technician came up and discovered it was the manager's fault. A user error per the IT technician. He also confirmed my computer had never been used for internet searches. Did I get an apology from the unit manager? No!

The manager returned the author's original works to me and told me to start over again. All I wanted to do was to go home, take a long hot bath, and crawl into bed. I did what I could until 4:30 pm. I then clocked out as overtime was not allowed in our division. I raced to my car and headed home. I pulled into the driveway, climbed out of my car, and gathered my mail. After letting myself in, I kicked off my shoes. What a relief. I threw the mail on the coffee table and headed for the bathroom.

As I sank into the tub of gloriously warm water, I could feel the tension ease. I was so glad it was Friday. At least I'd have two whole days to decompress before having to face that old office witch again. I didn't know how long I had soaked but decided to get out when the water had cooled and my finger looked like prunes.

I towel dried and applied some light powder. My friend Ali had given me the powder for my birthday. I would see Ali tomorrow. Although she was now married to Paul, she and I had kept our same ritual of treasure hunting for material at the flea market every Saturday. I brushed my hair until it was semi-dry. A grilled cheese sandwich and soup was on the menu for dinner tonight.

I liked to use Jarlesberg cheese with thin slices of pickle for my grilled cheese sandwiches. I finished my meal and went to the living room to relax. If I put in an hour or so on my newest quilt, I would be close to being finished. As I sat down, I realized I hadn't sorted through my mail. I knew my car payment would be due in a few weeks, so the bill should be in my collection of mail that now sat on the table.

Tons of advertising. Those went into the trash. Car payment set aside. Electric bill also set aside. Then I saw it. A letter from Lillian.

My dearest Emily,
Forgive an old woman for this out of the blue correspondence. I so meant to keep in touch. Time does seem to get away from me these days.

I hope this letter finds you well. I have been conversing with Elizabeth. She tells me that Daniel will be coming. She failed to elaborate on her announcement. I have no date when he will be coming or where for that matter. Elizabeth said I should pass this information on to you.

I am certain you will consider this situation carefully. I know it must be difficult to hear such news with no certainty.

If you are able to, and chose to come back to Sowerville, my home is open to you. I could arrange my driver to retrieve you from Thatcher town. It would be ever so lovely to have a house guest that also speaks to spirits. Please contact me to let me know, my dear, what your decision may be.

Affectionately,
Lillian

Huh? I wonder what all that is about. Now I was stumped. I had no idea what it meant. First, why would Elizabeth want me to know about Daniel? Wasn't she and Daniel married in the past? When would Daniel be coming? No one had a clue. Would he come here? Again, no one knew anything.

I sat there looking at Lillian's letter. I had no idea what I should do. I wasn't going to Sowerville and wait. That would drive me crazy. Of course, sitting and waiting here for some word of his arrival would make me crazy too. I decided to sleep on it. I have learned from past experiences that making snap decisions almost always turned out badly. Yes, careful thought is needed to make an intelligent decision. Boy could I use an intelligent decision now.

Chapter 44

I tossed and turned all night. I began dreaming of Daniel. In my dream, I saw him in the darkness. He was just out of reach. He kept saying, "I'm coming. Wait for me. I'm coming". When I woke up, I was more tired than when I had gone to bed. My bed looked like I had thrashed it. I called Ali.

"Can you come over?" I asked.

I had put on a fresh pot of coffee before Ali arrived. I put the last four donuts on a serving plate and waited. When Ali arrived, she took one look at me and said, "What happened?"

I gave Ali the letter to read.

"I don't even know what to make of this", said Ali, "there is no date or time. No assurance what so ever. And what does coming mean?"

"Want some coffee?" I asked.

"Yes, and the donut with the sprinkles too", she stated.

I smiled. It almost felt odd smiling. I had been frowning since I read Lillian's letter yesterday. "Boy, did I need you", I stated to Ali.

"Why didn't you call me yesterday when you got this stupid letter?" she asked.

"I wasn't certain how I felt about it. I thought I'd sleep on it", I explained.

Ali looked at my bed. "And how did that go?" she said.

We both laughed. Ali asked "What do you plan to do?"

After we devoured the donuts, I said, "I don't see any reason to do anything. I've come to same conclusion as yours. There isn't enough information to do or plan anything. I'll write Lillian and let her know I received her letter. Thank her for passing on the message and leave it at that".

Ali nodded her approval as she finished her coffee. I told Ali I would write a response and we could mail it on our way to the flea market. My response to Lillian was as follows:

Dear Lillian,

What a nice surprise to find your letter in my mail box. Please don't feel badly for not staying in touch. I am just as guilty as you for not corresponding.

Please let Elizabeth know you passed on the information. To be frank with you, I honestly don't know how to respond to that information. With that said, I promise to try and keep in touch more often.

I bet the foliage there is really beautiful this time of year. The memories of your countryside still frequent my thoughts, as does the wonderful time we spent together.

Take care,

Emily

I put Lillian's letter in my purse. "Ok, Ali, I'm ready", I said.
After Ali used the facilities, she and I were off.
It only took a moment to mail the letter. We were then off to the flea market.
Ali went directly to her favorite seller. She managed to buy bolts of fabric that really matched well.

I sadly walked past the table that Charlie use to use. Poor Charlie. A new seller was now in his place. The new seller was selling toys and baby items. I wandered down to the end of the row. Nothing but second hand items that were more for folks who did home canning and candy making.

I checked out the pole barn. I found a seller who had a zillion bots of fabric. The material had small flowers on it. I really enjoyed putting that pattern into a quilt. It gave the guilt more eye appeal.

When Ali and I finished loading our purchases into her car, we drove to a small café we had discovered last summer. Ali ordered the crock pot shredded beef and onions on a sesame roll with pickle and coleslaw on the side. A tall glass of ice tea filled with ice and a wedge of lemon.

I ordered the diced chicken with celery. My sandwich was also on a sesame bun with a slice of lettuce and a tomato on top. A side of multi-colored diced peppers marinated in a vinaigrette accompanied my sandwich. I ordered a tall glass of the flavored tea with mango.

After we had just about finished eating, Ali looked at me funny.
"What's with you?" I asked, "You keep looking at me in a funny way. Then you take a huge sip of your tea. Do I have mayo on my nose or something?"
Ali smiled. "No", she giggled.
"What?" I asked.

"I'm pregnant", she announced.

Tea squirted out of my nose and I started to choke. Ali grabbed my arms and held them above my head. I know my face must have been red. Not so much from the choking but the embarrassing way Ali had positioned my arms.

"Why did you hold my arms above my head?" I asked.

"I don't know. I've seen them do it in the movies for people who drown", she explained.

"Geez, Ali. You almost killed me twice", I said.

"Twice?" she questioned.

"First, by surprising me with your news and making me squirt tea out of my nose. Which burns by the way. Secondly, by raising my arms above my head", I blurted.

Ali grinned and said, "What do you think? About the baby I mean?"

"I think that's fantastic news. If I live, I'll spoil the little monkey", I stated.

Ali glowed. I was on the verge of tears. I was so happy for her.

"When are you due? "I asked.

"December 11", she replied.

"When do you want your baby shower?" I questioned.

"Well, my mom and my aunt want to throw it for me. Are you ok with that? If not, I'll tell them you are my best friend and they will just have to accept that", she said.

"I'd be just as happy going to the shower your mom and aunt are going to throw", I replied.

"I'm so happy to hear you say that. My mom already spoke with a restaurant in an area near her. She took one of their menus. She plans to make copies, label the tables with letters and mark the menus to correspond. The guest will be able to make their selection without verbally missing any of the shower activities", stated Ali.

"That is a brilliant idea. Your mom sure has things well in hand. What will your aunt be doing?" I asked.

"She's making the invitations, ordering the cake, and getting the game prizes together".

"Are you going to register at a few baby stores?" I asked.

"Oh, I hadn't thought of that. That is a good idea. Mom can put the store names in the invitations", replied Ali.

"What does Paul think of all this?" I asked.

"He's on cloud nine", beamed Ali.

We finished our lunch. We continued to talk about baby plans. Ali explained what she was doing to her guest room to turn it into a nursery. What names she and Paul had discussed to name the baby. She also mentioned they had planned to start a bank account for the baby's future college.

When the crowd started to thin out, Ali and I managed to finish our tea and leave. I carried all my bolts of fabric inside. I refused to allow Ali to carry any of the heavy bundles.

"I don't want you carrying in any of those bolts of fabric. You have Paul carry them in", I instructed.

"No worries", stated Ali, "Paul won't let me do anything these days. I'm lucky if I get to cook."

"Sounds like a man in love", I announced.

"I'll talk to you soon", she said and drove off.

.

Chapter 45

I went inside and sat down. Ali and I had a great time, but now, thanks to Lillian, thoughts of Daniel returned. "This is ridiculous", I said to myself, "I've gotten on with my life. Lillian didn't really have any concrete evidence or news that Daniel was really coming back. Elizabeth had spoken to Lillian but had not given her any real news".

Then I realized, Elizabeth had returned. My heart skipped a beat. Elizabeth was married to Daniel almost a century ago. She was sort of his sister. Her widowed mother, had married Daniel's father. Unfortunately, Elizabeth's mother died in child birth with a son. Daniel's father remarried and Daniel was born.

Lillian was Elizabeth's great-great granddaughter. Lillian and I had met when Daniel and I were trying to free him from the ring. So, Elizabeth was able to come back. Maybe Daniel could too.

I needed to stay busy. I pulled out my cutting board and scissors. I began measuring and cutting fabric squares. Ali and I competed on our quilts. We would both design quilts and compare our completed quilts to see whose design was the best. Ali always thought mine were. We donated our quilts to the church to raffle off. The proceeds went to help the homeless or families who needed a helping hand.

When my stomach growled, I looked at the clock. It was almost 8 pm. I had no idea what to make for dinner. I stretched. I had been cutting for almost four and a half hours. I ordered a pizza and put my material away. Material and grease didn't get along.

After indulging in four slices of pizza and a full glass of milk, I was stuffed. I went back to the sofa. I picked up my most recent quilt. I had used various colors of solid material. I centered a yellow square, surrounded it with an orange square. Then I surrounded the orange square with brown squares. Then surrounded the brown squares with red. Each section of joined squares were surrounded by white stripes of material. I liked to use white satin hemming for the outside border.

I only needed to secure the material with small stitches around each square on the border. Most of the material had been secured by quilted stitches. I put various colors of thin ribbon inside each square and tied them into a bow. When I finished the bows, I was pleased with how the quilt had turned out.

I climbed into my pajamas and sat reading a quilting magazine. I sipped on a cup of decaffeinated tea. I nearly jumped out of my skin when I heard, "Hasn't he come yet?"

My heart was beating faster than the music in "Flight of the bumble bees".

I slowly turned my head. There stood Sondra. Sondra was of the spirit world. She had been the one delivering messages to me when Daniel was in jail.

"Did he talk to you?" I asked.

"Not personally. I heard through the grape vine he was coming", stated Sondra.

"What does that mean, exactly?" I asked.

"You'll see", she laughed and said, then she disappeared through the wall.

"Argh!" I muttered. Why couldn't I get the information I wanted?

Chapter 46

I didn't sleep well again. My mind wouldn't shut off. I was angry that I couldn't get any answers. I came to the conclusion that Daniel would return to England because that was his home. Sondra had said she had heard Daniel would be coming through the grapevine.

I had considered traveling back to England to meet with Elizabeth. I wasn't certain if after all the expense and trouble of arranging airfare and that trip there that I would know any more than I did right now.

I thought about how Daniel must be feeling. He's trying to get back to me. Am I the same person I was? I needed to do some really indepth soul searching. I know I must sound fickle. Last year, I was so in love with Daniel. He disappeared and my heart broke. I was broken. I struggled to move onward without him. I succeeded. Now I was closing in on a cross road.

Thinking back, I was once willing to die to be with Daniel. I came close to it too. I also remember the loneliness I felt for days and nights on end after he left. Did I want to risk any of that again? How long would Daniel stay this time? What if he can't come? What if he can? I hadn't realized it but sometime during the late hours of the night, I had dozed off.

When the alarm clock sounded I had very little energy or motivation to get out of bed. Then I gave myself an extra ten minutes doze time. When the clock sounded again, I slid out of the covers. I needed to get ready for church. Today was the day I would donate my recently finished quilt.

I quickly showered and nibbled on a piece of cold pizza. Washed my hands and gathered up my stuff. I wrapped my newly finished quilt in a clean storage bag. I planned on showing the quilt to Ali before church services began.

The parking lot of our small church was always two thirds full. The town wasn't that big but our pastor was a good speaker. People came from quite a distance to hear him speak each Sunday. I had parked and had just opened the back of my SUV when Pastor Ryan spoke.

"I'm glad you are a bit early today, Emily. I was hoping to introduce Waynne to a few of our members more his own age", stated Pastor Ryan.

I turned to see a six foot one man with dreamy blue eyes. When he smiled, his dimples appeared and sent the warmth of his smile to his eyes. "Emily, I'd like you to meet Waynne. Waynne, this is Emily. Emily and her friend Ali make and donate quilts for the church to raffle. The proceeds go to help our homeless and less fortunate church members.

"Nice to meet you, Emily", Waynne said as he reached to shake my hand. I lost my grip on my quilt and as the quilt began to fall, Waynne and I both lunged for it. We bumped heads in the process. Pastor Ryan smiled and said, "Well, that is one way to get together". Waynne's face turned beet read. My scalp was throbbing from the encounter.

"Are you new to the community or just the church?" I asked. "Both. My job relocated me here. They just opened up a new office down town", he said.

"What do you do?" I asked as I locked my car.

Waynne smiled and gripped my quilt, "Allow me", he said. Pastor Ryan waved to more members and raced off to chat, leaving Waynne in my care.

"Your job is?" I asked as I began to walk towards the church entrance.

"I work for J and J electronics. They install surveillance equipment for homes and businesses. I manage their new office", stated Waynne.

"Interesting", I said.

"Sometimes. Most often its billing, accounting, and computer work. We have staff that monitor the computers, salesmen who sell the products, and of course installers. Funny it started out as a one man operation. The owner, Jody, worked his tail off to get the company off the ground. Now it's nationwide", stated Waynne.

"Excuse me a minute Waynne. I need to talk to Ali for a minute", I explained.

Waynne smiled and stood in place. I took my quilt from him and headed for Ali. "Ali, I brought my quilt. I finished it last night. I am going to put it in Pastor Ryan's office. Did you want to see it first?" I asked.

Ali smiled and said, "I finished mine too. Paul helped with this one". Ali nudged Paul. Paul opened up the large duffle bag he was carrying. The quilt was blue and white stripes. The quilt was beautiful. I showed Ali my quilt and she frowned. "You win again", she said.

"No," I replied, "You win this time". I didn't notice but Waynne had walked up behind me. I turned to go fetch Waynne to introduce him to Ali and Paul. When I turned, I walked right into Waynne's arms.

Waynne held me to prevent me from falling. His arms were strong and warm. He wore a short sleeve polo shirt. I could feel the hair on his arms against my skin. It felt soft, like kitty fur. I could smell the scent of fresh clean soap too. He smiled and his dimples appeared.

"I think you and I should notify each other of our moves before we kill each other", I said.

Ali gave Paul a look and a smile. "Why don't you introduce us to your friend?" stated Ali.

"Ali, Paul, this is Waynne. Waynne, I'd like you to meet my friend Ali and her husband Paul", I stated.

I had noticed since Ali had gotten married, she was more aggressive when it came to situations that use to make her cower back or cringe. "As I told Pastor Ryan and Emily, I recently relocated. I was hoping to find a small church nearby. Pastor Ryan suggested I arrive early so he could show me around. I didn't realize he was going to dump me on Emily", explained Waynne.

"Pastor Ryan just wanted to ensure you knew a few people before sitting down for services. Often people don't readily invite someone they don't know into the fold. Pastor Ryan knows how to prevent anyone from feeling lonely or left out", Ali stated.

"Waynne, why don't you join Ali and Paul while I go drop off the quilts", I said.

Ali handed me her quilt. "I can carry these for you if you don't mind me being your beast of burden", suggested Waynne.

"I wouldn't hear of it", I said, "Ali will you show Waynne where to pick up the latest church bulletin newsletter?" I turned and headed for Pastor Ryan's office. It only took me a moment to drop off the quilts. I adjusted my slacks and top, then headed back to the pews.

Ali and Paul were talking to Waynne. Waynne was looking over the church newsletter. "Hymns for this week are on the back side of this week's newsletter", said Paul.

Waynne turned the newsletter over. He picked up one of the hymn books from the book holder in front of him. He thumbed through the pages to the first hymn. I saw his brow furrow.

"Anything wrong?" I asked.

"I'm not familiar with the first hymn", he announced.

"No problem. Just move your lips while listening to the tune. You'll come to know it over time", I said.

"Oh", said Ali, "I invited Waynne to join us after church. I thought we could go to that family restaurant down the street".

"I don't want to intrude if you don't want me forcing myself into your group", stated Waynne.

"You aren't forcing yourself on us", I said.

"Besides", stated Paul, "I'm usually outnumbered. At least now I'll have a sporting chance".

Before anyone could reply, the pastor walked up to the podium. Church members began rushing to sit. A small child ran from his mother and headed for the front of the church. The mom chased and caught him. I sat down next to Waynne. Waynne smiled and looked forward.

It seemed services went quickly. I soon found myself sitting at the table with Paul to my left, and Waynne on my right. Ali sat opposite of me and kept smiling. I knew what she was doing. She was playing match maker.

We ordered our chosen selections and drilled Waynne for more information. He was twenty eight years old and single. He had two brothers and his parents traveled continuously since they retired. He loved opera, sports, and music.

"Was your girlfriend upset about you relocating?" asked Ali.

"What girlfriend" questioned Waynne?

"A good-looking man like you and no girlfriend?" questioned Ali.

"Hey", said Paul, "Remember you are married".

"I'm shy", replied Waynne.

"If I had a nickel for every time a man said they were shy", I countered.

"It's true", defended Waynne, "If Pastor Ryan hadn't introduced us, I would have been sitting in church alone".

It was kind of sad to think there are people out there somewhere who are crippled by shyness.

"Are you really that shy?" I asked.

"Yes", he replied. I noticed his face had turned red and he was trying to change the subject by asking, "Do you always come here after church?"

"We usually stop by each other's place and munch", stated Paul.

"Maybe, if you like us, you'll join our little gang", stated Ali as she smiled at me.

Waynne turned red again and looked at me. "I think it would depend on if you liked me", Waynne replied. We had finished our lunch and had been sitting and talking. The waitress kept eyeing us.

"I think the waitress is hoping we'll leave. We are keeping her from more customers", I said.

"Emily, why don't you give Waynne your telephone number too? Paul already gave him ours. Just in case he has questions or needs something", suggested Ali.

I had planned to offer Waynne my telephone number. There is nothing like feeling pressured or forced into doing something you already plan to do. I gave Waynne my home and work number. I explained that my work number could only be used for emergencies. He acknowledged my concerns and in turn gave me his work and home telephone numbers.

We all walked back to the church parking lot. We got into our perspective cars and drove away. I had barely gotten in the door when my telephone rang.

"Hello", I said.

"Well, what do you thing?" asked Ali.

"About?" I questioned.

"Waynne of course. He seems like a nice enough guy", Ali stated.

"Geez, Ali. I just met the man. Before you say anything else, I want it clear that I do not want you playing match maker", I instructed.

"Oh, Pooh", said Ali.

"I mean it", I enforced.

"Well, I did invite him to go with us to the flea market on Saturday. I told him to meet us at your house around eight in the morning. I hope you don't mind me giving him your address", countered Ali.

"Geez, Ali. He could be a slasher. We don't know him well enough to give him our personal information", I stated.

"Don't be silly", replied Ali, "he actually moved in down the street from you".

"He did?" I questioned.

"Yeah. He moved into that brick house on the corner", replied Ali.

"I did notice the sign said sold", I replied.

"Anyway, I'll bring Paul with me on Saturday. Maybe we can go to our favorite café too", suggested Ali.

"Good idea to bring Paul. Changing the subject, did you start your next quilt yet?" I asked

"I didn't start sewing yet but I do have my new pattern in mind. I cut the material out last night", stated Ali.

"Game on", I stated and laughed.

"Game on", replied Ali. We said our good byes and hung up.

I ironed my blouse for work tomorrow. I made out my grocery list. I took out the trash for pick-up tomorrow, then began my new quilt. I had decided on triangles for the quilt. I would mix solid colors with a patterned triangle. I managed to match the solid material to a color in the pattern material. This quilt would take a little more time, but it would be worth the extra effort.

Chapter 47

The next day, work dragged by. I had to keep myself from rushing through the editing changes on the book I had already edited once before. The office manager stayed more to her own office while I re-edited. I wonder how the unit manager was going to justify the delay on this book or cover for the extra time spent on editing.

I stopped by the grocery store on my way home. I always tried to save gas by planning errands and other needed task to complete in the same trip when I know I will be out and about. As I pulled into my driveway, I noticed something yellow on my front door. I finished lugging in the groceries. I put the perishables away and then went to the retrieve the yellow item which turned out to be an envelope. The envelope was addressed to me in handwriting with no stamp or street address. I opened it up and found a beautiful card inside. The front of the card had a picture of a tea cup. There was a slit in the card which housed a tea bag. The inside had been blank but the following was written;

Dear Emily,

I wanted to thank-you for including me in your group yesterday. I know it isn't pleasant having someone forced on you. Ali invited me to join your gang on Saturday. I don't want to impose but would enjoy visiting a flea market. I've yet to try one. So if it's alright with you, I will plan on meeting you at your home on Saturday. If you'd rather keep your group without any new members, you need only to call and let me know.

Affectionately,

Waynne

P.S. I hope you like the tea

I smiled. The card was very thoughtful. It was nice of Pastor Ryan to try and make his new members feel welcome by introducing them to current members. Ali, however, was attempting to play matchmaker. I think Waynne could see Ali's motivation too. So I picked up the telephone and dialed Waynne's telephone number.

"Hello", he answered in a question like tone.

"Waynne?" I asked.

"Yes", he responded.

"Hi, it's me, Emily", I stated.

"Oh, hello", he said.

"I just wanted to call and thank-you for the nice card. You really didn't have to go through all that trouble", I stated.

"It seemed proper etiquette. I did enjoy being part of your group", he admitted.

"Well, I think Ali is playing matchmaker. I wanted to let you know. You are more than welcome to join us on Saturday. The flea market can be very addictive. With what I believe are Ali's intentions, I wanted to give you a choice to bow out", I said.

"I kind of figured that's what she was up too. I hope there is no harm in hoping to become friends", he asked.

"Not at all. In that case, I'll see you Saturday", I stated and ended our conversation.

The week went by and I could hardly believe it was Friday. The office manager was out sick. Someone said she had a head cold. The manager had appointed one of her minions to monitor the unit while she was out. This particular minion was a snitch to beat all snitches. She would walk around to see if each employee was working. If a person was on the telephone, she wrote down the time the call began and when it ended. If someone was on the internet, she wrote that down too. She wrote down if someone went to the bathroom, listing the time the person departed for the bathroom and the return time.

When the day was finally over, I was happy. It gets tiring having to be on guard of your every move. Not that I did anything wrong, but it's strange how some people may perceive things the wrong way.

As I pulled into the driveway, I realized I should have stopped to pick up something for dinner. I didn't feel like driving back to the store now. After letting myself inside, I kicked off my shoes and made a pot of coffee. I sorted through a stack of takeout menus. I decided on Chinese. I called in my order for Singapore rice noodles then jumped into my pajamas. My Chinese orders always seemed to be delivered so quickly, it was almost as if they cooked the food in the car.

I soon heard a knock on my door. I raced to my purse. When I opened the door, I was surprised to see Waynne standing on my stoop.

"Oh, I thought you were the delivery guy", I said.

"Well, in a way I am. I was hoping I could catch you before you started cooking". He held up two bags of Chinese food. I had to laugh.

"Come in before my order comes. They'll think I'm a real pig", I said.

Waynne walked in and continued to my kitchen. "I didn't know what you liked, so I ordered a little bit of several different things". He said.

"I'm a bit confused", I said.

"About?" he questioned.

"Why are you actually here? Aren't we suppose to meet tomorrow?" I asked.

"Well, to be honest with you. I wanted to repay you for you allowing me to be a part of your group", he stated.

"That really is not a big deal", I replied.

"Actually, it is. If your friend is playing matchmaker, that puts you in a precarious position", he stated.

"I don't follow you", I said.

"Ali is married to Paul, right?" he asked.

"Yes", I answered.

"Well, then knowing what she is up to, and still allowing me , a single man into your group could cause you problems. You would have to try and stop your friend from setting you up or risk causing a problem in your friendship. You could be facing being placed in a very stressful situation if you are stuck in a group with someone you don't particularly like. Especially if Ali keeps playing the role of match maker with any single man she meets. Well, at least the single men that Ali believes qualifies or meets the criteria she is using for your perspective suitors", he divulged.

A knock at the door halted our conversation. I paid the delivery man and added my order to the buffet of Chinese food that lined my kitchen counter.

"We should eat while it's warm", I stated.

"Good idea. I'm starved", Waynne replied as he began looking in my cabinets for plates. I pointed to the right cabinet while I reached for the necessary silverware. Within moments, we were sitting at the dining table with two eggrolls on each of our plates. Waynne opened up two packages of the hot Chinese mustard and squeezed it on his first eggroll.

I knew the mustard must be hot because Waynne's face turned a bright shade of red over his sinus area and beads of sweat appeared on his forehead. After he managed to swallow he said, "I forgot the most important part of eating food with hot mustard, don't breath or it goes right up your sinuses and burns like fire". I had to smile. Waynne looked at me and smiled back.

"When you smile with eggroll in your cheek, you look like a chipmunk", he said.

I almost choked from laughing so hard. I had forgotten how annoyed I was that he had just showed up on my doorstop.

"Are you trying to kill me?" I asked.

"Well it would get you out of being set up by a matchmaker", he replied with a huge grin on his face. His dimples appeared and made him look even more handsome than before.

I had to smile and tried to change the topic. "Would you be looking for anything special at the flea market tomorrow?" I asked.

"I've never been to one. It sounds like an adventure", he replied.

"I always find something. There is such a variety of things", I stated. Waynne nodded in agreement as he began opening up the containers of Chinese food.

"Ok", he said, "This one has sweet and sour chicken, the next pepper steak, and continuing down the line, sesame chicken, Kung pow chicken, vegetable fried rice, just in case you are were vegetarian, and general Tao's tofu".

"I am not a vegetarian but I do like veggies. Mind if I try a little of each?" I asked.

"You better", he said with a grin.

"Oh, don't forget to aid my rice noodles to the group", I said.

"I really love Chinese food. They make it quickly, it's affordable, and they deliver. What more do you need?" Waynne commented.

"Dessert", I stated.

"I didn't think of dessert", replied Waynne.

"After trying all this food, I don't think we'll have any room for dessert", I replied.

"I can always find room for dessert", teased Waynne.

We managed to put a dent in the food. I packaged everything up and placed it in the refrigerator. "Would you like some coffee?" I asked.

"No", stated Waynne, "I'm a tea person".

"Then let me offer you some tea", I replied.

The tea kettle was soon whistling. I poured the hot water into his cup. While his tea was steeping, I reheated my coffee. Although the night started out awkward, Waynne and I managed to talk the night away. Before I realized it, it was well after midnight.

"I guess I should head home", stated Waynne.

"Let me package up your Chinese food to take with you", I said.

"Possession is nine tenths of the law", He said and smiled.

"There is way too much food for one person", I said as I reached for a grocery bag.

"Why don't we save it for dinner tomorrow? Unless you're tired of Chinese food or me", he said.

I felt a little bit pressured but realized how lonely Waynne must be in a town with no one he really knew.

"Ok", I agreed.

I walked Waynne to the door I flicked on my porch light. "I'll see you tomorrow morning at eight", Waynne said. I smiled and replied, "Thank you again for dinner. I'll see you soon".

I brushed my teeth and jumped into bed. It didn't dawn on me until I was about to drift off, that I had spent the entire night entertaining in my pajamas. Now it was my turn for my face to turn red.

Chapter 48

The alarm went off at six forty five. I put on a fresh pot of coffee and jumped in the shower. I dressed in jeans and a tee shirt. I pulled my hair into a ponytail and then glanced at the clock. It was seven twenty. I poured me a cup of coffee, a glass of orange juice, and grabbed a breakfast pastry.

At seven forty, I brushed my teeth, cleared the table, and gathered up what I had planned to take to the flea market. At seven fifty-five, I heard Ali's car. I opened the door to find Waynne sitting on my front step. As Ali and Paul walked forward toward my house, I asked Waynne, "How long have you been sitting there?"

"About a half hour or so", Waynne replied.

Didn't this man ever sleep? I thought to myself.

"Emily, I need to use your bathroom before we leave", stated Ali.

I invited everyone inside. "Would anyone like something to drink before we leave?" I asked.

I saw Paul look at Waynne. Waynne shook his head no. Paul stated, "We're good".

Ali joined us and we all headed out. I turned to lock the door. Waynne stopped to wait for me. When we went to get into the car, Waynne stood by my door and waited to close it for me. He then walked around and got in on the other side of the car.

"Hey, you're making me look bad", Paul jokingly said to Waynne.

"Sorry, my mother made certain her boys had manners", Replied Waynne.

Ali looked at me and winked. Oh for goodness sake, I thought.

It didn't take long to get to the flea market. Waynne and Paul had discussed sports in route. Waynne favored the Patriots and Red Sox. Paul smiled and admitted they were good teams. Paul parked further away than Ali and I usually did. We had barely gotten out of the car when Ali grabbed Paul's hand and raced to her favorite shopping spot.

I explained the layout of the flea market to Waynne. "Would you mind if I walked along with you?" Waynne asked.

"You won't find anything of interest if you shop with me. I shop for sewing supplies", I explained.

"You never know", he said.

"Suit yourself", I replied as I headed to the tables. I found some small flowered material, three spools of good quilting thread, and some batting. I paid for my purchases and tucked the items into my oversized bag. Waynne patiently walked beside me. He glanced from table to table. I could tell the market was a new adventure for him. I just couldn't tell if he thought it was a good or a bad adventure.

Ali had Paul loaded down with several bolts of fabric. Waynne walked up to Paul and offered to help carry the bolts of fabric to the car. Ali and I continued to shop.

"You and Waynne seem to be getting along pretty well", said Ali.

"I am simply shopping. He is walking nearby and looking around", I stated. I looked up to see that Paul and Waynne were standing by Ali's car and talking.

"Ok, I can't hold it in. Do you like him?" asked Ali.

"He seems like a nice guy", I answered.

"You know what I mean", stated Ali.

"Ali, I am not looking for another relationship. You can stop your match making. Waynne and I talked and we are working on becoming friends. Friends only", I said. I could see Ali was disappointed.

"I'm sorry, Em. I just wish you had a good man in your life, like I do", she said.

"I know, but I don't know if I'm over Daniel yet. And you know, you can't force love on someone", I said.

"I know. Ok, I promise I will let things take their own course", stated Ali.

"Thanks, I really appreciate you saying that", I replied.

Ali looked for a bathroom while I continued to look around. I walked into the large building. I saw the collection of multiple bolts of fabric. I pulled one out, then another. Before I knew it, I had five bolts of fabric in one hand but had caused an unbalance in the remaining stock.

As I attempted to straighten the remaining pile, I lost my grip on the bolts of fabric I had chosen. As I attempted to catch my chosen bolts of fabric, I had let go of the remaining stock. With my grip no longer stabilizing the remaining stock, the bolts began to tumble downward. Behind the remaining bolts was a large section of wood. The wood was not secured to the wall and began to fall as well.

I hadn't seen the wood. I did know the remaining bolts of fabric would fall, but fabric was soft. I knew if it fell and hit me, I may be sore but basically unhurt. I didn't realize the wood hit me. I also didn't realize Waynne would dig me out and carry my unconscious body outside the building. I didn't hear the ambulance. I didn't feel Waynne's hand in mine in the ambulance ride or in the emergency room.

I was still out during the ordered CAT scan. When I finally started to wake up, Waynne was at my side. I discovered he had been sitting beside me for almost an hour and a half. The nurse said I had been in and out of consciousness but hadn't effectively sustained wakefulness until now.

The doctor came in to examine me. After blinding me with his flashlight, in each eye, he said," We're going to hold you in our observation unit for a few hours. We'll get a repeat CAT scan. If everything looks ok, we'll let you go home".

"How long will this head feel like it's going to explode", I asked.

"We'll get you something for the headache. I'll let the nurse know what you can have. In the meantime, I'll leave you in your boyfriend's capable hands", replied the doctor as he turned and walked away.

I leaned up to speak. I was going to correct the doctor but my head stopped me. The pain was so intense. I put my hand to my head and must have moaned in the process. Waynne was beside me in a flash. "Let me put the call bell on and get your nurse in here", Waynne said.

I laid back onto my pillow. My brain throbbed. Moments later, the nurse appeared and said, "I bet you signaled me for pain medication".

"Actually, she moaned and had a look of intense pain on her face when she sat up", stated Waynne.

"Emily, I'm going to put the top of the gurney a little higher. Then we will give you some pain medication", explained the nurse. The nurse handed me a small cup with two pills in it. She then handed me a glass of water.

"What is this?" I asked.

"Oxycodone", was the nurse's reply.

I swallowed the pills and rested. I don't know why but closing my eyes seemed to help. I felt a cool cloth being applied to my forehead. I briefly opened my eyes to see Waynne smiling at me while he held the cool cloth. I closed my eyes and slept.

The pain medication knocked me out. When the transport team came to take me for the repeat CAT scan, I could barely focus my eyes. Waynne said he didn't want to alarm me, but told me I was snoring loud enough to rattle the windows. He said it with a grin so I wasn't certain if he was teasing or happy he discovered a flaw in me.

The doctor returned several hours after the repeat CAT scan. He informed me the results were unchanged. He agreed to allow me to go home if I had someone who could stay with me all night and make certain I could be awakened ever couple of hours. I agreed. I called Ali.

"I want to help", stated Ali, "but with my morning sickness, I take this pill at night and sleep hard".

"Do you think Paul would mind?" I asked.

"He's working", replied Ali.

"I guess I'm stuck", I said.

"I'm really sorry Emily. I wish I could skip the pill, but if I do, I'm sick all day".

"No worries", I said, "One day in the hospital can't be that bad, right?"

"I can monitor you", stated Waynne.

"I can't ask that of you", I replied.

"You didn't ask", he said.

"You'd be wasting your entire night and probably most of tomorrow", I explained.

"It sounds like you want to stay her tonight", he said.

"Not really, but you and I really haven't known each other very long", I said.

"You just met the doctors and nurses and they have all seen you naked. So your point is?" he replied. He had a point. Maybe I was being overly cautious.

"Ok, but remember, you offered", I said. The doctor gave me a prescription for Tylenol #3 and Zofran 4 milligram tablets for nausea. Instructions to rest for five days and see my regular physician on day six. The doctor gave Waynne the following instructions:

1. Bedrest. Up to use the bathroom only. Waynne was to walk me to the bathroom to ensure I didn't fall.
2. Eat small light meals. Include fiber to prevent straining on bowel movements. How embarrassing.

3. Wake me up every couple of hours to ensure my condition had not gotten worse.
4. No sexual activity until cleared by my primary physician. As if the fiber thing wasn't enough to embarrass me to death.
5. No driving for the next five days.

Waynne called for a cab. I was soon wheeled to the curb like a princess in her chariot. I felt so sleepy. I dozed off in the cab and awoke with my head on Waynne's chest and him holding me. I slowly leaned up to a sitting position.
"I'm sorry", I said.
"For what", he asked.
"For not drooling", I replied with a sickly grin. Waynne smiled back.

Chapter 49

We soon arrived at my house. Waynne paid the cab driver. "Oh", I said with surprise", what happened to my wallet and bag?" "Ali and Paul took it with them. Ali told me she'd drop them off tomorrow", Waynne explained.

My walk was stumbly. I walked like a man who had drank a whole pint of whiskey. Waynne put his arm around my waist to steady me. Then it occurred to me. How would we get into my house? Waynne must have realized it too.

"Do you have a safety key outside?" he asked.

"Nope", I replied.

"I guess you're staying the night at my house then", he exclaimed. He slowly walked us in the direction of his house. My legs felt like rubber bands. I started to stumble but Waynne caught me and swooped me up into his arms. Although I felt embarrassed, it felt good to be in his arms. I laid my head on his shoulder and once again fell asleep.

I don't know how Waynne managed to unlock the door with me in his arms. I didn't wake up when he turned on his lights. I barely stirred when he gently laid me on the futon. Two hours later, Waynne woke me up. He had prepared some soup and a grilled cheese sandwich. He had a juice glass with prune juice and a glass of ice tea. All these items were on a tray and sitting on the table in front of me.

"I thought you may be a bit peckish", he said.

I was hungry. "Thank-you", I said as I slowly sat up. I could feel my heart beat in my head, if that's even possible.

"Do you need help eating?" asked Waynne.

"I never need help eating", I stated.

The soup was really good. I'd have to ask him what kind it was when I knew I was alert enough to remember. Waynne insisted, backed up by the doctor's orders, so I drank the prune juice. I took a few bites of the grilled cheese sandwich but without pickles it just lacked something. I thanked Waynne and asked if I could use his bathroom.

He literally lifted me up from a sitting position to a standing position. I took a few steps. My legs felt better. I told Waynne I felt I could walk alright. I only needed directions but he insisted on walking nearby to ensure my safety. He was really taking those instructions seriously.

I used the facilities, washed my hands, and started out of the bathroom only to find Waynne standing right outside the door.

"Oh, you startled me", I said.

"Sorry, but I wanted to be nearby just in case you needed help", he explained.

I could feel his hand behind my back as I walked back to the futon.

"What time is it? "I asked.

"Around eleven pm", he answered.

I laid back down on the futon. Waynne sat in a chair nearby.

"Aren't you going to sleep?" I asked.

"I need to wake you up in two hours. Its better just to stay awake", he replied.

I closed my eyes for a few minutes. When I opened them again, Waynne was watching me.

"Are you going to stare at me all night?" I asked.

"No", he smiled, "but if you can't sleep, you can watch television or a DVD from my collection".

"I think I can sleep, if no one is staring at me", I smiled and said.

He came over and started tucking in the blanket he had placed over me.

"You do know, I'm not three years old, right?" I said.

"Sleep tight", he said and returned to his chair.

I closed my eyes and drifted off to sleep.

"Emily, Emily. Wakey, wakey", Waynne said. I forced my eyes to open.

"What time is it?" I asked.

It's nine am", Waynne replied. Waynne had woken me up at one, three, five, seven and now nine. I felt as though I hadn't slept at all.

"When do we get to stop these every two hour wake up calls?" I asked.

"We probably could have stopped at seven but I wanted to make certain you were alright", Waynne replied.

"Then we can actually sleep now, Right?" I asked.

"Yes, I guess we can", replied Waynne.

"Now maybe you'll go to bed. I feel so badly about you staying awake all night", I stated.

"While you were resting, I went and picked up your prescription. I thought you may have a headache when you woke up", state Waynne.

Waynne was right. My head pounded. I could even feel it throbbing in my eyes. I knew if I took two of those pain pills, I would be out for hours.

"Why don't I take one tablet and see how it goes", I said.

Waynne rushed to the kitchen and brought back a large glass of ice cold water.

"Would you want something to eat before you fall asleep?" Waynne asked.

I nodded yes and said, "Let me help you".

"No, you rest while I fix us something", replied Waynne.

"You've got to be tired. Why don't you let me help?" I asked.

"You are the patient. I'll cook then we'll both get some sleep", he stated.

It wasn't long before a plate of fried ham steak and scrambled eggs was set in front of me. Waynne sat on the futon beside me with a plate too. We both ate. Waynne jumped up and poured us both a large glass of orange juice. It was all so tasty. I didn't realize how hungry I was. My plate was clean in what seemed like on moments.

Waynne cleared our plates and glasses off the table.

"Would you prefer to sleep in my bed", Waynne asked.

"No", I replied, "I felt bad enough you've lost a night's sleep. I slept fine on the futon so far."

"Ok, But if you need me for anything, please don't hesitate to wake me up", Waynne instructed.

Waynne was soon in bed. Only a crack in the door separated us. I put my head down on the pillow and closed my eyes.

Chapter 50

When I woke up, it was dark. No lights were on and I could hear Waynne snoring. The poor man had gone over twenty four hours without sleep. I stood up. My balance was ok. I needed to use the bathroom. I tried to be as quiet as I could. I tip toed to the bathroom. I had just finished washing my hands and I heard an odd noise. I opened the door to find Waynne standing in the hallway.

"I didn't mean to wake you up", I said.

"Are you alright?" he asked.

"Yes, I just needed to use the bathroom", I explained.

"How is your head feeling?" he asked

"My head still aches but it feels better than it has been", I replied.

"I should probable get some food in you", Waynne stated.

"What time is it?" I asked.

Waynne looked at his watch and said, "Six thirty pm. Why don't I order some Chinese food?"

Waynne ordered Chinese food and set a plate for each of us on the coffee table. While we waited for our delivery, Waynne brewed some tea. Soon tall glasses of ice tea and plates of pepper steak sat in front of us. Waynne handed me my prescription bottle and said, "You may want to wait until you are finished eating before taking your medication. It seems to make you really sleepy."

It was true. I nodded as I ate. Then I realized, I'd be sleeping but Wayne wouldn't be tired "Maybe I should head for home. I'd hate to tie up your Livingroom sleeping and preventing you from watching your television", I said.

"I don't watch much television and you still seem to bear watching", stated Waynne.

"I think the worst of the situation has past. I really do appreciate everything you've done but I should get home", I said. The truth was, I wanted to take a shower and brush my teeth.

"How will you get into your house?" asked Waynne.

"I forgot about that. I can call Ali and see if she can drop my things off", I explained.

"I really don't mind monitoring you another day", said Waynne.

"Well, let's see if I can get a hold of Ali", I said.

Waynne handed me his cordless phone. I managed to reach Ali. She would meet me at my house in thirty minutes.

I informed Waynne that I would need to meet Ali at my house. Waynne put one of his jackets on me and insisted on walking me home. He carried my prescription bottle for me and held on to my arm as we walked. We sat down on my front stoop. We waited for Ali to arrive. Ali finally pulled into my driveway.

"How are you feeling?" asked Ali.

"Still have a bit of a headache but Waynne has been taking excellent care of me", I replied.

"I told her she should allow me to monitor her for another day, just in case", Waynne voiced with concern.

"It may be a good idea, Emily, if he watches for another day", replied Ali.

"Right now, I need a shower and to brush my teeth", I replied.

"I need a shower too", added Waynne

"Why don't you go home and take your shower. I'll stay here with Emily while she takes her shower. Then we can all sit down and decide the best plan of action", suggested Ali.

I was too tired to stand and argue so I nodded yes and took my stuff from Ali. I opened my door and went in. Ali followed me. Waynne turned and walked in the direction of his home.

Chapter 51

"I'll make some tea while you take your shower. Are you hungry?" asked Ali.

"No, Waynne and I ate Chinese food. I'll be out in a bit. I really want a long hot shower", I replied.

The warm water felt so good. I even enjoyed watching the soap bubbles slide down my body to the tub and slip slowly down the drain. I could feel the lump on my scalp. It was still really tender. I managed to wash my hair without further increasing my headache. I finally felt warm and clean. I stepped out of the shower and had just wrapped the towel around me when Sondra appeared. I stifled a scream and almost fell into the tub.

"You do take a long shower, don't you?" Sondra stated more than asked.

"Why are you here?" I asked her.

"I came to see if you have heard anything regarding Daniel", she stated.

"What do you mean?" I asked.

"I haven't heard anything from the grapevine. Have you gotten any word lately, when Daniel may show up?" Sondra asked.

"I haven't received any news from human or ghost on Daniel's status. I'm not sure I will", I stated.

"I'll keep checking in", stated Sondra.

"Why?" I asked.

Sondra hesitated then said, "In time", she smiled then disappeared. I finished dressing. I took a long time brushing my hair. My scalp was extremely sensative. When I came out of the bathroom, Ali and Waynne were sitting drinking ice tea and conversing. Waynne stood as I entered the room. He did have manners.

"I've been talking to Waynne. We both feel you should have someone around for the next several days", stated Ali.

"Why?" I asked.

"You can't see your doctor for several days. You've barely made the twenty-four hour mark, and it is better to have someone around just in case", stated Ali firmly.

I could see her point. I felt alright but if this had happened to Ali, I'd want to make certain she was safe too.

"I can take the couch", stated Waynne with a smile.

First the pastor forces him on me, then Ali. Now he's volunteering. He may be a nice guy but I wasn't feeling especially receptive. "Couldn't you just call and check on me?" I directed my question at Ali. I could see the disappointment in Waynne's face that I had basically requested he not be here.

"With a head injury, who is to say, you'd be able to answer or call if there were a problem?" argued Ali.

"I'm feeling much better. The pain medication just makes me sleepy", I explained.

"The doctor did say you were supposed to be on bedrest. You did walk home. I don't know if that would make any difference", stated Waynne.

I could feel my blood pressure rising. I could feel my heartbeat in my head from the pressure.

"I will take my pain pills and sleep. It's almost nine pm. I don't need to wake up every couple of hours. I think you two are just overly cautious", I said.

"Emily", stated Ali, "I'd feel better knowing you have someone monitoring you. I'd do it myself but like I mentioned before, I get morning sickness so badly if I don't take my own medication. The medication knocks me out. I'm useless."

I realized I wasn't going to talk anyone out of this. "Fine", I snapped.

I uncapped the prescription bottle and took out two tablets. My head was throbbing now and I only wanted to sleep. I swallowed the tablets with a big gulp of ice tea. I looked at Waynne. I could see the sadness in his eyes.

"I'm sorry", I said, "I get cranky when I'm tired".

"No need to apologize", he said, "I'm the one that over stepped my boundaries".

I gave Waynne a pillow and a blanket. I hugged Ali and told her to go home and get some rest. I sat my glass of tea on my bedside table, climbed into bed, and buried myself under my covers. It didn't take long for the pain medication to put me to sleep.

After Ali left, Waynne locked my door. Waynne had the foresight to bring a book to read. He slipped off his shoes and laid on the couch. Waynne must have fallen asleep late that night. He didn't notice the face peeking into my front window. Around three am, I turned over. My stomach lunged. I threw back the covers and raced for the bathroom. I don't know how long I was vomiting but

Waynne was by my side. He held my hair out of my face, put a cool wash cloth on my forehead, and even called the doctor to notify him of my recent symptom.

Waynne held my waist as he walked me back to bed. My head felt like it would explode. Waynne propped me up on several pillows. "The doctor believes the pain medication caused the nausea. He called in a different prescription for an antiemetic medication", Waynne explained.

"Who is open this late at night?" I asked.
"There is always a pharmacy open twenty-four hours", Waynne stated, "I'll need to drive there. It may take me an hours or so. Will you be alright while I'm gone?"
"I'm dying. What makes you think I won't be alright?" I said.
Waynne smiled and said, "Can I have your house key so I can get back inside?" I pointed to the kitchen counter and then closed my eyes. I heard the key in the lock as Waynne left. I dozed off. I woke up when Waynne returned. The prescription was for a medication called Compazine. I took it and it did help. Waynne made me a hot cup of tea and some toast. He made me laugh when he placed a brown grocery bag with a plastic trash bag inside next to the bed. "In case you feel sick", he said.

The toast and tea, along with the Compazine helped. I managed to doze back off. When I woke up, Waynne had laid back down. He was snoring loudly. I glanced at my clock. It was eight am. I would need to call work. I tip toed to the bathroom. I used the facilities and I even managed to brush my teeth. When I came out of the bathroom, Waynne had woken up and had put on some coffee for me. He looked fatigued. I felt ashamed of myself for feeling so resentful towards him before. I guess anyone would be angry if they repetitively had been pushed into including a person into their social gatherings. I had felt my arm had been twisted several times to include Waynne. Now I felt guilty that I had those nasty thoughts. Waynne had been so kind to offer his own time to help me.
"I should call work and also make an appointment with my doctor", I said.
"I could call them for you", suggested Waynne.
"That is awfully kind of you. I do hate speaking to our office manager. She can be a real dragon", I stated.
"Then let me call", he said, "What is the number.

I gave Waynne the number and told him the unit manager's name. I was impressed by how Waynne handled the conversation. He explained I had been injured and taken to the hospital. He also mentioned how I was being monitored by members of the church. He explained my return would be next Monday unless my doctor felt it necessary for additional recovery time. He then called my doctor's office and made an appointment for Friday.

"Don't you have to work today?" I asked.

"I am taking comp hours. How are you feeling now?" he asked.

"Much better, thank you. What are comp hours?" I asked.

"When you are in an exempt status or in management, you may have to put in over-time hours. Because I am salary, I don't get paid over-time. I get to take equal amount of hours off whenever I need to do so", he explained.

"So you could take a nice vacation instead of babysitting me", I said.

"I plan vacations but use comp hours when I need some R & R", he stated.

"Should we heat up some of that Chinese food for an early lunch?" I asked Waynne.

He smiled and said, "Now you are talking my language".

Chapter 52

Gail thought back at how she had seen Waynne sleeping on Emily's couch.

"So she thinks she can steal Waynne from me does she? She will learn how wrong she is", said Gail, "Yes, she will definitely learn he is mine". Gail smiled and recalled how easily her knife had cut slits into Emily's tires. All four tires to be exact. The stale air hissing as each tire slowly flattened gave Gail an excited feeling inside.

Gail knew Emily must have lured Waynne to stay the night. IF she didn't do something soon, Waynne may fall victim to Emily's tricks. Waynne needed to love Gail. It was Gail who always came into work when Waynne needed her. It was Gail who always made cookies and brought them to Waynne with a cup of his favorite tea made just the way he liked it.

Emily wouldn't know how Waynne liked his tea. Yes, Waynne needed to be hers. Emily would have to be set straight. Gail would set Emily straight and very soon.

Chapter 53

Emily felt much better. Waynne left to go home, take a shower and then return to drive Emily to the store. She needed groceries for the next few days and the doctor's order stated that she couldn't drive for three or four days. Waynne had offered to drive her to the store. Waynne had said he needed a few things too. Emily agreed to go with Waynne instead of calling a taxi.

Emily showered. Her scalp was still very tender but the headaches had become controlled with plain over-the-counter pain relievers. Soon she was dressed and making out a short grocery list. When Waynne knocked on the door, he had an odd look on his face.

"What's wrong", I asked.

"Did you notice anything wrong with your car when we waited for Ali to arrive yesterday?" he asked.

"No, why?" I asked.

"All four of your tires are flat", Waynne announced.

I walked outside. Sure enough, all four tires were flat.

"That's impossible for all four tires to go flat at the same time, isn't it?" I asked.

Waynne investigated further and stated, "We need to call the police. Your tires have been slashed".

A police car arrived less than an hour later. They asked several questions. When did I use the car last? When had I visually observed the tires were undamaged? Did I have anyone who may be angry with me? Did we have any unruly teenagers in the vicinity? I answered all the questions. The police gave me a business card and told me when I could pick-up the report. Then the police car left. I called a local auto tire store. Explained my situation. They arranged for a service technician to arrive tomorrow morning and replace my tires.

Waynne said, "I'll get my car and we can get our shopping done". I nodded in agreement.

Waynne and I drove in silence. I couldn't understand why my luck had been so bad lately. I had no clue who would have slashed my tires.

"I've been thinking. I'm going to put surveillance equipment up around your house", state Waynne.

"Do you think that it's really necessary?" I asked, "I'm sure it is some unruly teenagers, like the police mentioned".

"I was awake until two-thirty am. I don't know any teenagers that would be out that late on a school night. If they were teenagers and unruly, why was only your car tires slashed and no one else in the neighborhood?" Waynne asked.

Waynne had a point and it was a good one. Now I began to worry. When we returned to my house, I looked around to see if anything else had changed. Nothing. It seemed my vandal only worked at night. At least so far.

After dropping me off, Waynne drove himself home. I managed to put all my groceries away and started a nice spaghetti dinner. I knew Waynne would be back. I really didn't need a babysitter but Ali was so worried about me. I didn't want to add to her worries. She was pregnant and had her own issues to deal with. Morning sickness every day and a husband who was a policeman. That was enough stress for anyone.

My spaghetti sauce was almost done when Waynne knocked. I opened the door to find Waynne holding a large box of electronic gizmos and cables.

"What is all that?" I asked.

"Monitoring equipment", he explained.

"Is this stuff going to change my home in anyway?" I asked.

"No! I have remote cameras that can be placed in various areas. They are battery run, sort of like cell phones. They transmit to my computer system", Waynne explained further.

I watched as Waynne nested a camera on my window sill facing toward my car. He then placed one of the tiny cameras in a window facing each side of my house. When he finished placing the cameras, we ate dinner. I then loaded the dishwasher while he linked the cameras up to his computer.

When I had finished tiding up the kitchen, Waynne flagged me over to the coffee table. His computer was set up. He showed me how he could record what each camera was viewing. I felt safer. I gave Waynne his pillow and blanket. I got ready for bed. Although I hadn't done much, I felt extremely tired.

Chapter 54

The next morning Waynne and I woke up to a knock at my door. I opened the door to see the tire technician.

"Ma 'me, I'm here to put your new tires on your car", the technician said.

"Thank-You", I replied. I jumped in the shower and dressed quickly. Waynne was looking at his computer screen when I exited the bathroom.

"You need to see this", Waynne stated. I sat down beside Waynne.

"Here, watch", he said.

A figure walked onto my lawn. The person was pouring something. I couldn't tell if the person was a man or a woman.

"Could the person be dumping out their coffee or something?" I asked.

"It looks like a bottle of bleach", replied Waynne.

"Bleach?" I questioned.

"Bleach will burn your grass", replied Waynne.

After Waynne and I watched the unknown person pour the liquid onto my yard, the video feed showed that the person left my yard. Heading down the street in the direction of Waynne's house, the figure disappeared from view. Since the camera was aimed at my car, the person walked off camera and out of sight. There was no way to tell if the person kept walking or had a car parked nearby. The camera on the side of my house recorded my side yard and part of my neighbor's home.

"I'll rig up a camera to the inside of your car. We can put one aiming in each direction of the street so we can see where this person comes from or goes to. Maybe we can catch this person going into a home or a car", stated Waynne.

It was difficult to tell if this vandal was a man or a woman. Jean, sneakers, and a hoodie. It looked like a teenager, but with a hoodie who could tell if the person was young or old. After we had viewed all the camera footage, Waynne and I walked outside. The grass looked the same at this point. If it was bleach, we would see what damage was done in a few days. Waynne dug through his stash of electronics and produced two small items that looked like pencils.

"These are the smallest cameras I own. I will tape them inside your car after the tires are replaced", stated Waynne.

I paid the tire technician and he left, taking with him my four ruined tires. Waynne fixed the cameras so one faced each direction of the street. Now we only needed to do was wait. I kept racking my brain. I had no one that I could think of that was angry or upset with me. Maybe it was an error made on the part of the vandal. There are a lot of Wells. I could ask Paul to check to see if anyone else named Wells in the area was getting harassed.

Waynne read his book while I worked on my quilt. I had a habit of looking out the window more frequently now even though I knew all the damaged occurred in the wee morning hours. Waynne had gone home and showered but had returned an hour later. He said he had given a copy of camera recording the vandal to the police. I had started dinner. I thought a nice meatloaf would be tasty. I peeled some potatoes as my meatloaf baked. Soon I had potatoes boiling, meatloaf baking and I washed and sliced some large tomatoes. I had picked up a fresh baked loaf of multi-seed bread and some whipped butter at the store yesterday. I thought they would go well with dinner.

The aroma of the meatloaf made my stomach start to growl. I mashed the potatoes and set the table. I called Waynne over and we ate. I could see the fatigue on his face. I know he was trying to catch this vandal.

"Waynne, let's let the cameras do their job and we both get a good night sleep tonight. What do you say?" I asked.

"It sounds like a good idea. The police have been making frequent rounds. The cameras are recording. We're doing everything we can at this point", he replied.

We finished dinner. Waynne helped me load the dish washer. I worked on my quilt while he fiddled with the computer. I think he was setting the camera recordings. We both decided to make it an early night. I did have my doctor's appointment early in the morning.

"Do you want me to set the clock to a half hours earlier than I normally would so you'll have time to go home and shower?" I asked.

"That would be great", he replied.

Chapter 55

The alarm clock went off as planned. Waynne went home to shower. I jumped in the shower. I was dressed and had coffee made by the time Waynne returned.

"How about I treat you to breakfast after my doctor's visit?" I suggested.

"Ok", he said with a smile.

Waynne drove me to the doctors. The doctor looked me over. He flashed a bright light into my eyes, held up two fingers, and tested my hand grasps, besides testing my balance and memory. The doctor approved my returning to work on Monday. I paid my co-pay on my doctor bill and then Waynne drove us to a local family restaurant.

As I sat sipping on my coffee, Waynne looked puzzled.

"Ok, what's going on?" I asked. I knew something was troubling him. It showed on his face.

"I'm worried about you", he replied.

"The doctor said I was fine", I replied.

"I'm not talking about your accident. Someone has a grudge against you", he stated.

"I can't think of anyone that would be angry with me. Even the few friends who do have teenagers, their children have been well mannered and very polite", I explained.

"That may be, but someone has targeted you. The damage to your tires and your lawn are not things that a normal person would do. I can't imagine what may be planned next", stated Waynne.

"There is no reason to keep worrying about it. That's like living through it twice. I'll just have to face whatever happens, if and when it does", I replied.

I paid for breakfast, as promised and then Waynne drove me home. I told Waynne that I would treat him to lunch after church Sunday for all the care and monitoring he had done. That and the monitoring of my safety. Waynne followed me into my house, gathered up his laptop and then headed home.

I called Ali to see if she wanted to go to the flea market tomorrow. She declined my offer. Paul was off and they made plans to visit Paul's parents who lived up state. They even discussed taking a ferry from Ludington to Wisconsin to eat at Joey's seafood. A family restaurant that Paul and his family had stumbled on during one of their excursions. The food was great and the owners, Jim and Laurie Knop the nicest people you could meet.

I'd be on my own tonight and throughout the weekend. I hated to admit it, but I wished Waynne would be here too. I thought if I kept busy, I wouldn't be so fixated on the vandal. I pulled out my quilt pieces. I worked on putting some strips together. My pattern was coming together nicely. I hadn't noticed the hours passing until my stomach started to growl. The clock read two pm. I decided to make a grilled cheese sandwich. I know a lot of cheese isn't good for a person, but a grilled cheese sandwich was a favorite lunch for me.

I heated up a can of tomato soup. There was nothing better than tomato soup and a grilled cheese sandwich. Yum! With my stomach appeased, I decided to take a break from sewing. I carefully put my quilt pieces away. I had a book I had begun reading and was anxious to get to the plot of the story.

A young woman named Linda in love discovered the man she loved was not in love with her. They had made love but the man whose name was Paul, said it was only passion. Linda knew it was love. Unfortunately, a rich woman named Gail was threatening to ruin Linda's family if Linda didn't exit from Paul's life. It seemed Gail wanted Paul and needed Linda out of the way. I was hoping Linda found a way to get Paul and pay back Gail. I laid on my bed and began reading. When shadows appeared, I flicked on my lights.

I decided to ask Waynne if I could put my porch lights on without interfering with his surveillance cameras. I sat on my bed and dialed Waynne's number.

"Hello", answered Waynne.

"I hate to bother you. I wanted to ask you if it would be alright to turn on my porchlight for a little extra security. I mean, would it interfere with your cameras?" I asked. Before Waynne could answer my question, a rock broke through my front window. I screamed. The rock landed somewhere in my living room. I could see glass slivers and large shards of glass on my carpet and furniture. I was trembling. Then I heard banging on my front door.

"Emily, it's me, Waynne. Open up", he demanded. I don't know how I managed to walk to the door. My legs were shaking so badly but soon I was in Waynne's arms. I felt safe again. He held me until the police arrived.

"I called the police before I left my house", Waynne explained. Waynne spoke to the police. He explained how he and I had been on the phone when he heard the window break and me scream. He headed to my house while calling the police. He also explained how my house had been vandalized twice before tonight.

Waynne got on my telephone while I gave the police my account of the situation. When the police left, Waynne had stayed. He heated up my coffee and sat with me at the kitchen table. I looked at all the broken glass. I was glad I had put my quilting away. It would have been ruined.

"I called a window replacement company to replace the window. I also called a cleaning crew to remove all the glass", stated Waynne.

"This vandal is costing me a lot of money", I admitted.

"Your home owner policy will pay for the destruction that occurred tonight. When the window is fixed, we'll go to my house and view the camera feed", Waynne stated.

It was almost midnight when the cleaning crew finished vacuuming and ridding my home of all the broken glass. The window repair company had replaced the glass and suggested I consider triple pan windows. Right now, I was considering moving.

"Why don't we plan on you staying at my place tonight", stated Waynne. I nodded yes.

"You look pretty frazzled. We can view the camera feed tomorrow", he finished.

We locked my door and walked to Waynne's house. Waynne offered me his bed but I refused. I told Waynne I would sleep on the futon or go back home. Waynne brought in a pillow and some blankets. He then went into his kitchen and returned with two glasses of wine. He sat down on the futon next to me. The wine made me feel more relaxed.

"It's kind of warm in here, isn't it", I asked.

Waynne kept looking at me. I finished my glass and felt less afraid. Waynne put his arms around me. I moved into him. His lips were soft and warm when he pressed them against mine. I could taste the wine on his mouth.

"I think we should get some sleep", he suggested.

"So soon?" I questioned.

"We have a lot to do tomorrow", he said.

"Ok", I replied. I laid down and pulled a blanket over me. Waynne turned the lights off. I did notice he left his bedroom door open a crack.

Chapter 56

I awoke to the aroma of bacon.

"Oh, you're awake', said Waynne.

"What time is it?" I asked

"Almost ten am", he said. My stomach growled. Waynne smiled.

"Come on, breakfast is ready but I only have instant coffee", he confessed.

"Beggars can't be choosers", I said.

Bacon, eggs, toast, orange juice, instant coffee and hot tea. Soon I was stuffed. I helped Waynne clear the table. I began washing the dishes while Waynne set up his lap top.

Waynne began viewing what the cameras had recorded yesterday. I had finished the dishes and poured myself another glass of orange juice when Waynne called me. We both sat and watched as a person on a bike rode to my house. The person wearing jeans and a hoodie, picked up a rock and threw the rock through my front window. The person got quickly onto the bike and rode off.

"It looks like a woman", said Waynne.

"How can you tell?" I asked.

"The way the rock is thrown. The hoodie tightens and female breasts can be seen. Luckily the street lights were on and we were able to get a better view of the vandal", Waynne explained.

"Can you see where the bike went?" I asked.

"Unfortunately, she rode away from my house. If she had come my way, I would have seen her and possible stopped her", he replied.

"Waynne, I'm frightened. I don't know when this will end or how it will end", I confessed.

Waynne put his arms around me. "We'll catch her", he said.

"You have a life. I can't expect you to spend your life rescuing me. Who knows when this person will be stopped?" I stated.

"I know you haven't known me very long and I am usually too shy to start a conversation. I am developing feelings for you", Waynne admitted.

I didn't know what to say exactly. I tried to put my feelings into words that wouldn't hurt him.

"I know I wasn't very friendly to you when we first met but I've come to enjoy your company. I am still recovering from a broken relationship. It's only been over for a year and I don't want to rush into anything. I think this situation has made me more dependent on you than I would have been otherwise. I trust you and that has made me feel as though I need you. I won't deny I wish I had a nice man in my life. I admit, I need your help now and I feel safe in your arms. I don't want a stressful situation to create false feelings for both of us", I blurted out.

Waynne smiled at me and said, "Take your time. I'm not going anywhere". He pulled me close and gave me one of his warm soft kisses. I kissed him back. When we parted, I quickly said, "I need to go home and take a shower".

"I'll walk you home", he said.

After we made it to my house, Waynne walked around the house. He inspected my car, the doors, windows, and the yard. He sat on the couch and called the police while I took my shower. I felt safer with Waynne watching over me. I made us some ice tea.

"I'll make a copy of the footage from last night and take it to the police station. Would you like to come with me when I deliver the footage?" Waynne asked.

"Actually, I have some things I need to get done so I'll be ready for work on Monday. Besides, nothing seems to happen during the day time", I said.

I could see my response disappointed Waynne but he was a good sport about it.

"Make certain you lock your doors. Stay away from the windows, and make certain you turn your porch lights on when it begins to get dark outside", he instructed.

"Won't you be back before it gets dark?" I asked.

Waynne smiled, "I should only be a couple hours. Why don't I pick up some take out on my way back and we can have lunch together".

"I should treat you", I stated.

"You can treat for dinner", he said as he walked toward my door. I locked my front door and pulled out my ironing board. I finished my ironing my clothes and soon had everything ready for work. I was making another pitcher of tea when a noise behind me startled me. I turned slowly. Daniel stood before me.

I was stunned. Words wouldn't come. I grappled for a chair. Daniel stepped toward me. I stepped back. Daniel stopped. I could see the confusion in his eyes.

"I thought you would be happy to see me", he said.

"Sondra has been waiting to see you. She keeps popping in here asking me if I've heard from you", I stated.

"You sound angry, Emily", replied Daniel.

"You left me. You left me alone in England. It took me a long time to get over that loss. I don't know if I want to open myself up to that again", I explained.

"I don't have the energy to stay long, but I'd like to talk to you about our future when I visit next", Daniel said. I could see the sadness in his facial expressions but I was still angry. Sondra appearing anytime she chose too, and no guarantee of any future with Daniel.

"Yes, we do have some things to discuss", I replied. Daniel was going to respond but a frantic knock came on my front door. Daniel disappeared. When I opened the door, Waynne bolted in.

"Where is he?" Waynne asked.

"Who?" I replied as if I didn't know.

"The man I saw arguing with you", Waynne explained.

"There's no one here", I confessed.

Waynne tossed a take-out bag on the table then checked the back door. The door was locked. No one was in the bathroom. He turned and had an odd expression on his face.

"I could have sworn I saw a man standing in front of the window. It looked like he was arguing with you", stated Waynne still looking around.

"You are the only flesh and blood man that has been in my home today", I stated honestly.

I could see the relief on Waynne's face. I know he wasn't certain what had happened but at least I had dodged that bullet.

Waynne and I ate our lunch. Waynne liked my ice tea. I enjoyed the battered fish and coleslaw he had purchased. Waynne and I cleared the table when we had finished our meals. With the take out containers, we had no dishes to wash. That was always a plus. We took our ice tea into the living room.

"You'll need to call your home insurance company", instructed Waynne.

"I'll call them on Monday on my lunch hour. I'll need to get the complaint number from the police department first", I said.

"The police said they would make more frequent passes past your house during the night. Will you be ok here at night without me here? "Asked Waynne.

I would feel a whole lot better if Waynne was here but now that Daniel was making appearances, I couldn't risk Waynne staying overnight.

"I'll be ok", I said.

"I'll keep my phone on my bedside table. Don't hesitate to call if you need me", Waynne offered.

"Thanks for everything, Waynne. I don't think I could have gotten through these assaults if you weren't here to help me", I confessed.

"Well, I guess I'd better head home", Waynne said.

I was not happy. I had a lot of thinking to do. Waynne kissed me goodbye. It was a quick peck on the cheek kind of kiss. What was I going to do? I had once been so in love with Daniel. We **HAD** loved each other. Then I discovered I looked exactly like Daniel's wife, when Daniel was alive. Daniel was a spirit that had been anchored to me because of a ring I owned. We thought him leaving would be eternal. Now we found that Daniel had found a way to return to the world of the living. Yes, Daniel returned just as I started having feelings toward Waynne. In time, my feelings for Waynne could grow stronger. If our feelings grew stronger then Waynne and I could have a life together. What kind of a life could I have with Daniel?

Funny. I once thought my life was over because I had lost Daniel. Daniel would never age. We could never be married. We could never have children. What would happen when I grew old and Daniel remained young? I still cared for Daniel and didn't want to hurt him.

I wasn't hungry when dinner time rolled around. I called Waynne to thank him for all the support and protection this week. I could hear the relief in his voice.

"Are you going to bed now?" Waynne asked.

"Yes, I know it's only nine thirty pm. Will you be at church tomorrow?" I asked.

"Would you like to ride with me?" asked Waynne.

"Yes", I replied.

"Make certain your porch lights are on. If you can, sleep with it on, keep your television on too. You can mute the sound. It could make your vandal believe you are still awake", Waynne suggested.

"Great idea", I said. We said our good byes. The television had a sleep mode built into its programming. I set the television to run for six hours. If I calculated it correctly, the television would shut itself off around four am. The neighborhood came alive around four thirty. Paper delivery cars, and we had a few nurses in the neighborhood who were up and out early in the morning.

Chapter 57

I laid in bed for hours. I don't know when I finally fell asleep but I awoke when the alarm clock rang. I showered and dressed. I sipped on some coffee. I nibbled on a breakfast bar. I grabbed my purse, locked my front door and walked down the street to Waynne's house. Waynne answered the door and smiled, "I'm running late", he said as he finished buttoning his shirt.

I stepped inside. Waynne shoved his wallet and change into his pockets. A handkerchief and his keys were tucked into another pocket. Then off we went. Church services were inspiring. Ali and Paul were still out of town so Waynne and I went to the restaurant down the block together.

"I dread going back to work", I said.

"I thought you enjoyed reading new authors works before they become famous", stated Waynne.

"I've enjoyed being away from the office Nazi", I said with a smile.

"Is it that bad?" he asked.

"Some days can be", I admitted.

"Have you thought about changing jobs", he asked.

"No. The office manager is doing the job the only way she knows how. She really isn't a leader so she has to bully people", I explained.

"Could she be our vandal?" Waynne asked.

"No. She doesn't even know where any of her workers live. She is trying to work her way up the ladder. She spends all her extra time finding ways to make herself look better to her bosses", I stated.

"I guess we'll have to keep working on who could that vandal be", Waynne stated.

"I hope the police can find the vandal", I stated.

"Would you be interested in coming over tonight for Chinese?" asked Waynne.

"I'd like that", I replied. We walked back to the church parking lot. There was a note on Waynne's windshield. The note read: ***Don't be fooled. The woman is trash!***

I blushed. Waynne reached for his cell phone. He called the police station and informed the detective he had been working with that between the camera recordings and this note, I had a stalker.

I don't know why, but I started shaking. I guess I was hyperventilating too because Waynne sat me inside his car. He looked around for a bag of some sort. He couldn't find one so he kissed me. When our lips parted he said, "I didn't have a bag for you to breathe in so I thought maybe I could slow your breathing down with a kiss".

I began to laugh. Waynne did too. We drove to the police department. Waynne led me to Detective Triplett's office. When Detective Triplett saw me, I could see the look of shock on his face.

Detective Triplett opened up the file. Four flattened tires, property damage, and now stalking. So far no injuries to me but was it just a matter of time? Waynne and Detective Triplett discussed potential scenarios while I sat and listened. Then Waynne drove me home. He first checked around my house, inside and out, made me lock the door before he would leave. I poured myself a glass of tea and sat in the living room. Daniel appeared.

"It seems the time that has passed has caused your feelings toward me to change", Daniel said.

"It's not that Daniel. I still care for you. But you were married or are married to a woman who I look like. A woman who's spirit still lingers on earth. It makes me wonder if you aren't misplacing your feelings", I explained.

"I have fallen in love with you", stated Daniel.

"And when I grow old", I questioned.

"Our love will grow even more", Daniel claimed.

"We could never marry or have children", I said.

"Actually, I have discovered, I can enter a body and live through that person", stated Daniel.

I could feel the blood drain from my face. "What do you mean, you could live through another person?"

"I can live again. We could be together", Daniel stated, "We could marry, make love, have children and grow old together".

"By cheating someone else out of their own life?" I asked.

"I had not considered that. I was thinking only of us", stated Daniel.

"I have known you Daniel. I thought of you as honorable. I can't believe you would take someone else's life for your own benefit", I said.

"You have given me something to contemplate. I will mull this over and return when I have thought this through", Daniel said sadly. He then placed a light kiss on my cheek and disappeared.

I shivered. How frightening. A spirit being able to take over someone's body. I jumped when the telephone rang. It was Waynne. Waynne called to confirm our dinner time. We decided on six pm. I changed from my church clothes into a pair of tan slacks and a white silk blouse. A splash of perfume and I was ready. I read my book until five-forty-five. I turned on the porchlights, I checked to make certain the windows and doors were locked. I kept the television on and after locking the door behind me, I walked down the street to Waynne's house.

I was just reaching to knock on Waynne's door when I felt something hit me hard in the back, again and again. I screamed. Waynne opened the door just in time to see an old car squeal away. Waynne's neighbors had come out to see what all the hullaballoo was. Waynne helped me inside. He grabbed a shirt and told me to change my top. I went into the bathroom. I noticed large red paint splatters on my silk blouse. I glanced over my shoulder into the mirror above the sink. Huge welts were appearing on my back.

When I rejoined Waynne, he informed me that he had called Detective Triplett. Apparently, I had been shot multiple times with a paint ball gun. Had it been a real gun, I would have been killed. When Detective Triplett showed up, he also had a police woman with a camera with him. The police woman had me go into Waynne's bedroom and take off the shirt Waynne had given me to wear. She took pictures of my back and my silk blouse. When we were finished, I joined Waynne and Detective Triplett.
"This is definitely more than a mere vandal case", stated the Detective.
I could see the look of concern on Waynne's face.
"What do you suggest we do?" Waynne asked.
"I'm assigning a police officer to Miss Wells", stated the Detective.
"What does that mean?" I asked.
"An officer will be at your side twenty-four-seven", the detective replied, "Until we can find the perpetrator".
At that moment, I felt safe and fretful. I would no longer have a private moment. Waynne and I ate our dinner with a police car parked out in front of Waynne's home. I didn't feel social. My back ached. I felt an odd sense of loss.

I really enjoyed being with Waynne. He was doing everything he could to protect me. Cameras had been placed inside and outside my home by him in efforts to catch the vandal. I could see Waynne glance repetitively out the window to ensure the police officer was still at hand.

After dinner, Waynne turned on his computer and attempted to zoom in on the car that had been driven by the person who had fired the paint gun at me. The license plates had been covered with a plastic bag. The head rest in the car had hidden the driver's head. I could see the frustration on Waynne's face. "Damn", he said.

At nine-thirty, Waynne escorted me to my home. He did his usual check of the house, inside and outside before saying his goodbye. The police car sat in front of my house now.

I turned the television off, climbed into my pajamas, and went to bed. When the alarm rang, I was a bit disoriented. Then it occurred to me, I had to go to work. I took a long hot shower. My back was still really sore. After eating breakfast, I took a couple aspirins to ease the back ache. I wasn't sure how this police presence was going to affect me and my job.

I grabbed my purse and jacket, locked the front door, then walked to my car. I wasn't certain if the police person was going to follow me or go in my car with me. My question was answered when a light tap was placed on my window. I lowered the window and the police officer spoke, "Mame, I will be following you to work. There is another officer in my vehicle that will accompany you to your office. He will keep in contact with our headquarters throughout the day".

"Thank-you", I said as I started the car. When I arrived at work, the police officer stood in the aisle. The office manager came up to me. "What is all this about, Ms. Wells? "She asked.

"I'm under police protection. Someone fired some shots at me yesterday", I explained.

"If this situation causes any disruption in the work force, we may have to make other arrangements!" stated the manager as she turned and walked away.

Chapter 58

I hadn't noticed that sometime before my lunch break, the police officers had changed out. Where a male police officer once stood, now was a female officer. I had stashed a peanut butter sandwich and an apple in my purse in preparation for today's workday. I had left a bottle of water in my desk for emergencies. I ate quickly and returned to my tasks at hand.

The day ended none too soon. When I arrived to my car, a huge yellow envelope was under my windshield wipers. The police officer called headquarters and informed Detective Triplett of the event. I was told to follow the officer to the police department. After testing the envelope to ensure there was nothing on or inside that would cause harm, the letter inside was read.

Heed my warning. Stop now or else!

The police tested for fingerprints but none were there.

"Detective, I have no idea what this person is wanting me to stop doing. Could this be a case of mistaken identity?" I asked.

"We've been investigating several angles on this situation. At this time, we have no other persons with the name Wells having problems like this", said Detective Triplett", we are connecting street cameras in your area with what your neighbors surveillance cameras have shown".

I thanked the detective, shook his hand, and then left. The police car followed me home. The young officer exited his car and assessed my home and yard before allowing me to enter my house. I kicked off my shoes and collapsed on the couch. Just as I was feeling the stress dissipate, my telephone rang. It was Waynne. "I'd like to come by, if it's alright", he said.

My heart skipped a beat. "Sure. How about I treat to Chinese? "I asked.

"Deal", Waynne said, "I'll see you soon".

Waynne arrived within the hour. He had brought his laptop with him. "I thought we could view today's recordings after dinner", he said. Our poor delivery guy had to go through the police officers questioning and inspection before he was allowed to deliver our food. I gave the delivery guy an extra five dollars for his delay.

We ate quickly, then settled into the couch to view the camera recordings. I told Waynne about the envelope that someone had left on my windshield. We watched as numerous staff members walked pass my car. Then suddenly a hooded figure came into view. A woman with brown curly hair approached my car. She placed the envelope under the wiper, then an odd thing occurred. She looked straight at the camera and blanched.

"The camera must have moved out of place while you were driving. One camera is still facing sideways but this camera is facing forward", stated Waynne.

"I wonder who she is. I don't recognize her", I stated.

"I'm afraid I do know her", said Waynne.

"You do?" I asked.

"Of course, he does", stated Gail as she walked into my house with a gun in her hand. This gun didn't look like a paint pellet gun.

"Gail, what have you done? "Asked Waynne.

I looked out the window. The police car was still there but I couldn't see the officer.

"He won't be of help to you", Gail said, looking straight at me. I couldn't imagine what she could have done to that young officer.

"Gail, it's not too late. If you give yourself up now", stated Waynne.

I was lost. "Just who are you and why have you been targeting me?" I asked.

"I've warned you time and time again to stop bothering Waynne. You failed to heed my warnings. Now I will have to stop you myself", declared Gail.

"Gail, you are only an employee at the company", Waynne stated.

"Don't be silly," said Gail, "You and I both know I am your girlfriend. Don't I bring you goodies to nibble on when you work late? Don't I work extra hours when you need someone? Of course, I do. Only your girlfriend would go to those extra efforts I do for you".

Waynne reached for his cell phone.

"I think you need help Gail. Let me call a friend for you", Waynne said.

Gail shook her head no and grabbed the phone from Waynne's hand. She threw the phone on the floor and crushed it beneath her foot.

"You", Gail said, pointing her gun at me, "Get over there".

I stood up slowly. My legs were wobbly. I tried to walk towards the area Gail had pointed to but I was having trouble.

"Turn around", instructed Gail. I slowly turned to face Gail. Gail aimed her gun at me. My heart was racing. I closed my eyes. I heard

Gail laugh then the gun fired. I heard a scream and a loud thud. I opened my eyes to see Waynne lying on the floor bleeding profusely. Daniel had arrived and somehow knocked Gail out.

I grabbed my telephone and dialed nine-one-one. I told the person that answered my call to send an ambulance. I explained an officer and my friend had both been injured. Waynne was unconscious. I grabbed a clean towel and applied to Waynne's chest. I saw a whole lot of bright red blood oozing through Waynne's shirt where the bullet had hit. I applied pressure and began to pray. The towel was turning red. Blood was oozing rapidly from Waynne's body.

"I can save him", stated Daniel.

"What? How?" I asked.

"I can save him if I enter his body. I can give him my life's force. I can either take over his body, or I can let him take over my life's energy", stated Daniel.

"Who would survive? You or him?" I asked.

"Who do you want to survive?" Daniel asked.

I couldn't think. I couldn't wrap my head around it. Daniel must have realized I wasn't begging him to survive. Then Daniel said, "I would die in his place".

Daniel was dead but he had a life force. Of course, he had a life force. How was it he was able to come back to me?

"I love you, Emily. I wanted to give you happiness. I wanted to be with you forever. This way, I can give you everything you've dreamed of. A man to love. Someone you can marry and have a family with", stated Daniel. Then Daniel laid down on top of Waynne. It looked as if Daniel's body was being absorbed by Waynne's body.

I could hear sirens approaching. The bleeding began to slow. Suddenly my living room exploded with activity. An EMS crew arrived with a gurney. The moved me out of the way. A flock of police officers came rushing in. Gail was cuffed and escorted out. Detective Triplett walked me to the sink. He helped me wash my hands, then had another EMS crew member sit me on the couch and assess me.

"I think she is in shock", the EMS member said to Detective Triplett.

"Take her to the emergency room too", instructed Detective Triplett.

Chapter 59

The emergency room doctor had the nurse give me a sedative. When I woke up, Waynne had gone through surgery and had been admitted to the intensive care unit. Detective Triplett arrived and asked the doctor if he could take me to the intensive care unit to see Waynne. Moments later, I sat in a wheelchair at Waynne's bedside.

The nurse came in and said, "I gave him some pain medication about an hour ago. He may still be pretty sedated".

I held Waynne's hand. I stared at his pale face. His breathing was slow but regular. His hand was cool and lifeless. The nurse said his blood pressure was stable. I asked Detective Triplett if I could remain at Waynne's bedside at least until he woke up. Detective Triplett nodded yes.

I don't know how long I sat by Waynne's bedside. I laid my head down on his hand. I wanted to feel close to him. I must have fallen back to sleep. I awoke when I felt a small nudge on my shoulder. I opened my eyes. Waynne was awake and smiling at me. I started to cry. My eyes wouldn't stop. Waynne lifted up my chin and said, "Well, I usually take a vitamin to get my iron".

Now I was crying harder but sort of laughing too. Waynne recovered from his injuries. The bullet had entered his chest and nicked a major blood vessel. The bullet had also bounced around and fractured two ribs. Waynne had to go through days of being in the hospital. He progressed so quickly that they moved him from the intensive care unit to a regular medical-surgical floor only two days after surgery. Once the danger of opening up his sutures was removed, he was discharged home. I took time off work to take care of him. It may take months to totally recover and get back on his feet, but Waynne and I managed to get him back to work and progress each day. I'm sure the office manager wasn't happy about me taking time off but I didn't care. I helped Waynne bath. I helped him cook and clean. I helped him as he had helped me. Then Paul called.

Waynne rested at his home while I visited Ali in the hospital. The baby was so beautiful. It is amazing how wonderful babies smell. I returned home. I called Waynne. His phone went to voice mail so I assumed he was sleeping. I stretched. I could feel the fatigue catching up with me. I laid down on my bed and dozed off. I woke up several hours later by someone knocking on my door. I stumbled to the door. When I opened the door, a huge bouquet of red roses were on my porch.

I looked around through sleepy eyes. I didn't see anyone. I brought the flowers inside. It looked like three dozen roses in a huge crystal vase. I sat the roses on the table. I pulled the small envelope free from the branches of the roses. I removed the card and read:

A dozen roses for each month you have been in my life.
There was no signature but I had to assume they were from Waynne. I had barely read the card when another knock came to my door. I was stunned when I opened the door. A group of caters rushed inside. They placed a white table cloth on my table. Next candle holders and candles appeared. Plates, goblets, silverware, cloth napkins, and a bucket of ice with a bottle of champaign.

I could see salads being placed inside the refrigerator. Warm food in the oven with the settings placed to warm. Another envelope was handed to me as the catering crew exited my house.
What is going on?
I opened the card.
A special dinner for a special woman!

I sat on the couch. Then I heard music. I stood. I was afraid to look. I peeked around the curtain. A violinist, a man with a key board, a girl with a clarinet, and a guitarist stood in my driveway playing love songs. I could see some of my neighbors coming outside to see what happening.

Then came another knock. I opened the door and there stood Waynne.
"May I come in?" Waynne asked.
"Sure. Maybe you can tell me what's going on", I said.
Waynne walked me over to the couch and said, "Even though we have only known each other for six months, we have gone through a lot together. I believe these odd and crazy situations have brought us closer. I know you want to take things slow but do you think you could take it slow wearing this ring?" He removed an old looking jewelry box from his pocket.
"I was walking to the new jewelry store and passed an antique store. I stopped at the antique store instead. I saw this ring and thought you might like it".

I opened the box with shaking fingers. It was a gold ring with a beautiful red stone shaped like a heart. Diamonds surrounded the red heart and there were gold leaves that circled the finger portion of the ring. Waynne kneeled down on one knee and said, "I fell in love with you the first moment I laid eyes on you. Your selflessness and your generosity along with the caring you give to others makes my heart crave you all the more. Emily, I want to spend the rest of my life with you. Will you marry me?"

I couldn't deny I had feelings for Waynne but three months is not a long time. Suddenly Waynne stood up, he took me in his arms, and kissed me. A long, warm kiss. My heart began to race. He hugged me tightly. The he whispered in my ear, "Emily, I gave this man my life's force so you could have a happy ever after. He's a good man and he truly loves you".

"Daniel?"

"Wow, I must be tired. I zoned out", stated Waynne.

I saw the anxiousness in his eyes.

"Yes", I said softly.

Waynne hugged me so hard I thought my ribs would break. Then Waynne moved back, took the ring and placed it on my ring finger. The music continued to play. Waynne lite the candles, popped the cork on the champaign, and said, "Let's celebrate, the first official day of us being a couple". Waynne smiled. His blue eyes shined brightly as he raised his glass to clinch with mine.

I can't believe so many years have passed since then. Waynne and I were married. We had a baby daughter a week after our first wedding anniversary. We named her Lillian Elizabeth. I think of Daniel often. I wonder if he appears in Waynne when I'm not looking. I did realize that life can be lived in a safe, cozy little world. Or you can have adventures and make wonderful memories. I highly recommend the latter.

My name is Emily and this is my adventure.

The End….until the next adventure!

Made in the USA
Lexington, KY
09 August 2016